OF TERAVINEA

THE PROPHECY

D. Maria Trimble

ISBN-10: 0985575328
ISBN-13: 978-0-9855753-2-8

To my family — my support.

Contents

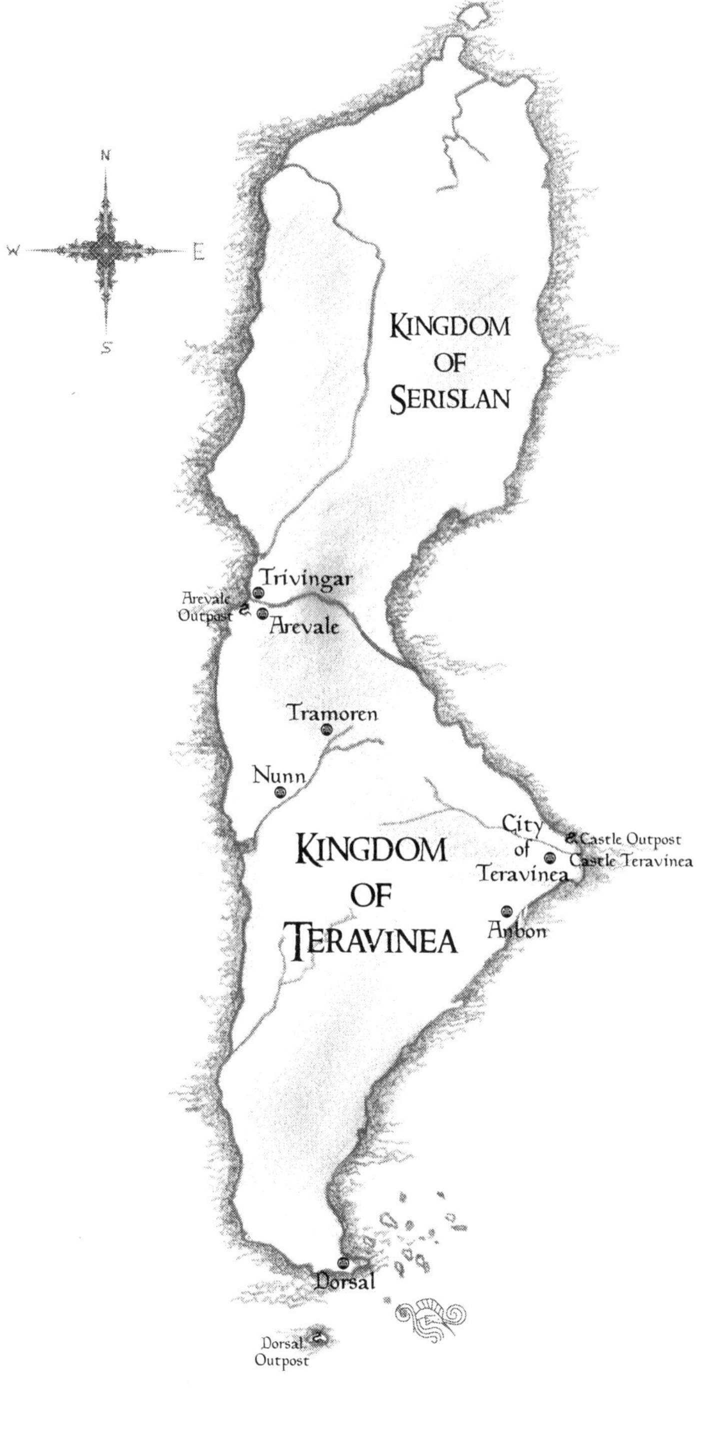
N
W
E
S
KINGDOM
OF
SERISLAN
Trivingar
Arevale
Outpost
Arevale
Tramoren
Nunn
KINGDOM
OF
TERAVINEA
City
of
Teravinea
Castle Outpost
Castle Teravinea
Anbon
Dorsal
Dorsal
Outpost

From the Guild of Clay she shall emerge
The Kingdom's bane in hopes to purge.
Tip of the Kingdom shall shield the One
Will it be daughter, will it be son?
Twice-Linked this hero be
Convincing all that it is he,
Who gains an Egg containing gold.
The mystery to at last unfold.
The Rider, the Hope, shall hold the key
Thus ringing true the prophecy
That fire and water will take to air
to crown Drekinn, the rightful heir

~ The Prophecy

Chapter One

I chose the blue silk ribbon because it matched my gown perfectly. Braiding a section of my hair on each side, I pulled both strands together and held them with a clip, letting the rest of my hair fall down my back. Thankfully, my young age allowed me to wear my hair loose.

As I wove the silk ribbon through one of the braids, I wished for my mother to help me. But that was not possible. I was preparing to attend the Life Celebration Gathering, honoring those who now rested with our ancestors. I would be walking alone in the ceremony to accept my mother's ashes.

There was an ache in my heart I wouldn't have been able to bear if I didn't have my dragon, Eshshah, humming a soothing tune to comfort me. My dragon, my strength, my love. But of course she could not accompany me to the Gathering. There were no dragons left in all of the Kingdom of Teravinea, and hadn't been for almost eighteen years — or so it was thought — we had to keep it that way.

I was now a ward of the Healer, my mother's closest friend. The Healer's dragon, Torin, was the last of the noble creatures that once filled the skies of Teravinea. At that time the Healer was known as Nara, the greatest dragon rider that had ever ridden.

Standing back from the looking glass, I appraised my progress. Taking in the full view, I didn't recognize the girl who looked back at me. Never before had I worn such finery. My eyes swept over the beautiful blue gown — more costly than most people in Dorsal could afford on a year's wages. Overly extravagant, I felt quite guilty wearing it here, but it was a gift.

It had been about five weeks since Eshshah and I returned from the Arevale Outpost. Outposts were small dragon rider strongholds located throughout the realm. Arevale was at the very northwestern corner of our kingdom, just on the border between Teravinea and the Kingdom of Serislan. It was about a four-hour flight to the outpost, where Eshshah and I had transported Ansel, the Healer's nephew. More than that, he was the son of the late King Emeric of the Royal House of Drekinn and rightful heir to the throne of Teravinea. He had started a new life in exile across the border in the Kingdom of Serislan. King Tynan had allowed him one of his manors in the southwest corner of his kingdom. The king knew Ansel only as a young noble whose lands had been confiscated by our present ruler, the usurping King Galtero — Ansel's great uncle. King Tynan had not been made aware of Ansel's true identity.

I became close friends with Ansel after Eshshah and I rescued him from the dungeons of Castle Teravinea. It would be the perfect friendship if he could keep it only at the friendship level — he cared about me more than I wanted to allow. It was the only chink in the armor of our relationship, and the cause of our strained parting when we saw each other last.

Since that farewell at the Arevale Outpost, I'd carefully built a fortress around my heart to keep my feelings guarded within, and his affections out. It was necessary, because in two weeks' time Eshshah and I would travel to Ansel's manor in Trivingar for his eighteenth birthday ball and the Dragon Rider's Council Meeting.

I poured myself into my fighting practice for most of the past several weeks — training with a feverish intensity. Not only did my life depend upon it to stay in top form, but it kept me occupied, and prevented me from thinking too much about Ansel. I could not jeopardize my intended quest to procure a dragon egg — I could not get emotionally involved with him. Ansel and I had been over this discussion on more than one occasion. He didn't want me to risk my life for his throne. I, on the other hand was bound by duty to help obtain it — no matter the cost. Two weeks didn't leave me much time to make ready my emotions.

The communication disc posed a problem in my efforts to keep my distance from Ansel. The device consisted of a thick glass disc, about two hands-width in diameter, mounted on an ornate wooden background. Behind the glass was an inlay of three dragon scales in a triangular formation. Below the glass was a brass knob. When a rider placed their hand on the knob, they would whisper the name, "Gyan," and then the proper name of the rider they wish to contact. The glass would shimmer and the rider's image would appear in the glass. It was an ingenious device created by Gallen, the Healer's assistant and closest friend. This device kept the dragon riders throughout the kingdom in contact with each other — and with Ansel. I found a pattern when Ansel and the Healer would communicate and I made it a point to be unavailable at those times. I retreated to the barn or rushed to my chambers each time I anticipated they would contact each other. There were a few occasions where I had no choice but to show myself at the disc. With some effort, I managed to pull myself together to speak with him — slightly distracted by my sweaty palms and racing heart.

I secured the first ribbon in my hair as my thoughts drifted back to a week ago.

"Amáne!" Gallen called. "A package just came for you. Take a break. Come in and open it."

I'd never received a delivery from anyone in my life. I ran into the kitchen after stopping at the laver outside to wash the dirt and sweat from my face and hands, anxious to see what had arrived.

On the kitchen table sat a rather large fabric bundle. It looked like the same cloth of which ship's sails are made. The package was tied securely with leather thongs.

"What is it?" I looked at Gallen and the Healer.

"We won't know until you open it," said Gallen.

After struggling with the knots in the leather, I finally just drew my dagger and carefully cut through them. Shaking with anticipation, I managed to release the bundle from the thongs and began to unroll it. The sail cloth fell open and revealed the most beautiful blue silk gown I'd ever seen. I gasped, afraid to even touch it. My eyes wide, I looked at Gallen and the Healer in bewilderment.

"Lift it up, Amáne. It's not going to bite you," Gallen laughed.

I held the gown up against me so we could admire the full length. As I did so, a piece of parchment dropped to the ground. Gallen picked it up and handed it to me. Without thinking, I read it out loud.

My Dear Amáne

I know that shortly you will be going to the Life Celebration Gathering. I sincerely wished that I could be with you when you accept your mother's ashes, but I am sad to say that you'll have to walk alone. Please accept this gown to accompany you in my stead. Its style is not too extravagant, as I know you would not have approved otherwise. I thought of your eyes the moment I saw the blue fabric, and knew it was meant for you.

Your Friend,

Ansel

Thankful I was still flush from the exertions of my practice, I hoped the red that began to rise in my face was not noticeable.

"Ansel certainly has a perfect memory. That gown is the exact match to your eyes, Amáne," said Gallen.

I held it up again as the Healer and Gallen nodded in approval.

"I can't accept this, can I? It doesn't seem proper — I really haven't known him for that long. And it's too fine to wear in Dorsal."

The Healer and Gallen disagreed.

Coming out of my reverie, I refocused on my reflection in the glass and thought of Ansel's sweet gesture to help me through this difficult day. *He really is a true friend*, I thought, as I followed the tear that slowly made its way down my cheek.

I wondered if he really knew how frightened I was of walking alone in the Receiving of the Ashes Ceremony. I don't like drawing attention to myself — the entire township of Dorsal would be watching me, talking about me or pitying me. Just thinking about it made me nauseous.

Others attending the ceremony would be walking with their family members, but my family had consisted only of myself and my mother, Catriona. The Healer and Gallen were the closest I had to family, but they were presiding over the Life Celebration Ceremony and wouldn't be able to accompany me. I had no choice but to walk alone.

My stomach churned as more tears escaped. It was rather ironic that I would feel this way over something as mundane as walking in front of the townspeople who had known me since I was born. My fear made no sense when I considered some of the recent events in my life that would paralyze any normal person. Eshshah and I had shared quite a few harrowing experiences that would make walking in the ceremony seem like a pleasant day at the cove. Nevertheless, I was terrified.

As I worked on weaving the silk ribbon in the second braid, my mind went back to review my resolution regarding my heart — that it was not to be given to anyone. I had to shield it before I saw Ansel again. I returned to the same conclusion — two weeks was just not long enough to prepare.

Chapter Two

"Amáne, hurry up. We need to leave soon." The Healer called up to me.

"Yes, Healer, I'm coming."

With one last glance at myself in the glass, I gathered my skirts and bounded down the first flight of stairs to the landing. I turned quickly for the second flight and got halfway down, when I froze and caught my breath. My knees weakened, my mouth went dry. My heart beat like thunder in my chest — demolishing the barrier I had been constructing around it.

"Ansel!"

He stood at the foot of the stairs as he gazed up at me. So handsome, dressed in emerald green, which made his eyes even more green than I remembered. My surprise was not well-masked. He looked pleased with my reaction.

The intensity of my feelings upon seeing him frightened me. I found myself not yet ready to test my resolve. I swallowed hard, took a deep breath and composed myself. After retrieving my heart, I managed to repair the wall around it. I tucked it away in a safe place. The hope that illuminated in his eyes told me my recovery was not quite fast enough.

Being a gentleman, Ansel followed my lead and appeared to put up his guard as well. He recovered more quickly than I.

Forming a "d" with his thumb and forefinger, he placed it on his heart and gave me the dragon salute. "Greetings, Amáne, and my greetings to the lovely Eshshah."

I nodded back in the correct response to the salute. "Greetings, Ansel, from both of us." My knuckles turned white, holding fast to the railings, lest I tumble down the last few steps.

"The gown," he smiled approvingly, "— you look ravishing!"

I clenched my teeth, narrowed my eyes and curtsied deeply, "Thank you, Your Grace," knowing this action annoyed him as much as his compliment annoyed me.

"Okay, we're even," he laughed, holding his hands up in surrender. "No more curtsies."

"No more personal compliments," I countered.

"Deal."

"Deal. But I do want to thank you for the beautiful gift. Truthfully, I do love it."

In control of my emotions, I practically flew down the remainder of the stairs and we hugged each other as close friends.

He held me a little longer than necessary with his face buried at my neck. I figured out why and pushed him away, "Stop that!"

On more than one occasion I'd caught Ansel enjoying the scent of my hair, which had a spicy fragrance to it, similar to Eshshah's delicious scent. It was either because I had her venom running in my veins or because I was always around her — or a combination of the two. He never missed an opportunity to inhale the aroma.

Ansel laughed, took my face in his hands, kissed my forehead, then one cheek, followed by the other. I stiffened ready to push him away again should he go for my lips. But he didn't. He pulled away and announced, "This is how friends greet one another in the Kingdom of Serislan, my new home."

"I'm happy to hear that you've learned the local customs," I said. "But what are you doing here? And how did Braonàn ever allow you out of his sight, or let you travel alone?"

He explained that he decided to personally deliver some documents to the Healer, so he sailed down on a merchant ship from Trivingar. "Don't worry, Braonàn thoroughly searched the ship and sent guards along, posing as hired ship's hands."

He tilted his head. "So, you see, I've been delivered safely, and here I am in time to accompany you to the gathering today. I assumed you wouldn't mind someone walking with you in the Ashes Ceremony. I'd like to be your support and your family, if that's okay with you."

I was touched. *How could he have known that I'd practically made myself sick anticipating that walk by myself?* Now, he would take all of the attention off of me as everyone in Dorsal tried to figure out who he was ... especially since he was much more interesting to look at than I.

I didn't know what to say. A lump formed in my throat.

"The only catch is that I have to beg a ride from you and Eshshah back up to the Arevale Outpost tonight after dark."

"Eshshah and I have been wanting to go on an extended flight for a long time. We'd be more than happy to take you."

I paused and pursed my lips, "But I wouldn't be opposed to seeing you beg first,"

We both laughed.

"Amáne! Ansel! I'll leave without you if you don't come out now." The Healer called.

We found her already seated in her cart, with reins in hand when we ran out to the courtyard. I said farewell to Eshshah as Ansel helped me up on the seat next to the Healer. He climbed in beside me, and we were on our way.

My relief at having someone with me at the gathering was immense. I turned to Ansel to thank him, but quickly looked away when I caught him gazing at me intensely.

We were still very early when we arrived at the gathering grounds south of the town walls — the sun just began to rise. Gallen had been there since the early morning hours setting up the tent and all the necessities for the Life Celebration Ceremony. We helped the Healer unload the urns and other items from her cart.

The Celebration was full of festivities and music, scattered with colorful booths offering food and drink and other wares from the town's vendors. The smells, colors and excitement helped me to forget my apprehensions from this morning. We had a while before the ceremony began, so Ansel and I wandered the aisles as the peddlers set their booths up for the day.

I enjoyed the looks directed at Ansel. The fine quality and style of his clothing made it obvious that he was not from around here. I admired his talent at ignoring the stares. Certainly he had been accustomed to having eyes on him all his life — being a noble and a very good looking one at that.

The sun continued its arc in the sky. It promised to be a very hot day.

Ansel and I made our way back to the ceremony location and joined the group that would be walking in the Receiving of the Ashes. It had been a relatively safe year and there were only about twenty families that would walk. I was relieved, because in bad years we've been known to have more than a hundred families. Those occasions made it so very sad, but it also made the length of the ceremony almost unbearable.

The Healer and Gallen led us all in memorial and life celebration songs, as well as other traditional ballads. We were accompanied by minstrels playing lutes and recorders. It was truly a moving part of the ceremony.

Those of us who had ashes to receive waited on benches under a shade tent. When the Healer called our loved one's name, the family walked a path from the tent, then up a middle aisle to accept the urn that contained the ashes. As the relatives walked, the townspeople were led in a song chosen by the family. Most of the time only a verse or two would be sung, but large families often meant that the entire ballad or song would be completed — even a second or third time until all of the family members made it up the aisle.

While we waited, I observed the glances we continued to receive. The combination of Ansel's striking looks, and me in a silk gown — when I usually dressed very plain — caused more than a few people to point at us.

Finally, I heard my mother's name called. The musicians struck up the tune of the "Battle of Sregor's Field." My mother had taught me that ballad. It remained one of my favorites. It told of Nara, rider of Torin — the Healer and her late dragon. More than once, the Healer pressed me to confirm that it was indeed the ballad I wanted sung. I insisted it was, unless it would upset her. She eventually acquiesced, and I believe she even felt honored, as my mother had been her close friend.

When I heard Catriona's name, I squeezed Ansel's arm

nervously — probably a little too hard. He winced and gave me a look. We stood up, I put my arm in his, and slowly we started our walk to receive my mother's ashes. As we walked, I could hear whispers and comments from the crowd. Sometimes my extraordinary hearing was a blessing, but at times like this, it just hurt.

"Who is that walking with Amáne? If that's a marriage arrangement by the Healer, I can't imagine why he would stoop so low."

"I wonder what Amáne offers him to accompany her [snickers]. You know she could never afford that gown on her own."

"He is obviously of a much higher class than she. How embarrassing for him."

I wanted to shout at them to mind their own business, but my recent training focused on the ability to exercise self control. It wasn't easy, but for now I managed to hold my tongue. How hurtful people can be.

We made our way up to the Healer who then handed me my mother's ashes in a ceramic urn. Catriona spent her life as a potter. I had selected one of her pieces that I loved since I was a small child — fascinated, as it depicted scenes from the City of Teravinea in its days of dragons. My mother made it a point to save that urn for me. *Did she anticipate it would be used to house her ashes?*

The urn was heavy, not just because it was ceramic, but the ashes themselves weighted it. I had to let go of Ansel's arm in order to carry it with both hands, for fear of dropping my mother's remains.

As we walked back down the aisle, my ankle — the one with the hideous linking mark of the black lizard who had bitten me — suddenly flared up in a shot of pain. I stumbled. Thankfully, Ansel caught me by my elbow and I recovered. But not before half the town noticed, fueling additional opinions and whispered discussions.

The sudden pain confused me. The venomous bite from the black lizard creature had been healed for weeks. I thought I'd successfully put behind me that harrowing experience in the dungeons of Castle Teravinea. But the sharp stab brought it all back. Ansel could see my distress and I hoped that he believed it was because of my embarrassment by my near fall. I didn't want to burden him with my fear and my pain.

He kept a hold on my arm, and a pleasant look on his face so as not to magnify the attention as he whispered to me, "Are you okay, Amáne?"

"Yes, I think so. Thanks." I succeeded in keeping a neutral expression, not entirely sure of how okay I truly was. My ankle heated up. My head hurt. *Why now?*

The comments from the crowd again drifted my way. I was thankful that Ansel could not hear them.

"He doesn't know what he has agreed upon. She's quite the odd one."

"She always was a little off. No wonder the Healer had to go outside of Dorsal to find someone for her."

Even the kinder remarks were not easy for me to bear.

"Wow, that's Amáne, Catriona's daughter? I never knew she was so beautiful."

"Why did she always hide her beauty?"

"My, how she's changed."

Accepting compliments was difficult, and added embarrassment to my current troubles.

We finally made it back to the benches under the tent. I lowered myself slowly. A cold wave of fear went through me as I tried to understand what could have triggered the sudden pain.

Ansel looked at me with concern, but I managed what I hoped was a reassuring smile. As long as it didn't get any worse, I should be able to endure it. We still had to go through the reception segment, where closer friends would offer their stories and memories of the loved ones who had passed.

The last urn was accepted and we were moved to our respective places to receive our friends and fellow celebrators of life. The queues started forming and for some reason there were quite a few people lined up to offer their condolences to me. Much more than I anticipated. My mother was loved in Dorsal, and most knew her, but when I surveyed the people in my queue, I saw many that I was sure were not close. Then I noticed that quite a few of them were women and young girls, and I suppressed a smile as I guessed that they all just wanted a closer look at Ansel. He seemed to have drawn the town's attention.

My headache and my ankle continued to throb on and off in waves. At times I hardly noticed, and at other times I could hardly bear it. Meanwhile, I acknowledged, kissed and hugged countless townsfolk, each uttering their version of "May she find happiness with her ancestors," and "Peace to Catriona," and "May she rest in joy." The ones that knew my mother well offered a short narrative about her from their memories. If they had a longer story, they presented it to me on a piece of parchment to read later.

Ansel was gracious enough to act as a member of my family and participate in the reception queue alongside of me — shaking the well-wisher's hands or nodding politely. No one seemed to be really sure of his relationship with either my mother or myself. I preferred to leave it that way. It intrigued me the way the ladies and young girls batted their eyes at him. This was another of those feminine practices that remained foreign to me. *How could a female's blinking eyes gain the attention of males?* It was beyond my comprehension.

Finally, people I knew and cared for. Fiona made her way to the front of the queue with her twin sisters, Rio and Mila. The little girls hugged me, but immediately their fascination of my gown got the better of them.

One on either side of me, they ran their dainty hands over my sleeves, enjoying the feel of the silk. "Amáne ..." they said with honest feeling, "may your mother find happiness with her ancestors." Unable to suppress their interest in my gown, they had to add, "How beautiful you look in this silk."

"I see your sister has trained you well, you two," I said, allowing a smile.

They handed me a rolled-up parchment. "This is a story we wrote for you. It's about how your mother helped the Healer when we were born. Our mother said if Catriona were not there helping at our birth, we both might not be here today."

"Thank you. I look forward to reading it." I was truly touched that they took the time to write something that meant so much to me. A wave of regret flowed through me as I once again lamented the fact that I was an only child — no one to share my grief. Fiona was truly blessed with these girls.

"Amáne, peace to your mother," said Fiona with sincerity as she hugged me. But neither could she contain her curiosity, "Don't tell me this is Serislan silk?"

"I ... er ..." I snuck a side look at Ansel, having no idea what kind of silk I wore. He thankfully had heard the question and gave me an almost imperceptible nod and a smile. I turned back to Fiona and assured her that it was.

Fiona smiled. She'd caught my ignorance. "Serislan silk is the finest you can buy. The Kingdom of Serislan is known for their extraordinary silk."

With a quick glance at Ansel, she said to me, "I see the Healer has finally made some arrangement for you." She showed more than the necessary amount of enthusiasm. Always obsessed with marriage and marriage arrangements and betrothals, naturally this would be her first assumption.

"Fiona, let me introduce Ansel, the Healer's nephew and friend of mine. We are just friends — no arrangements." I emphasized the word *friend* both times.

She held her hand to Ansel. He took it in his, bowed, and pressed a kiss upon it. I thought she was going to collapse in front of me as she tried to hide her blush. He took Rio and Mila's hands as well, and kissed them. They looked as though this would be a moment in their lives they would never forget. I mouthed a thank you to Ansel for including them in his attentions.

Fiona then pulled me closer and in a reprimanding tone, said, "Nonsense, Amáne! Just friends? Are you blind? Do you not see how he looks at you? You're breaking that boy's heart!"

"I am not!" I said a little too defensively.

Fiona became distracted when she saw her betrothed further back in the queue. She called him up to the front to join her. I noticed Ansel raise his eyebrows when she called Kail's name. I glared at Ansel as a warning not to say anything embarrassing to him. Unfortunately, he missed my clue. When we were at the Dorsal Outpost, after Ansel's rescue, Kail's name came up a couple of times. Ansel did not have a positive impression of him.

"Kail, I want you to meet Amáne's *friend*, Ansel." Fiona said, tilting her head and drawing out the word *friend* a little longer than necessary.

"I've heard a lot about you, Kail." Ansel said as they each nodded their greeting.

"Yes," I jumped in before Ansel could say any more, "I've told Ansel how you and I used to spar. You taught me a lot about swordplay over the years." I gave Ansel a 'watch what you say' glare and noted that he caught it this time.

"She's actually pretty good," said Kail, "... for a girl." A knowing tip of his head to Ansel, like a private joke for men only.

'For a girl?' How dare he? I no longer had any interest in protecting Kail. I would have run him through myself if I'd had the energy — and if my head wasn't ready to explode.

"Amáne," Kail continued, oblivious to my anger, "we haven't practiced in a long time. You wouldn't want to lose your skills. Let me know if you need me to work with you sometime. I'll be fighting in the games later today if you care to watch."

Ansel just barely disguised his laugh with a cough. I flashed him a seething look and he quickly hid his amusement.

Knowing I couldn't very well teach Kail a lesson here and now, in front of all these people, I gathered myself once more to practice self restraint. I took in a deep breath and with an even tone that actually surprised me, I said, "Thank you, Kail. I'll let you know if I need your help."

Fiona acknowledged the remaining well-wishers who had become impatient with her for taking so long at the front of the queue. Even still, she didn't miss the interchange between Kail and me.

Realizing that the love of her life had angered me, she gave me an apologetic look, and then said to her little group, "All right, Kail, Rio, Mila, we must be going."

Turning back to me, she grabbed my arm. "Amáne," she whispered as she cocked her head towards Ansel, "do not disappoint him. He's meant for you."

Chapter Three

At last there was one person left in my reception queue, but my stomach turned as I saw who it was — Jeslyn, a girl a little older than I, who lived only to attract men's attentions. She had broken many a heart in Dorsal and was one of my least favorite people. There she stood purposely last to greet me, but with her eyes focused on Ansel. It added to my irritation. Jeslyn was no threat to me of course, because Ansel and I were just friends. Besides that, she embodied the type of female of whom he was weary — 'weak, oblivious to anything outside her small circle of concerns,' as he once put it.

She approached, "Peace to your mother." Her words came without any sincerity. Brushing past me, she moved directly to Ansel as she turned on her smile. I praised him to myself when he lightly took her offered hand and tilted his head in acknowledgment, but did not kiss it.

Jeslyn regarded me and said, "Amáne, you look horribly tired. I'll be happy to take your friend around the Gathering and show him how we celebrate life here in Dorsal. I'm sure you won't mind."

Hmm, I could only imagine the way she'd like to show him how we celebrate life.

Word had obviously gotten to her that I introduced him as my friend. Before I could respond, she took his arm and pulled him in the direction of the main festivities. The pain in my ankle continued to increase, my head felt like a battle raged inside. I did nothing to stop her.

I grudgingly admitted that Jeslyn was right, although my teeth were clenched in reaction to the way that she said it. I felt exhausted, and probably did look it — I couldn't stand up for one minute longer. Making my way to the nearest bench, I sat heavily. A twinge of pity went through me as Ansel — having been tugged at quite a distance already — turned with a 'help me' look on his face. I looked at him and could only shrug my shoulders, mouthing the words, 'I'm sorry' as she drug him away.

I became immediately angry with myself that I had let him leave so easily. Then I turned my anger at him for allowing himself to be led away so easily. Perhaps he was not as weary of that kind of person as he had me believe. I could have used his support — I was scared. But on the other hand, I didn't want him to be aware of my pain. In fact I applauded myself that I managed to hide it so well. Ansel had a way of reading me that was uncanny. Besides, I had Eshshah's support, and that was all I really needed.

Maybe it was the heat of the day, but now my head felt about to explode. My throat became dry. I had no choice but to find the Master Brewer's tent and get some watered ale. I limped painfully, wishing I had my walking stick that Ansel had made with Eshshah's likeness carved at the top.

As I arrived at the Brewer's tent, three men pounded past me on horseback, and nearly ran me over. They charged through much faster than they should have in the middle of a crowded gathering. The explosive sound of the horses' hooves striking the ground reverberated in my head as they galloped by. My pain increased. Thunder went off in my ears and flashes of lightning behind my eyelids. I squeezed my eyes closed and put my hands over my ears, barely able to prevent the scream in my throat from escaping my lips. Something compelled me to turn towards them and watch as they passed. A chill like icy fingers went up my spine as the three horsemen slowed their pace. Inexplicably, one of the three — a most horrid looking man — turned his head towards me and caught my gaze, holding it for just a brief moment before continuing on their way. His piercing stare left me shaking in terror. *Who were these men?*

Disoriented, I stumbled into the tent ready to collapse, when the Brewer's wife came to my aid.

"Amáne, you don't look well. Come in, dear. Sit down."

"Thank you. I'm okay, I just need to rest for a minute." She eyed me doubtfully.

I let her lead me to a table where she sat me down. Immediately, she brought me a tankard of watered ale.

"Drink this, it'll make you feel better." I fumbled with the drawstrings of my coin purse. "Keep your coins, Amáne. If I could not offer an ailing neighbor a drink without charging her, then what kind of person would I be?"

I could barely utter a thank you as I struggled to lift the mug to my lips. Although I was parched, all I could get down was one small sip, which I hoped would stay down.

Crossing my arms on the table, I rested my head for just a minute.

From far away I heard my name, but couldn't answer. I felt a hand on my shoulder and flinched.

"Amáne!" I heard the concern in Ansel's voice as I made an effort to lift my head. It felt like it weighed about five times as much as it should have. I managed to raise it enough to follow the direction of his voice, but I couldn't see him. He gently pushed my hair back from where it stuck to the moisture on my fevered face. At last he came into view.

"She came stumbling in here about an hour ago," said the Brewer's wife, "I couldn't get her to take more than a small sip of ale. I let her sleep. The poor thing probably had too much going on for her today in this heat."

"Thank you, madam. I've been looking all over for her. I'll get her to the Healer."

He turned to me. "What happened?"

"It's my ... my ankle — the one with the scar."

His face went pale as he figured out which "scar" I meant. Then annoyance flashed in his eyes. "Why didn't you tell me? I thought maybe you were tired and needed a break. Otherwise, I wouldn't have let that girl drag me away."

I shrugged.

"Come on. Let's go. The Healer needs to know." Ansel bent down to pick me up, but I protested.

"No, no ... I can walk, please, Ansel. Don't pick me up." I would have been mortified.

I closed my eyes and whispered to Eshshah.

"I'm with you, Amáne," she said

Her strength flowed into my body. With an exasperated sigh, Ansel held his hand our for me as I rose from the chair. I breathed deeply. Even with Eshshah's help, I barely managed to suppress the pain in my head as well as my ankle. With great effort I willed one foot in front of the other, mumbling my gratitude to the Brewer's wife as we left the tent.

I found myself no longer able to hide my pain from Ansel. I forced myself to stay upright as we went to find the Healer.

"You shouldn't be walking. I should be carrying you. I don't know why I even listen to you, Amáne."

"Maybe because of my extraordinary powers of persuasion?" I offered, trying my best to make light of the situation and relieve him of his worry.

He just shook his head. "Don't ever keep something like that from me again. I should have paid more attention. I'm sorry."

"Ansel, you have nothing to be sorry for."

We made our way to the Healer. One quick glance at my face and she sat me immediately.

"I can't very well examine your ankle here," the Healer said, "there are too many people around. I don't know why this is happening now — it's been healed for weeks." She took my face in her hands and studied my eyes. Hers reflected serious concern.

"Lord Ansel, take my horse and get her back home," Gallen said. "I'll ride home in the cart with the Healer."

"Remove her boot as soon as you get there and have Eshshah treat her," the Healer instructed.

Ansel retrieved Gallen's horse and brought him to where I waited, "Sit in the saddle, Amáne, I'll sit behind you and make sure you don't fall." Ansel said as he cupped his hands to give me a leg up.

"No, Ansel. I'll sit behind you."

"Get up in the saddle, Amáne," he repeated. Since I had no fight left in me, I obliged. He lifted me up to the saddle. I didn't sit like a lady in a nice gown with both legs on the same side as I should have, but swung my leg over. Manners were not a priority at that moment.

Ansel mounted up behind me and put one arm around my waist as he took the reins in his other hand. I gritted my teeth, shut my eyes tight, and melded with Eshshah to keep from screaming as the horse's gait jostled me in the saddle.

When we were about halfway home, I noticed my headache had receded. The pain in my ankle diminished to a dull throb. Several minutes later all that was left of my suffering was but a memory. Except that I felt a bit fatigued, it was almost like it had never happened. I was baffled. Eshshah could offer no justification for my sudden recovery.

I turned around to Ansel and announced, "My pain is gone. I'm starting to feel much better."

He looked at me with pity, like he thought my fever gave me hallucinations.

"Truly, Ansel, it's hard to believe, but I feel like I was never in any pain at all. I'm sorry I made you leave the Gathering before you saw everything. I'll be happy to go back with you, if you want."

"I'm relieved to hear it, but how could you feel fine already? And, no, I don't need to see any more of the Gathering. Remember, your friend was kind enough to show me around." There was a good amount of sarcasm in his voice as well as mock irritation.

"She's not my friend."

We rode into the Healer's courtyard and dismounted. Ansel stared at me, observing my every move. I think he was unwilling to believe my illness had disappeared. Less than an hour before, he had felt my fever and seen the pain in my face. I was at a loss for an explanation. Rather than draw any more concern from Ansel, I turned away and dismissed any further discussion with a wave of my hand.

I greeted Eshshah with a hug, "Eshshah, please let the Healer know that I'm fine. I don't want her to worry."

After a pause, Eshshah relayed, "She was hard to convince, but I finally assured her that you are well. As if she didn't know a dragon cannot lie."

I was famished, not having eaten since earlier that morning. Stopping at the laver, I washed off the sweat and dust from my miserable morning. My beautiful silk gown would need some attention, but for now all I could think about was making my way into the kitchen. After cutting a wedge of cheese from the wheel, I grabbed a small loaf of bread and a piece of smoked fish. I snuck a bite of the bread as I set everything on the table, along with ale for Ansel and tea for me.

Ansel came in from taking care of the horse. He sat across from me.

"I'm so sorry I ruined the first half of your day." I said.

"You didn't ruin my day." Our eyes met, and I could see that he meant it. He looked as if he may have had more to say, but left it at that.

Still feeling guilty, I wanted to try to make it up to him. "What would you like to do for the rest of the day?" I asked.

He raised his eyebrows.

I rolled my eyes.

Then he lit up and said, "I know what we can do — first, are you sure you're okay?"

"I feel perfectly fine — truly, I do."

"Do you remember our deal when you challenged me at the Dorsal Outpost?"

I thought for a moment, "I do remember! It feels like so long ago. I taunted you that I could wield a blade better than you. And, that as soon as my ankle healed, I'd be happy to take you on. What a great idea! I almost forgot about that."

A thrill went through me at getting a chance to try my skills against his. Aside from fighting the lazy guards at the castle, since linking with Eshshah, I'd never practiced with a regular human — all my training had been against dragon riders.

I don't think he expected such enthusiasm. My confidence might have made him doubt if he should even have brought it up. But he did — and I answered the challenge.

After we finished our meal, I found some clothing for Ansel to change into. Gallen wouldn't mind me lending them. Rushing to my chambers, I changed out of my gown and into my usual boys' clothing — a tunic and tights.

I examined the linking mark on my ankle from the black lizard. Its likeness staring up at me brought a wave of revulsion, as it always did. But it looked the same as it had since it healed. The mark was no longer swollen or hot, or anything other than the hideous reminder it would always be.

Was I truly linked to that vile creature from the dungeons of the castle? What did that mean? Why did it give me so much pain just a short while ago?

Chapter Four

Ansel and I met in the courtyard. Eshshah accompanied us to the area in front of the barn. She settled herself in a comfortable position, eyeing us with interest and amusement.

We elected to fight with partial armor and unsharpened metal practice swords. Instead of my dragon-scale-lined breastplate and my own equipment, I decided to choose from the same supplies Ansel had to use. Of course, he wouldn't have his personal armor here, and I wanted to make our fight more even. He protested, saying I took the challenge too seriously. I don't think he understood the unfair advantage I had with Eshshah's venom running in my veins.

We helped each other with our armor. Each selected a sword. We chose to use bucklers instead of the full-size shields.

"Okay, I have a quick rule," I said.

"Oh, now you have rules for us to follow?"

"Only that you should know I won't call upon Eshshah for help. The fight is just you and me."

"I wouldn't expect anything less."

And so we launched into our contest. At first he hesitated. Gentleman that he was, he wouldn't strike first — probably afraid of hurting me. He obviously didn't understand that I was used to sparring with dragon riders, and even though they held back some, they weren't afraid to throw a hard blow.

If he wasn't going to make the first move, I would. I lunged. He parried but didn't have time to counter because I rushed him again with a series of strikes that kept him busy parrying. Ansel had skill and strength. He moved fast, but I was faster and more agile. I didn't push myself very hard, but decided that he not discover that fact. We settled into our practice as our swords clashed and the dust rose — sweat ran down my face.

Facing each other for a yet another bout, Ansel lunged first. Seeing an opportunity, I swept my leg around to take advantage of his exposed knee. He went down backwards. As he fell, he managed to hook his buckler under mine. I was pulled down on top of him, both of our lungs emptying in a loud huff. He caught his breath as our eyes met. Neither of us having face shields on our helmets, we found our lips just inches apart.

He broke into a smile. His eyes danced as he said, "I'll take the extra point for this round."

The heat rose in my face. I made an effort to escape my awkward position. He laughed at my difficulty as we realized that in the collision my pauldron — shoulder protector — had cracked and had caught on his. The more I struggled, the more the metal from the overused armor would not release me. To my mortification, he had to roll us both over before I was finally freed from the humiliating equipment disaster.

He took his time getting up — still smiling as I seethed under him.

"Get off of me!" I yelled. Not too kindly, I shoved him off, rolled to my hands and knees and rose to my feet. The practice armor, much heavier than my dragon-scale gear, kept me from moving as fast as I wanted. I stood over him and glared as he utterly enjoyed my embarrassing predicament. Unable to hide his laughter, it took a few minutes before he finally gained control of himself. He stood up, still snickering.

I should have been ashamed of myself for my lack of etiquette when I raised my blade and advanced on him before I should have. He wasn't really ready ... but oh well, ... at least I waited until he picked up his sword.

He recovered and made a valiant effort to defend himself, but I gave him a small taste of my true skills. It took only seconds to disarm him. I shot him a smoldering look so he understood I hadn't found my armor dysfunction humorous in the least. He didn't seem affected by my intended lesson — the smirk still on his face.

Irritated, I called an end to the practice, and took my helmet off. I spun around and headed off to the barn. He hurried up to me, "So, you were holding back all this time, Amáne. I thought as much."

To my surprise, my aggravation receded. I felt a bit of remorse that he had discovered my self-restraint. Another black mark against my hot temper.

I stopped and turned to him, "I think I'd like you to help me with the long bow."

I knew he was skilled in this discipline. Archery took more skill than speed or strength.

He eyed me with suspicion and pursed his lips, surely aware I'd changed the subject. I wondered how he recognized I wasn't fighting to my fullest abilities — how he had read me so well. He had an uncanny way of being able to figure me out.

From the start Ansel and I had a connection that I could only attribute to my linking with Eshshah. Her line intertwined in a complicated tapestry with the Royal House of Drekinn — Ansel's family. It remained the source of our bond.

We helped each other remove our armor. As he unbuckled the sides of my breastplate, he said, "Well done, Amáne. I apologize for frustrating you." He shrugged his shoulders, "I can't help it that I enjoyed that round — or at least the conclusion of it. I'll concede to the fact that I was beaten by a girl. But my pride is not harmed, taking into consideration, the girl. You're amazing."

"No, Ansel, you are. Your skill is remarkable. I just have an unfair advantage, and it's connected with this." I pointed at my linking mark from Eshshah.

"Yes, but even without that mark, I'm sure I would still be impressed with your abilities."

I smiled tipping my head.

"So, you want to work on your bow skills?" he asked.

"Yes, I heard you're good with the long bow and I think maybe you can show me a few things. But that's okay, if you'd rather do something else. I've already taken advantage of you, I'm sorry. You're here for such a short period of time. I'd hate for you to think I was a poor hostess. What would you like to do? It's your decision."

He turned to me with a devious smile — our eyes locked. Stepping closer, he pushed an errant strand of hair behind my ear and then glanced at my lips before he returned to my eyes. I couldn't bring myself to move.

"Well, since you ask, I feel I must tell you the truth. What I would really like to do is kiss you. But, I don't feel like being slammed on my back, staring at the sky, wondering what hit me. I'll go with your suggestion and we'll empty some quivers."

My heart leaped out of my chest as the heat rose in my face. "Uh ... er ... let's see if we can find a bow that suits you." I turned quickly to seek one out.

CHAPTER FIVE

When the Healer and Gallen rode into the courtyard, Ansel and I were washing up at the laver. He had outshot me with the long bow. I found his teaching skills to be exceptional as he shared his knowledge with such patience.

They brought home some roasted turkey legs and Dorsal's native dish of potatoes with chili peppers already prepared from one of the booths at the Gathering. Ravenous, we made short work of it.

Afterwards, we sat at the table and talked about the upcoming Dragon Rider Council, which was to take place the day after Ansel's eighteenth birthday ball at his manor in two weeks.

I was excited for the council. Eshshah and I would be officially sworn in as dragon and rider for the Royal House of Drekinn. The ball, on the other hand, scared me speechless. I'd never dreamed of attending a high social event. The thought of mixing company with the aristocracy terrified me. I voiced my fear.

"You have nothing to worry about, Amáne." Ansel assured, with a warm smile. "Trust me, you'll be the envy of all. And, you forget your position as dragon rider. You need to understand that Eshshah is of the royal dragon line. There is no dragon that ranks higher. Being her rider ranks you above all but a few of the riders. My aunt and Gallen both rode dragons of her line. Dorjan's Unule, who I'm sure was beautiful, was a common dragon in service to the king. Your station is above Dorjan. Unless King Tynan graces us with his presence, which is not likely, very few guests will outrank you."

"That might be fine, if it was publicized that I'm a rider. I'm a commoner as far as anyone there will know." I protested.

"No matter. The fact still remains." Ansel responded. "I don't care what the other guests say or think."

"But —"

Gallen broke in and changed the subject, "So, Lord Ansel, tell us, have you had the chance to speak with King Tynan and get an idea on his position? Will he join forces with us, you think?"

"I haven't had the opportunity yet to have an audience with him. My father and he were allies. I have no doubt that when the time is right and I reveal myself to him, he will lend us the help we need to overthrow Galtero."

Further discussion of petitioning King Tynan ensued. Ansel then told us about his involvement in the silk-growing business. Serislan is famous for their excellent quality of silk — a significant source of trade. The wealth of Serislan was largely built on textiles, mostly silk. King Tynan allowed Ansel his manor in exchange for overseeing the monarch's silk production business at that location. He'd done such a fine job that he drew the notice of the king. No doubt he would be summoned by him and could then disclose his true identity.

The conversation shifted once again, and to my dismay, I became the subject of our discussion. Gallen proudly informed Ansel, "You'll be happy to know that Amáne has been putting a lot of time and effort into her practice. Her skills have improved remarkably since you last saw her."

"I found that out first-hand today. She truly has mastered the defensive arts." He looked over at me and winked. I felt the heat rise in my face.

Before I could stop him, Gallen went on, "You don't know how much she's looking forward to procuring a dragon egg. She's been studying the maps of the castle every day with Dorjan. I think she knows that place as well as he does." I couldn't catch his eye in time, and I didn't feel it was good manners to kick him under the table, as I so wanted to do.

Ansel's face hardened; my chest constricted.

Gallen had no idea of Ansel's strong opposition to putting me into danger on such a quest. Sending me back into Castle Teravinea, after we barely escaped the last time, became a heated subject between us. I had done my best to avoid this topic today. Ansel's stay was so brief, I didn't want any item of contention to mar his visit — I planned to take it up with him during my visit to Trivingar.

Plans were already being formulated to get me back inside the castle. The Healer needed a dragon egg from the hatching grounds, and Eshshah and I were the only ones who could procure one for her. She had to determine what was preventing the eggs from hatching. The Healer, Gallen, Dorjan and Bern, another rider who lived near the City of Teravinea, were working with me. We had the start of a workable plan but we were not going to reveal it until the Council. I certainly would not even hint of our plans to Ansel before that time

Poor Gallen was quite uncomfortable when he noticed the expressions on Ansel's and my face. He realized he had moved to an unpleasant topic. The Healer quickly jumped in, "How are the plans for the festivities going for your upcoming birthday ball?"

It took a moment for Ansel to gather himself — I was still struggling to breathe.

With remarkable control in his voice, he answered, "My staff has been working on the final arrangements. I get the feeling they want very little input from me, which is the way I prefer. Festivities and balls are not activities I enjoy planning. I told them to just tell me what to wear and when to show up, and I'd be happy with whatever they came up with."

"Well," said the Healer, "I'm sure it will be magnificent. We're all very excited to come and celebrate with you, and to see your new home." Then standing up and taking the plates off the table, she said, "It will be dark soon. You should probably be preparing for your trip, Amáne. Is Eshshah going to hunt before you leave?"

"Yes, she said she'll fish and eat light before we go. She's leaving soon."

Gallen leapt up to help her clear the table. I shot him an angry glare as that left me sitting alone with Ansel. It was an awkward moment. I stole a glance at him. My heart melted as I caught him staring at his hands, brooding.

I put my hand gently on his arm. "Ansel, I'm sorry Gallen brought that subject up. Please don't worry. Everything is going to work out fine. I promise."

He turned to me and our eyes met. Managing a small smile, he put his hand on top of mine. It felt so warm and strong, like that's where it belonged.

I swallowed hard and willed my heart to be still as I eased my hand out from under his. "You'd better gather your things. We'll be leaving as soon as Eshshah comes back."

Rising from the table, I retreated to my chambers to change into warm clothing — we would be flying high in the frigid air. Two riders are no problem for Eshshah, but with the distance, it's easier for her to fly where the air is thinner. This time I wanted to be prepared for the cold. I had experienced more than one trip where my teeth chattered so badly, I was afraid they would break.

Pulling out the cloak that Ansel had found at the Dorsal Outpost, I smiled, recalling how regal he had looked in it. I closed my eyes, and held it to my face — his scent still lingered — a warmth rose in my chest as I remembered how he had shared it with me on our last flight, when I was numb from the freezing temperature. The heat from his body remained very alive in my memory. But, what was I thinking bringing that event back to mind? It weakened my resolve and reminded me that the walls around my heart were not nearly strong enough. I needed to make more of an effort to stand strong.

I wanted Ansel as a friend — I needed him as a friend, but the kingdom of Teravinea held me to my duty. Getting Ansel to the throne came first — before my happiness — even if it meant sacrificing our friendship.

I still had to consider my vow that I uttered in front of Dorjan and Gallen — that I would never fall in love. I must not give my heart to anyone, even to Ansel. Gallen told me at the time to keep an open mind, because trying to control my heart would be more difficult even than trying to control my temper — but I had to try. I couldn't jeopardize our quest. If Eshshah and I are successful and return with a dragon egg, then just maybe I'll rethink my vow. Until then, my feelings would stay in check.

Chapter Six

Eshshah brought me out of my thoughts, and let me know she had returned from her hunt. As usual, she was a part of my personal monologue and disagreed with my assessment. She felt the Healer had a point when she once told me that there is a fine line between happiness and duty. I, however, could not find that line.

I grabbed my own cloak as well as Ansel's and headed towards the kitchen.

"Here, I kept your cloak for you." I handed it to him.

He looked at me and his face lit up.

Then I held up my own cloak. "And look, now I have one as well."

His expression dimmed, like a flame that had been blown out. My heart wrenched. I realized he too must have been reminded of our last journey. *Did he entertain hopes of sharing it with me again?*

Fiona's words came back to me, "You are breaking that boy's heart!"

I looked at him ruefully and could only mouth, "I'm sorry."

He shrugged and forced a smile.

Eshshah waited for me in the courtyard, ready to be saddled. Gallen had a great idea to put wheels on the saddle stands to make it easier to bring them from their storage to the courtyard. It allowed me to get the saddle closer to Eshshah before I had to pick it up to throw on her. The double saddle was quite heavy and very awkward for me to handle — getting it from my small height up to the height of her shoulders. I could put any of the single saddles on easily, but I knew it would take a few tries to toss up the larger one.

My first attempt was unsuccessful. Eshshah did her best to help me by crouching low. After several failings, she suggested that I ask someone to help me. I was too stubborn, of course. I would rather do it myself than ask, so I continued to struggle.

Just as Ansel came out to the courtyard looking for me, I flung the saddle with all my might. This time it landed squarely on Eshshah's shoulders. Before I could glow in my accomplishment, one of the straps whipped back and lashed at my face, the buckle sliced a gash above my eye.

I grabbed my forehead and swallowed my cry of pain.

"Amáne! Are you okay?" Eshshah and Ansel asked simultaneously.

"That seems to be the question of the day." I mumbled.

Removing my hand, I inspected my blood-smeared fingers and said, "That's probably going to leave a scar."

Ansel brushed my hair away from my bloody face to inspect the gash. "It's not as bad as it looks." He shook his head and added, "I would ask why you didn't call Gallen or me to saddle Eshshah for you, but I already know the answer. You are the most obstinate person I've ever met."

"Annoying isn't it?" I offered.

"Very much so."

Eshshah then turned her head and breathed her healing warmth on my cut. She was just as irritated with me.

I ran in to wash up and left Ansel to finish securing the saddle. The Healer had filled a water skin, wrapped some travel cakes in parchment and packed them in a small satchel. It was time for us to leave. Eshshah's and my excitement was obvious. It had been a while since we had been on a flight of any distance. Flying together was our expression of true freedom.

I bid Gallen good bye and he kissed my forehead, then whispered an apology for bringing up a sore subject at the table.

"I forgive you." I whispered back, took his face and kissed both cheeks — a new custom for me that Ansel had started.

I gave the Healer a hug, kissed her cheeks, and then turned and mounted. I reached down and locked wrists with Ansel. He swung into the saddle. We buckled up, put on our helmets and lowered the eye shields as I gave Eshshah the word. She launched into the air in an upward spiral, and headed for the Arevale Outpost.

Waiting until we reached a height that was out of earshot from land, I closed my eyes, breathed in the fresh air and laughed out as loud as I could. I didn't care if Ansel thought I'd gone mad. Flying just had that effect on me. Eshshah rumbled her laughing sound and soon Ansel joined in. We were whooping and laughing until we were hoarse.

Eventually, we calmed down. Eshshah climbed to the frigid heights where it was easier for her to fly. I buried my face in my cloak and settled in for the long cold ride.

CHAPTER SEVEN

Eshshah woke me as we approached the Arevale Outpost. She started her descent while I shook off my stupor. I found I had dozed against Ansel.

"Sorry," I said over my shoulder, loud enough to be heard over the wind. "You must have been uncomfortable with me leaning back on you."

"Not at all." I heard the smile in his voice.

"If you and Eshshah are too tired to fly back to Dorsal, I have plenty of room in my apartments at the manor. I'm sure any of the women on my staff could get you whatever you need, and you can fly home tomorrow night." He sounded hopeful.

"Thank you, that's a very kind offer, but Eshshah is fine with flying back tonight. And besides, we'll be back here in two weeks."

I wasn't sure I could take him up on his offer anyway. My defenses had weakened and I needed to distance myself from Ansel. Should we have decided not to go home that night, Eshshah and I had the accommodations of the Arevale Outpost, which would have been more than comfortable for us.

The grassy field near the outpost appeared before us. We soared across the expanse that ended abruptly in a drop-off to a beach far below. Eshshah flew over the water before she banked right and headed back towards the cliffs. She found the push-rock that opened the stone door into the entry cavern of the outpost, and we flew in.

I whispered "Sitara" to illuminate the dragon scale light shields — the same lighting devices that hung in all of the outposts. We dismounted. As Eshshah curled up to nap near the ledge, Ansel and I proceeded to the library to contact Braonàn. I put my hand on the brass knob of the communication device and whispered, "Gyan," and then, "Yaron," Braonàn's true name as a dragon rider. Soon the disc shimmered with the colors of a prism, and then cleared to reveal Braonàn, rider of the late Volkan. He saluted.

"Greetings, Lord Ansel. Amáne. I'm thankful you've come back safely. The horses are ready. I'll be there in less than half an hour. Amáne, will you be accompanying us to the manor?"

"No, thank you, Braonàn. Eshshah and I are flying back to Dorsal tonight."

He gave Ansel a look that was supposed to mean something between them, but I couldn't decipher it. We signed off and went back to the entrance cavern.

Ansel and I sat on one of the stone couches and shared the travel cakes and water. We ate in the comfort of our silence. He and I had no need to speak, but only enjoy our last few minutes together.

Finally, I stood up and said, "Okay, Braonàn should be close. Are you ready to go?"

"No." He said quietly. He glanced up at me and opened his mouth as if to tell me something, but changed his mind. I looked at him, tilting my head, curious as to what he was about to say, but he just said, "All right, let's go."

I went over to Eshshah, rubbed her jaws and gave her a kiss. I asked in thought transference if she was up to flying back now or if she wanted to stay here for a couple of hours rest. We would still have enough darkness to make it home.

"I could fly all day and all night and not be weary, but you might want to consider Lord Ansel's offer. In two weeks he'll have a houseful of guests and won't be able to give you much attention. Don't you want to stay for just one night?"

"No!" I said out loud, without meaning to.

"I thought you said it was time to go," Ansel said, probably thinking I was responding to his 'Let's go.'

"I'm sorry, I was speaking to Eshshah." My bad habit of speaking to her out loud still bit me.

We got back into the saddle and I whispered "Sitara" to turn off the lights. After closing the outpost, we flew to the empty field. Ansel and I dismounted and headed towards the lane where Braonàn would be arriving.

We only had a few more minutes together when Ansel turned slowly and faced me. He took my face in his strong hands. Kissing my forehead and both cheeks, he draped his arms loosely over my shoulders and asked, "So, how did I do?"

"With what?"

"Complying with your ridiculous request to carry on as 'friends only.' I tried to keep it simple for you. No pressure. You mean you didn't even notice?" His shoulders dropped.

"Yes, I did notice! Thank you. I appreciate it, Ansel. See how easy that was?"

"Trust me, Amáne, it was not easy. Can you truthfully tell me that it was easy for you?" He raised one eyebrow waiting for my answer.

I would never have admitted this out loud, and I rejected my own inclination to even think it, but he was right — it was not easy. It frightened me that my resolve was not at the strength I needed it to be.

As I bit my lip, my heart fought for dominance over my necessity to remain detached. Truly, it was no small feat for me to hide whatever fondness I had for him — to adhere to my own rules of remaining strictly on a friendship level. But it was necessary. This entire day, when I thought I'd been successful in my efforts, it appeared that he saw right through me — again.

I couldn't honestly answer his question. I tried to avoid his eyes. Too late. Looking up in a weak moment, I was drawn fully into his ardent gaze. The battlements I had so carefully built around my heart were breached, the white flag of defeat already being raised.

A soft smile turned the corners of his mouth as he pulled me close. He found the answer he sought — albeit a silent one.

"I didn't think so," he whispered as he tilted his head and pressed his lips to mine. The warmth of his kiss wafted around me, forcing me to surrender without even a fight.

Our lips separated. His eyes shone with pure joy. "I'll take the victory on this round, if you don't mind."

"I concede." I said, angry with myself, yet still weak-kneed. "I'll fight harder next time," I promised. Pushing him away good naturedly, I said, "Now, just go! Here's Braonàn. I'll see you for your birthday."

He kissed my forehead and my cheeks again, turned lightly and headed for his horse — victory showing in his every step. I stood there frustrated as I watched him go. I squeezed my eyes shut and shook my head, reprimanding myself.

Weak, weak, weak! I didn't even try!

Eshshah just looked at me with her golden eyes. I knew she was satisfied that her rider had lost this round.

Chapter Eight

Dipping my brush into the creamy ceramic glaze, I applied it onto the piece I had spent the last few weeks working on for Ansel's birthday. Unable to afford an expensive gift, I wanted to give him something more personal — just from me. What better offering could I give? Clay, potter's wheels, kilns and glazes had been a part of my life — it was in my blood. My mother was a potter. And before her, her family had run the potter's guild of the City of Teravinea for several generations.

I sat in my mother's studio at our cottage studying my creation — admiring the goblet I had thrown on her potter's wheel. I'd formed two dragons and had attached them to the bowl of the goblet, noses touching while their tails intertwined down the stem. Quite satisfied, I couldn't wait to see Ansel's face when he opened his gift. But this thought brought me back to my dilemma.

Eshshah and I used the long flight home from the Arevale Outpost the previous night to discuss my situation. We had gotten nowhere as she insisted that I follow my heart, and I was adamant that I procure the dragon egg before I even thought about giving my heart the reins. We arrived back at the Healer's at early morning, just before light. I threw myself in bed for a few hours rest before running here to finish my goblet.

My mother's cottage was about a fifteen minute run from the Healers — outside the walls of Dorsal. I came here every so often to take a break from my training, to think, to get away. It was my sanctuary.

The thought had crossed my mind that maybe I should opt out of the birthday ball and send the goblet with the Healer and Gallen. But the Dragon Rider Council was the day after the ball — and that, I could not miss. Besides, it would hurt Ansel if I didn't attend his eighteenth birthday. He was, after all, my best friend.

The heat of the day dried the glaze in a short time. I decided I would load my piece in the kiln to complete the one last glaze firing. As I arranged the wood, I felt a twinge of pain in my head. My ankle started prickling. My stomach lurched as fear gripped my heart.

"Eshshah!" I called silently. "I can hear hoofbeats and men approaching. I'm having the same symptoms that I had at the gathering yesterday."

"I'm with you, Amáne. Get out of there now!"

The closer the hoofbeats, the more pain I experienced, which slowed my actions. Eshshah gave me her strength as I hurried out of the studio and headed towards the large rocks behind the cottage. There was a path I knew well where I could stay hidden while I made my way to the town walls and safety.

I reached the concealment of the boulders just as three horsemen arrived at my mother's cottage. They were the same three that had galloped behind me at the Master Brewer's tent. My ankle burned. Fever threatened to slow me even more. I stopped to catch my breath, leaning against the cool side of the rock. Something compelled me to peek around it, just to get another glimpse of the men. As I craned my neck to see, one of them jerked his head in my direction — the evil looking one who had caught my gaze yesterday as they galloped by.

A sorcerer, I thought.

I ducked back behind the rock, hoping I wasn't spotted. My heart beat at an unheard of pace. The pain and fever drained my energy.

"Amáne, I've alerted the Healer," Eshshah's urgent thoughts informed me. "She's sending Gallen to get you. You must make it to the road that leads to the East Gate. I'll offer you more of my strength. I've never shared this amount. I'm not sure how it will affect you, but it's necessary to get you away from those men."

"Who are they and what do they want?" I asked her as I felt a surge of her power enter my body.

"The Healer believes they're Galtero's men searching for the 'man' that entered his castle to rescue Lord Ansel. She's just received reports of three horsemen terrorizing the people of Dorsal. There have been injuries to several who tried to defend their families. Word is that they will search every household until the thief is found and brought back to the king. The Healer suspects that something about a prophecy has brought them to Dorsal."

I moved along the path and made good time with Eshshah's extra strength. But I found myself short of breath. I couldn't get enough air — my chest tightened. When I shared this with Eshshah, I felt her concern.

"Then that's how my extra power is affecting you, Amáne. I'm not sure which will slow you more, difficulty in breathing or your pain and fever."

"I think I can go faster without the pain."

It seemed that the further I moved away from the men, the less I hurt. My guess was that the sorcerer was somehow the root of my pain.

As my distance from the men increased, Eshshah began to withdraw her strength. Breathing became easier. The pain continued to decrease as the space opened between the sorcerer and me. I made it to the main road and turned to head towards where I would meet with Gallen and safety.

Without warning, my head felt like it would explode. I heard horses coming up the road behind me.

"Eshshah!" I at least had sense to call her via thought transference. She poured out her extra strength once again. Although my head and ankle were now manageable, breathing was difficult again. I hoped Gallen would find me before I became too light-headed.

The horsemen quickly approached. My fear increased. I had nowhere to hide. An idea came to me when I looked down and noticed the herb, Valeriana Officinalis growing at the side of the road. I bent down and began to pick it, feigning concentration on my task. When the horsemen came close enough that I could hear their horses breathing, I turned, looking surprised as they pulled up. Rising slowly, I made a concentrated effort to avoid fainting as my head spun.

"Hello kind sirs," I said innocently as I curtsied. My voice came out in a whisper.

"What have we here?" said the man on the nearest horse, as he leered at me.

I hoped my disgust didn't show.

"A fine wench from this backward township you call Dorsal. I have to say that the women here are easy to look at, and —"

"Borgen, enough," said one of his companions.

I regretted that I only had my dagger hidden in the folds of my skirt. Borgen repulsed me. But truthfully, my fear began to rise. On a fair fighting field I could easily take him, but I could feel the eyes of the sorcerer as they bored into me. Because of him I would not have full use of my skills. I found myself at a dangerous disadvantage.

The sorcerer emanated an air of power — I could feel it. Only with Eshshah's additional strength did I avoid his intense stare. If I looked at him, I feared he would have discovered my identity — dragon rider and the subject of their search. However, resisting his pull, probably drew his attention as well. I preferred this alternative over the terror of his gaze.

Ignoring his companion, Borgen dismounted and stood in front of me — closer than was proper. "What are you doing here alone, m'love?"

Stepping back slowly, I suppressed a shudder as he looked me up and down. I managed to keep my jaw from clenching. I fought for control to maintain my innocent pretense.

"I am a healer's apprentice, sir. I came to pick Valerian for her. My father is meeting me here momentarily." Starved for air, my voice came out weak.

"What is Valerian used for, girl?" The gravel-like voice of the sorcerer tested.

"It's a powerful sedative and a tranquilizer, my lord." I kept my eyes lowered.

He pulled his horse up closer to scrutinize me. Thanks to Eshshah, I could endure his presence. But she had to increase her power to fight his. My chest tightened even more, my breathing more laborious. *Where was Gallen?* I was on the edge of panic.

Out of the corner of my eye I could see the sorcerer lift his nose and sniff the air.

What if he caught the scent of Eshshah that permeates my hair? Without detection, I began to break up the Valerian which has a putrid, rotted cheese odor. It filled the air around me. I fought to keep from gagging, but it did the trick.

"I thought I detected a familiar spicy scent." The sorcerer continued to test me.

"I am a healer's apprentice," I repeated. "There are countless herbs and spices that I am immersed in daily, my lord," I said, thankful that the pungent odor of the herb now overtook any scent of Eshshah. I vowed to myself I'll never complain again whenever the Healer asks me to pick Valerian.

Borgen took a step towards me and reached out his hand to touch my face. Slowly, I transferred the herb to my left hand and lowered my right closer to my dagger. I made calculations in my head, planning my strategy to fight. I doubted, though, that I had the strength. My difficulty in breathing would be a major issue. I couldn't be certain that I could take Borgen down successfully — let alone, his companions. My best option would be to continue to hold back and hope that Gallen would arrive soon. Patience was not one of my stronger qualities. I closed my eyes and bit my lip.

At last Gallen appeared. I stepped back, away from Borgen's reach and allowed a silent song of thanks to drift though my mind.

"Eshshah, please tell Gallen that I am his daughter, Siri, apprentice to the Healer, if he is asked."

Gallen pulled up and immediately dismounted. He moved to where I stood and stepped between Borgen and myself in a smooth and unthreatening maneuver, then turned to me.

"Siri, you were not to stay out this long searching for herbs." He sounded angry. "The Healer is not happy at your delay. I would appreciate it if you would stop shaming your father, and follow the Healer's instructions." Then turning to the three men, but not looking directly at the sorcerer, he said, "She is such a chore. Thank you, sirs, she will not be bothering you any longer."

Leaving a look of confusion on Borgen and his companions' faces, he then boosted me up into the saddle, swung on behind me and without another word or glance in their direction, spurred the horse towards home.

After we had ridden some distance, Eshshah withdrew her power slowly as the pain in my head and ankle began to lessen on its own. I could breath again. I gulped in as much air as I could.

Relieved that Gallen had arrived just in time to remove me from danger, I turned to thank him. Before I opened my mouth, the sound of an explosion filled the air. I wheeled my head towards the direction of the blast. In disbelief my eyes fixed on the black smoke that billowed up from the spot at which my mother's cottage had stood. My hand flew to my mouth and covered the scream I could not stop. I watched in horror as I tried to understand what had just happened. Tears blurred my vision, but there was no mistake that my mother's cottage no longer existed.

Gallen held me tighter and coaxed his horse faster. At last we arrived in the courtyard where Eshshah waited for me. I leapt off the horse, ran to her and pressed my forehead against her nose. I held her fangs and sobbed as she hummed a calming tune. I held her like that for a while until the Healer came out and put her arm around me. She gently led me inside.

"Amáne, you need to prepare to leave. You and Eshshah will fly to the Dorsal Outpost the moment it gets dark. I have no doubts those men will be here looking for you. I can only hope they have enough other households to search before they arrive here."

"I want to stay with you and fight. Please don't make us leave!"

She took my face in her hands and drew my full attention. "Amáne, we are not ready to expose you and Eshshah. They cannot find you here. You will leave at dark. That's less than two hours. Now go. Prepare."

Chapter Nine

Grabbing supplies as quickly as I could, I filled my satchel with cheese, bread and potatoes. My pack with my clothes and other necessities lay on the floor near the kitchen door. I threw on my warmer tunic and tights. At the Healer's recommendation, I donned my fighting gear — my dragonscale breastplate, helmet, a sword in its scabbard at my waist, and my dagger ready at my back. My glaive — my spear — leaned against the wall. If the men arrived before dark, I was prepared to fight.

A noise and commotion in the apothecary shop at the front of the house startled me. My adrenalin flowed as I grabbed for my spear. The Healer drew her sword. Gallen called for her help. We both ran to assist him. The Healer and I reached the shop and found Gallen holding a limp form in his arms. Behind him were Rio and Mila. Tears streamed down their faces — their mother wailed behind them. I looked again at the limp form and recognized the blond hair.

"Fiona!"

"Three men came to our home," said their mother between sobs. "They were looking for something or someone. Then one of them grabbed Fiona, he was horrible, he hurt her ... and ... and ... my husband was mortally wounded defending her honor. But not before he killed that evil man." She crumpled to the floor.

I dropped my glaive and rushed to her aid. Helping her up, I led her to another room and tried to make her comfortable.

"Keep your eyes on her," I told the twins. "I'm going to get her some tea to help her relax."

I caught the open-mouth stares from Rio and Mila as they took in my attire. The day before, they had seen me dressed in an expensive silk gown. Today, my clothing was as opposite as moon and sun. I offered no explanation, but rushed out of the room.

I brought back the tea and made sure the family was comfortable, then helped the Healer attend to Fiona. Another disturbance interrupted our efforts as bootsteps rang outside the door. Glaive in hand, I ran into the entry of the shop just as the door flung open. I crouched into my fighting stance as Gallen rushed to join me. I froze.

"Kail!"

Taken aback, he stared at me as I stood in front of him in full fighting gear. He could just barely get out my name.

Anger replaced my relief. "You could have at least tried to enter a little more civilly and not try to break the door down! We might have hurt you."

His face changed from bewilderment to one of concern. "Where's Fiona?"

"She's okay. The Healer is with her."

Kail tried to get past me, but I stepped in front of him, my spear up in a block. He seemed stunned by my action and stepped back.

"Amáne, I have to see her." He lost his strong façade and looked so vulnerable for a brief moment. "Did they hurt her? Did they touch her?"

"Kail, she's in good hands now," I said more gently, "but just so you know, her father now rests with his ancestors because he defended her honor. Believe me, Kail, he defended her well. She's a bit bruised and still in shock, but she'll be fine."

He made one more attempt to step around me. I held firm. "You know her well enough, Kail, do you think she would want you to see her now? Of course not. Her mother and sisters could use your support."

"I'll stay with them for a bit, but then I'm going to find those men and I'll slaughter them like the pigs they are." His face turned purple with rage. I knew what Kail was like when he was angry.

"You need to calm down Kail. You may not even have to go looking for them because we believe they'll be heading this way."

"What's going on, Amáne? What are they looking for and why are you dressed for battle? And since when have you fought with a spear?"

I turned to Gallen with a silent plea to help me out. He put his arm around Kail and led him to another room. I was free to finish my preparations for Eshshah's and my departure.

Chapter Ten

Eshshah was saddled and waiting for me in the courtyard. Everything was ready for us to leave, and darkness had finally fallen.

The Healer had contacted Dorjan who rushed over immediately. He whispered farewell to me, then occupied Kail in conversation while the Healer and Gallen walked me out to the courtyard.

"Healer, please let me stay and fight. I feel like such a coward, running." At that same moment, my head began to hurt and my ankle heated up.

"They're near!" My fingers pressed against my temples as I doubled over in pain.

"Amáne you would be of little help to us the way the sorcerer's powers affect you. And as I said before, we cannot risk exposure. Not yet." In a commanding voice, she said, "Mount up now and do not return until we contact you that it's safe. Let us know when you arrive."

They both kissed me on the forehead before Gallen helped me up in the saddle. I gave Eshshah the word, and we were off.

As soon as we arrived at the Dorsal Outpost, we rushed into the library. I put my hand on the knob of the communication disc and whispered, "Gyan," and then "Nara," for the Healer. I received no response. Then I tried "Gyan," and "Kaelem," for Gallen. Nothing. Lastly, I tried for Dorjan and still no shimmer from the disc. It had been less than half an hour. Why were they not answering? I tried to convince Eshshah that we had to fly back and see if they needed our help.

Panic rose in my chest. Not knowing what was going on at the Healer's was torture. I begged Eshshah to take me back home, but she could not be convinced. Instead she suggested I try to contact Braonàn. The Healer had advised him of the situation in Dorsal. He may have heard some news from them.

Braonàn's face appeared in the disc and we went through the formalities of saluting and greeting. He hadn't heard from the Healer, yet, either. I caught him up on the events that occurred before we departed and informed him that I needed to fly back to Dorsal.

Ansel appeared by Braonàn's side. I quickly dismissed my heart as it fluttered at the sight of him. This was not the time to deal with that issue. Ansel had heard my quick summary of how I'd escaped the Healer's. Concern shown on his face when I repeated that I couldn't make contact with anyone there.

"Ansel, I want to fly back to the Healer's. We have to help them."

"Did the Healer give you any instructions, Amáne?" he asked calmly.

I sighed, dropping my shoulders.

"She told me not to return until they contacted us that it's safe."

He shook his head and a corner of his mouth curved up. "I seem to recall an incident where you attempted to follow your friend's advice. What was it? — something like it's better to do what you want and ask for forgiveness after, than to ask for permission beforehand? Did you not learn anything from that fiasco? My advice is to follow the Healer's orders."

I wanted to snap back at him for reminding me of that event. That would have been disrespectful, especially in front of Braonàn, so I kept my temper in check. Even so, I couldn't control my tongue.

"But you have no idea how I feel hiding here, safe, in exile, while others risk their lives for me." Before the last word left my lips, I gasped, realizing what I'd just said. At the same moment his eyebrows raised and he opened his mouth to respond.

I cut him off, "Ansel. I'm so sorry. Of course you know." He had lived his entire life under this very same circumstance — others risking their lives for him. I silently reprimanded myself. My outburst didn't gain me any ground.

"So, you have a different perspective when the tables are turned, don't you, Amáne?" A 'now-you-see-how-I-feel' tone in his voice.

"But it's not the same, Ansel, I —"

"Amáne, I will not have this conversation with you now." He radiated an air of authority. I had to remind myself who he truly was — heir to the throne. Arguing with him was wrong. I had to bring that bad habit to an end.

"I'm sorry." I bowed my head, truly contrite and determined to show the respect he deserved. It was my duty. This contact should have nothing to do with me and my quest. It was about our concern for what was happening in Dorsal.

Ansel's face softened as he redirected our conversation, "I'm sure they're fine. Maybe the communication disc is not working. Just wait there until you hear from someone, all right?"

"Yes, Ansel."

"Amáne, promise me you will do as the Healer ordered." He tilted his head at me in an urgent plea.

"Yes," I closed my eyes, as I exhaled the word. "I promise."

"Thank you. They'll be fine, Amáne." He threw me a reassuring smile — it wasn't as genuine as he tried to make it. His anxiety showed through. "Please let me know when you hear from them, and when you leave the outpost."

We signed off and I went back to pacing — my stomach felt like I had swallowed a bucket of worms.

Chapter Eleven

The sorcerer shouted at me. His evil eyes penetrated into the very core of my identity — calling me out — exposing me as the thief. He repeated the same meaningless words in a grating, rasping voice. I awoke to find myself at a table in the library at the Dorsal Outpost. My head rested on my crossed arms. I couldn't believe I had dozed off. I realized that the unintelligible words were actually the communication disc buzzing. Shaking the fuzziness from my head, I rushed to the disc.

Dorjan appeared in the glass, and he looked dreadful. Burned and bruised, anguish written on his face.

"Dorjan! What's happened? Is everyone all right?"

"It's over, Amáne. The king's men are no longer a threat, but at no small cost."

My heart felt like someone had yanked it from my chest. My throat tightened.

"Gallen has been injured — perhaps mortally."

"No! Eshshah and I are leaving now! Please tell Ansel."

And with that, we signed off. I leaped up on the saddle, buckling in as Eshshah rushed to the entry and dove from the ledge. The communication disc barely had time to fade. Eshshah pushed herself to speeds she had never before attained. Sick with worry, we couldn't anticipate what we might find at the Healer's.

We arrived in no time and rushed into my chambers to find Gallen laid up in my bed — burned almost beyond recognition. The stench of burning flesh filled my sensitive nose. It took all of my concentration to keep from vomiting. The Healer, at his side, looked as battered as Dorjan. She held Gallen's right hand where there seemed to be the least damage. Gallen had burns over thirty percent of his body, mostly on his left side.

Kail sat silently in the corner with the same battle-worn appearance as the Healer and Dorjan. His jaw dropped when we ran in. Like me, he had believed in dragons — not fooled by the current teachings. Nevertheless, his head jerked at seeing a full-size one enter the room. He immediately jumped up and saluted us. Shocked that he knew the protocol, Eshshah and I both nodded back to him as we headed to Gallen's bedside.

Eshshah wasted no time. She directed her attention to the left side of his chest where the injury appeared most severe. Blackened flesh clung to his ribs — the damage deep. She breathed her healing breath on him as she hummed. I was drawn in to join her, and held my hands above his leg. Closing my eyes, I hummed with Eshshah, melding myself with her in hopes I could offer her my strength. Although a small offering, it came from my heart.

Energy radiated through my hands. I couldn't determine if it came from Eshshah or from me. The Healer silently cried while holding Gallen's hand to her lips. The intensity of the healing increased, as did Eshshah's and my concentration. My hands became uncomfortably warm, but I did not let up. The treatment went on for quite a while. My hands at first got red and then my palms began to blister.

"Amáne, you can stop if it's too much for you."

"No, Eshshah, I can take the pain, and if it will help Gallen, I won't stop."

Gallen, who at first had been moaning, now began to breathe more evenly and a sigh finally escaped. Eshshah eased up. She pulled away and I did the same. I felt drained, yet relieved to see a noticeable improvement in him. We were convinced he would live. I sung a silent song of thanks.

Eshshah then tended to my hands and advised I get some rest. We would need to do several treatments throughout the rest of the night. I didn't think I would be able to stay awake for much longer, but I needed to speak with Kail for a few minutes.

Kail had left my chambers earlier, while we were still tending to Gallen. I found him sitting on a surviving bench in the midst of the destruction that was once the Healer's beautiful library — a blank stare on his face. My heart sank as I saw so many of her books in ashes. Kail saw me coming and started to salute.

"Kail, you don't need to do that every time you see me."

"Wow, Amáne," he whispered, still in shock, "who are you?"

"I know, hard to believe, right?"

"I should have seen it coming all those years I worked with you," he said. "You were so different than anyone else. You always had a fire in you — a spirit that lit your eyes."

I'd heard a similar description of myself before, and my mouth lifted on one side in a barely perceptible smile.

"Gallen will live, Kail. Eshshah has remarkable healing powers."

Kail exhaled with relief.

I eased myself onto the bench next to him. Bending over, I picked up a charred map of Castle Teravinea that I had only recently been studying. It crumbled in my hand leaving a sooty stain on my palm. I examined the black smudge as I felt a tear trickle down my cheek.

Still studying my palm, I said, "Stop staring at me, Kail, I'm still the same Amáne you've always known."

"Sorry. It's just hard to take it all in — there's been three dragon riders living in Dorsal all my life and I never knew. And now I find out that you're one ..."

"No one knew ... and that fact still remains." I looked at him pointedly.

"Yes, I know, Dorjan already swore me to secrecy."

"So, Kail, tell me — what happened here?"

He took a deep jagged breath, "Not three minutes after you left the room, two men burst in the door of the shop. One of them was a sorcerer — the most wicked person I've ever seen or felt. Evil so strong, you could actually feel it."

I shuddered and nodded, fully aware of what he meant.

"Dorjan told me to take care of the sorcerer's companion who had drawn his sword as soon as he saw us. It looked like he hadn't been expecting a fight because he didn't have his shield. He fared well enough without it, though. That was the first time I was glad I had so many older brothers. They used me for fighting practice from the day I could walk. It only made me a better fighter. Even so, there were a few minutes that I doubted myself.

"Dorjan, Gallen and the Healer dealt with the sorcerer. That Healer can wield a blade. The sorcerer had a sword, but he also used some kind of dark magic. He started hurling balls of fire at them. How they avoided so many, I couldn't tell you — I was kind of busy myself. I finally got the advantage and dispatched my man."

Kail remained silent for a moment. "It was the first human life I've taken. I always thought I would feel powerful after I'd sent an enemy to their ancestors. But it didn't feel that way at all. I hope you never have to experience that, Amáne. I don't know if it gets easier, but you don't want to know."

A shadow crossed my face as I thought about the man in the guardroom of Castle Teravinea, what felt like so long ago. The look on his face when he realized he'd been defeated and would soon be meeting his ancestors. That vision will always haunt me. He was my first ... and no, it was not a good feeling. I remembered my nausea and emptying the contents of my stomach afterwards. My second and my third men — they were not easy either. I'm ashamed to admit they were different, almost not as hard. I assisted in taking one more life, and truthfully, I blocked any further feeling.

Kail noted that I struggled with my thoughts. I could tell he knew I understood what he spoke about. He didn't comment, but continued his story.

"I joined in their fight with the sorcerer and dodged a few fire balls myself. Then the sorcerer hurled one straight at the Healer. She lunged in the wrong direction and would have received a direct hit, but Gallen jumped in front of her and —" Kail's voice cut short as he fought for control. Horror showed on his face as he relived that moment. "He burst into flames. The smell of burning flesh ... I can still smell it. I remember yelling at the sorcerer and I did a stupid thing. I charged him. When he turned to look at me, it gave Dorjan an opening. I've never seen anyone move that fast. He leapt behind the sorcerer and ran him through." Kail demonstrated by plunging an imaginary sword with a thrusting motion.

He shook his head slowly. "I've always known him as the town blacksmith. I had no idea he held such power behind a sword."

I nodded. "Dorjan is a master swordsman."

Kail looked spent after relaying his story of the battle. He paused again and swallowed. He blinked hard in an effort to control the tears that filled his eyes. I put my hand on his arm and told him. "Go ahead, Kail, just let it out. It's cleansing."

I don't know why men can't understand that. I could see he was angry with himself and this unknown emotion. But he heeded my words, and dropped his head into his hands as his shoulders shook. I stroked his hair — the only way I knew to offer him support.

He sat up and wiped his dirty sleeves across his dirty face, smearing it more. Breathing a heavy sigh, he bent his head back and stared at the ceiling.

"Dorjan and I then carried Gallen to your chambers. Afterwards, we took the two bodies to the crematorium, and cleaned the blood off the floor. I didn't want Fiona or her family to see what we had done.

"Then Dorjan went home to contact you, since what he called the communication disc was disabled. He said he'll return later tomorrow — that would be today, I guess."

He looked at me, shrugged and said, "That's about it, Amáne. I thought you were going to fight with us. Where did you go?"

"I had to leave so I wouldn't get caught here. It would have ruined the plans that the riders have been working on for so long. Eshshah and I are basically in hiding. I felt awful leaving while you risked your lives for us, but I had to follow orders. Thank you, Kail."

"I'm glad I'm a part of whatever is going on. You can count me in." Then he turned to me and took in my appearance, "You look like you're ready to collapse, Amáne. Go get some rest."

Chapter Twelve

The remainder of the night passed in a blur, except for the last healing session near dawn. Eshshah and I had come to the end of Gallen's treatment and were happy with our progress. He was healing remarkably well.

Drained and exhausted, I wasn't sure I could even crawl back to my bedding on the floor with Eshshah.

Gallen stirred, and cried out, "Nara!"

"I'm here Kaelem," the Healer responded, as she sat on the bed next to him.

"Don't leave me, Nara."

"I won't."

I raised my eyebrows at that interchange but kept my thoughts to myself ... and Eshshah. I don't think they were aware that I was in the room.

I woke up a few hours later pleased to see Gallen sitting up in bed, the Healer beside him. They were deep in a quiet conversation. I couldn't make out their words — I wasn't fully awake. My eyelids, too heavy to hold open, closed as I fell back into my dreamless sleep.

At midday I awoke alone on the floor in my chamber. My bed was stripped and candles were lit— the scent of lemon grass, rosemary, sage and lavender oil filled the room. Eshshah sunned herself in the courtyard. She informed me that Dorjan had arrived while I slept. He and the Healer had helped Gallen upstairs to his room. Kail had taken Fiona and her family back to their home.

I made my way up to Gallen's chambers and found him with Dorjan and the Healer in serious discussion. Eshshah's healing powers had assured his recovery. It would probably take a while for his scars to heal completely. His handsome face had been spared. Hopefully, his once-beautiful blonde hair will grow back. I silently sang a song of thanks to see he had taken well to the treatments.

They stopped talking when I entered the room, which made me uncomfortable. Maybe they were having a discussion about me, or about something to which I was not privy. I excused myself and turned to leave.

"Amáne, don't leave, please come in," said Gallen. "I've thanked Eshshah a dozen times, but haven't had a chance to thank you for saving my life. You seem to have acquired the healing powers of your dragon."

"It wasn't me, it was all Eshshah, but I'm pleased to see you looking so well."

He shook his head, "No, Amáne. It was you, along with Eshshah. The two of you worked together and believe me, if it weren't for you two, I would either be with my ancestors, or wish I were. Thank you."

I didn't want to argue with him, and wasn't about to contradict his belief that I had any kind of healing powers. It was all Eshshah.

I just did what I could for him. I smiled, nodded and headed to his bedside to give him a gentle hug and a kiss. He kissed my forehead. The Healer looked at me with unprecedented gratitude. I felt a change in her. She looked younger at that moment. Moving to the other side of the large bed where she sat, I put my arms around her and gave her a long hug.

"The Dragon Rider Council is less than two weeks away," said Dorjan, "and we were just discussing that we need to finalize our plans to get you back into the castle for a dragon egg. We'll have to lay out our strategy to propose to Lord Ansel. We like your idea, Amáne, and Bern is already working on his part. You've met Bern on the communication disc. He's in Anbon, not far from the City of Teravinea and has started making the arrangements. We believe this can work.

"As I've mentioned before, we have a man inside. He's high up in Galtero's court. We don't know his identity, but Bern does. A short time after Galtero took the throne, this man, we only know him as Ellard, contacted Bern. He told him he's regretted playing a part in Galtero's plans when he took the throne. To make up for it, he decided he'd side with us, but remain in his position in the king's court. He's been an indispensable ally for many years in our efforts to end Galtero's reign. We plan to tell him soon that the heir to the throne lives and that there is now a dragon rider in Teravinea. Ellard will help us in your quest for the egg, Amáne." Dorjan continued. "Does this still sound like a mission to which you'd agree?"

"You know it does. I've never wanted anything more in my life. My only concern is that Ansel ... I mean Lord Ansel ... will overrule my quest. He's already said as much."

"Well, we'll have to ensure that won't happen. We'll be successful. Of that I'm certain."

Chapter Thirteen

I didn't even try to stop my flow of tears as I shuffled through the ashes of what was once my mother's cottage. I found hardly anything salvageable in all of the rubble. A few walls were left standing. They reminded me of the weathered rib bones of whales that had washed up on our shores. Most everything was destroyed. A half-melted piece of jewelry here, a broken piece of pottery there. Everything gone. My entire childhood — gone.

Dorjan had ridden to the cottage with me because the Healer wouldn't allow me to go alone. I needed to see what was left of my home — I had to face one more outrage after the terror of the last two days.

The cottage had been my last refuge where I could be close to my mother. I could sit at my table with a cup of tea and imagine that she sat with me. I could confide in her — where the sound of her voice still lingered. But now, just the muffled sound of my footsteps in the ashes remained.

As I surveyed the destruction, my mother's final blessing came back to me, "Amáne, accept whatever befalls you, in great misfortune be patient."

I let my head fall back and searched the sky, "How much misfortune do I have to endure before I no longer need to be patient?" I wanted to scream these words at the birds overhead, at the broken walls around me, at the boulders that had shielded me, but I felt it wasn't right to upset Dorjan. Already pacing anxiously, he looked unsure of how to handle my dark mood. So, instead, I swallowed the words and kept them to myself.

I felt myself easing into depression and self pity, and made no effort to stop it. Eshshah had allowed me to wallow, for which I was thankful. Wandering through the destruction, I found the spot where our kitchen table had been. I slumped down in the cinders. A little cloud of ash whirled up around me.

Many hours were spent at this table where my mother told me about her life in the city of Teravinea before she came here with my father, Duer. She had fallen in love with him and for some unknown reason Duer had taken her from the city she loved and brought her here to Dorsal, the farthest corner of the kingdom. To this place, where you had to be born to understand its harshness and its beauty. How difficult must that have been for her?

And then, as if that wasn't hard enough, he left. Whether or not he knew that I was conceived, he left her here, alone — and let her believe he had more important things to do in working for Galtero. He promised her he would return, and made her promise she would not leave Dorsal. She went to her ancestors still waiting for him. There were times when I caught a sadness in my mother's eyes that she couldn't hide. I believed that had he stayed, she wouldn't have had to work so hard. She would still be here, I would have siblings, we would have been the family I longed for. For these reasons I loathed the man. I never told my mother, but there was a vengeance buried deep in a small black corner of my heart, that if

I ever were to meet Duer, I would first make him understand what he had done — shown him what he had missed, and then I would gladly send him to his ancestors. No, I would wish that he never found his ancestors. I should have been ashamed that thought had ever crossed my mind, but at that moment, I had no remorse.

Were my feelings of abandonment related to the struggle I'd been having with my feelings for Ansel? I knew my quest had a lot to do with keeping him at a distance, but what if that was just a surface reason? What if my true fear lay in the possibility that he would abandon me after I'd fully given him my heart — like my father did to my mother? This thought struck me, heavily — my chest constricted, an iron fist gripped my heart. I couldn't breathe, and this time, I could not swallow my next word.

"No!" I cried out loud.

Dorjan rushed to my side, blade drawn. He scanned our surroundings and seeing that there was no danger present, he said, "Get up, Amáne. I'm taking you home, now."

Broken, I didn't argue. He pulled me to my feet. I didn't even dust the ashes off, but numbly allowed him to lead me to the horses.

After a deep breath, trying to pull myself together, I said, "Wait, Dorjan, let me just walk over here for a minute." Without waiting for his response, I pulled my hand out of his and headed towards the last place I had been that fateful day, before I had to run from the sorcerer and his companions. Poor Dorjan looked like he couldn't decide what to do with me, but he let me go without protest.

Walking in the ruin of my mother's studio, my boot kicked something solid. I stooped down and dug through the ashes. My heart lightened as hope began to show its rays. I blinked the tears away to see what I didn't think possible — in my hand was the dragon goblet on which I had worked so hard for Ansel's birthday. I couldn't believe it. I found it in near-perfect condition. Not broken. It's final firing completed by the inferno that had destroyed everything else. I used my skirt to wipe it off, and admired the effect the ashes had given the glaze — a unique dark finish.

I stood up slowly and held the goblet in front of me. The dark cloud that had been wrapped around me began to fade as I gazed upon the two dragons, nose to nose, having risen from the ashes.

"What did you find, Amáne?" Dorjan came over and I showed him the goblet.

"I made this for Ansel's ... Lord Ansel's birthday," I whispered, "and it survived." I hugged it to my chest. "I'm ready to go back to the Healer's now, Dorjan."

His face softened, "Amáne, when the time is right we'll help you rebuild this place."

I looked up at him as my eyes filled. Allowing a slight smile, I placed the goblet carefully in my satchel, then turned towards the horses.

Eshshah was waiting for me when we arrived back in the courtyard, concern in her thoughts. I hugged her tight, and she hummed to me.

"I don't like the dark spot on your heart that you've saved for Duer," Eshshah admonished, "nor the depths of where you've just been."

"I don't like it either, Eshshah, but I'm not sure what I can do about it."

"It's called forgiveness, Amáne."

I had no response.

We went straight to our chambers and I shared with Eshshah the few things I had salvaged. I washed the ashes off the goblet, set it on the table, and stepped back to gaze at it.

"It's beautiful. I know that Lord Ansel will love it," she said.

My mother's necklace beside the goblet still had a few stones left in it. It gave me a great idea. I replicated what Ansel had done with the walking stick he carved with Eshshah's likeness. I attached a set of green and amber stones to the eyes of the dragons. I nodded, quite pleased with the results.

Chapter Fourteen

The Healer, Gallen and Dorjan, along with his wife and young son, planned to leave the following day for Trivingar. It should take them four days on a fast merchant ship. The Healer had decided that it wouldn't be safe for Eshshah and me to remain in Dorsal by ourselves. We would leave tonight for the Dorsal Outpost. I didn't want to arrive at Ansel's manor too much in advance — the less I saw of him before the Council, the better I thought my chances that he would allow our quest. The first and most important priority was for the success of our mission to bring back a dragon egg.

Eshshah and I planned to stay at the Dorsal Outpost for five days and leave for the Arevale Outpost the day before the ball. I figured that day would find Ansel too busy to pay much attention to me. Then, of course, the ball would require his full attention, after which was the Rider's Council. If I could stay out of his way until the Council, I hoped he would give us his blessings — or at the least, his approval.

My desire was to see our quest completed before I could consider rethinking the contradictions of my heart. Suddenly, my fear of abandonment that had immobilized me that day at my mother's cottage returned. Before panic could set in, I took a deep breath and willed the doubts from my head. This was a matter that would have to reside in another corner of my heart, to be dealt with at a later time. It was hard to believe that Ansel's and my friendship had gotten even more complicated.

As we all gathered in the courtyard at dark to say farewell, Gallen put his arms around me and kissed my forehead and then saluted. I saluted him back, "Gallen, you don't know how happy I am that you've healed so well. If the Healer can spare you," I shot a smile at her, "please save a dance for me at the ball. I'll be your partner for a pavane. I think it's a slow enough dance, and if they don't elaborate, I might be able to perform it without tripping over my feet."

"It would be my pleasure. I'll make sure you don't miss a step."

The only evidence left from Gallen's brush with death was a slight limp and some scarring. We were all fortunate he would be making the trip in such good health. I shuddered as I recalled the condition in which we had found him only a short time ago.

Dorjan then gave me a strong fatherly hug, kissed my forehead and we saluted each other. "I think I might be jealous unless you promise me one dance. I'm sure my wife would appreciate the break. I'd prefer a little livelier dance than the pavane, though, maybe the galliard?"

I laughed and said, "I think that one might be a little difficult for me. You're forgetting I'm from Dorsal, and I've never been to a ball. I'm more comfortable with the jig. Do they play jigs at courtly balls?"

"Yes, they do. It would be a dull feast if they didn't. Then it's settled. I'll seek you out for the first jig."

"Deal."

Lastly, I gave the Healer a long hug and we kissed both cheeks.

"Please contact us when you arrive, Amáne and we'll do the same when we arrive in Trivingar."

Gallen gave me a leg up, I buckled in, gave the word and Eshshah and I were on our way. Excitement coursed through us as we headed to our outpost, looking forward to our time alone with each other. As usual, flying with Eshshah always exhilarated me. Nothing could compare. I held myself in check until we were over the water and far enough away from land, and then I let myself loose, whooping and screaming with the joy of our freedom.

Our days at the outpost went quickly. We were always busy. I worked on my strikes and thrusts with my spear, practicing on the poor scrub trees. I couldn't bring myself to use the dragon trees on the island for practice. They were too special to me, but the other trees and shrubs knew no mercy. I also practiced some shadow sparring. We ran through our tail mounts and wing mounts, ecstatic that we were able to take off after each one. Here, no one would see us and we could fly in broad daylight without a worry.

We swam in the warm waters, and I even managed to get some angling in. One of the days, we spent stranded inside as a Valaira reminded us of her fury. But I used that time to study the maps and castle floorplans that were in the library. I decided I'd have to bring some of the books and maps back to the Healer's to replace those that had been destroyed during the fight.

CHAPTER FIFTEEN

We traveled across the kingdom on a moonless flight towards the most northwestern corner of Teravinea. A few hours remained before dawn when we landed at the Arevale Outpost. We made our way to the first chamber and I fell into bed. Anxiety worked my stomach into knots as I anticipated the activities of the next few days. I didn't know what to expect at the manor, other than the fact that I would feel completely out of place. I was, in truth, quite ignorant of how to carry myself amongst nobility. I had rarely come into contact with the few who oversaw Dorsal. Sleep became difficult. When I finally closed my eyes, my nightmares returned with a vengeance. Fires, creatures, raging seas, and evil ladies dressed in finery. I was awakened by my own screams.

Eshshah soothed me. I fell back into a fitful sleep and awoke late morning to the sound of the communication disc buzzing in the distance. Still disoriented, I rushed to the library and put my hand on the knob. The Healer appeared with concern on her face, which shifted to relief when I came into view.

"Amáne, you were supposed to contact us when you arrived at Arevale."

"I'm sorry, Healer. We arrived in the middle of the night and I didn't want to disturb you. I had planned on contacting you as soon as it got light, but I guess I overslept."

She gave me a shake of her head, but only said, "I'll let Ansel know you've arrived."

My heart skipped at the mere mention of his name. I sincerely hoped I was ready to face him. I must confine my heart and strengthen my resolve. Our quest depended upon it.

Changing into one of my two best gowns, my stomach rippled in panic. I worried that they were too outdated. Never one to be concerned with fashion, now I couldn't help but feel inadequate and out of place when it came to dressing as a guest of a lord. *What if I embarrassed Ansel?* I wished I had confided in Fiona for her help in choosing something more befitting. It was too late for that. I brought my beautiful blue silk gown that Ansel had given me. I planned on wearing it for the ball tomorrow night, but what if that was too plain for the feast? My anxiety grew. I bit my lip as I gathered my pack and satchel and rode Eshshah bareback down to the field.

The sound of horses approaching triggered my heart to beat wildly. Closing my eyes, I breathed in and made an effort to calm myself. I fought for control of my unexpected anticipation of seeing Ansel again. More than just an eagerness to see a friend — it took me by surprise.

A devastating wave of disappointment shot through me as Braonàn appeared from around the bend ... alone, with only a horse for me. I felt out of control as my spirit shifted to fight the opposing emotion. Composing my face as quickly as I could, I saluted

Braonàn, and tried to convince myself that it was to my advantage that Ansel hadn't come.

"Greetings, Amáne. Lord Ansel sends his regrets that he couldn't be here to show you to his home. A rather troublesome guest required his attention and he could not evade her demand. He'll see you once you're settled."

I had to swallow the lump that rose in my throat. I somehow managed to nod and force a smile of understanding. Meanwhile, I questioned my emotions. *Why was I so upset?*

Braonàn dismounted, and after greeting Eshshah, took my pack and satchel, then looked around for more. "This is all you have? Just these two bags?" He was incredulous. "Perhaps our lady guests could use some instruction from you. The amount of trunks and bags for such a short stay have worn out the boys assigned to assist them." He boomed with laughter.

I groaned silently to Eshshah, dreading any contact with those ladies. Hugging her goodbye, I mounted the horse Braonàn held for me and we headed for Trivingar Manor.

We rode out of the woods, rounded a corner and the manor house came into view. It took my breath away — it was magnificent. Larger than anything in Dorsal. The red roof contrasted against the blue sky, and the two towers on either side with bluegreen domed roofs made the most striking impression.

A wave of nausea rolled through me as the towers loomed above. I found myself angry at the Healer for not training me in dealing with nobility. I fought the urge to turn my horse around and return to Eshshah. I'd always thought myself strong, but here I was cowering like a little girl. I took a deep breath and looked forward to the sanctuary of my chambers where I planned to hide until the ball the next night.

The doors swung open to the entry of the manor. My awe at the magnificent portal increased as I took in the interior — majestic as well as daunting. I felt my lowly position as Braonàn ushered me inside. We ascended the staircase to the left and proceeded down a long corridor. A young boy approached us, bowed to Braonàn, and after a hesitant glance up and down at me, he bowed to me as well. Evidently he decided that if I was accompanied by Braonàn, I might deserve a bow. I wanted to melt into the nearest tapestry.

The boy whispered something to Braonàn and then took his leave with one more quick bow in my direction. Braonàn turned to me and quite apologetic said, "Amáne, I'm so sorry, but something urgent has come up. Please wait here and I'll get someone to take your things and show you to your chambers."

"There's no need for that, Braonàn, just tell me where my room is and I'll find it." Already humiliated by my appearance, I couldn't bear for anyone else to scrutinize me. He hesitated, but didn't argue.

He pointed down the corridor and said, "Please forgive me, Amáne, but if you insist. The guest apartments are in that direction. At the next hallway, turn left and your chambers will be the last door on the left."

I thanked him, picked up my bags and hurried as fast as I could to find my room. Before I could get to the hallway where I was to turn left, I cringed. Heading towards me strolled an elegantly dressed young lady, maybe about my age, or a bit older. I wouldn't reach the turn before our paths crossed. My only hope was that she would think I belonged on the manor's staff and would ignore me. To my dismay, I realized she purposefully drifted to my side of the corridor. Her face, though it could be beautiful, looked quite hostile. I glanced behind me to see if maybe she was directing her stare at someone else. There was no one behind me.

The lady stopped in my path. She wore a beautiful silk gown that had a revealing neckline. It had a tight-fitting bodice that forced her ample breasts up to where more of hers was protruding than I could ever hope to have in total. She looked me up and down with utter disdain, shook her head and made a "tsk tsk" noise.

Tossing her hair back with her hand, she said, "You must be Amáne," she practically spat out my name. I'd never met this girl before. *What could be bothering her? Was her anger directed at me? How did she even know who I was?*

"Yes, and you are ...?" I was at a loss as to how to handle this situation. I did nothing to provoke her, but she continued to glower at me. Managing to maintain control of my temper, I forced a smile on my face — but my instincts kicked in. I needed to be on my guard. I lowered my bags to the floor in case I needed to defend myself. It occurred to me that this might be a silly overreaction — this was Ansel's home. I couldn't imagine any one of his guests, especially one of her station, initiating a fight. But I had to go with my gut feeling. She had a wild look in her eyes. I didn't trust her.

"Well, if you are truly Lord Ansel's *friend*," and she emphasized the word 'friend,' "he certainly has told you about me."

Unable to find my voice, I shrugged and shook my head. I could not recall him talking about any lady in particular.

She continued, "I am to be the future lady of this manor. My mother is finalizing the betrothal negotiations with Lord Ansel at this moment. You may call me Lady Kalonice."

In an instant I felt as if all the air had been sucked out of the hallway. My head spun. I couldn't breathe. My heart had been ripped out. Abandonment — my worst fear had been realized. I knew I had held Ansel's attentions at bay. I hadn't truly committed myself to him, other than friendship, yet I couldn't help but feel I had been cast aside. Should I be thankful that this truth came out before I had taken that next step? I couldn't keep the shock from showing on my face.

"Eshshah!" I silently screamed.

"I'm with you Amáne." She was as confused as I.

Clearly shaken, I managed to close my mouth. Evidently it was the reaction Kalonice had tried to achieve. Pleased with herself, she pulled her shoulders back, tilted her nose up and glared down at me wickedly.

"Oh?" She stroked her hair. "I see by your blank stare that maybe he hasn't told you our plans. I thought maybe you were better friends. We will announce our betrothal tomorrow at his birthday ball."

Still unable to take a breath, my throat tightened — I grew light headed. This didn't make any sense. *Why wouldn't Ansel have told me such an important part of his life?* My first inclination was to believe that this girl had gone mad and had lied to me for some evil reason. But then I recalled a couple occasions where it seemed he'd tried to tell me something and then changed his mind.

Had he been trying to find the right time to tell me he was to be betrothed? Then what was he doing with me all this time? He had me convinced that he had feelings for me. I'd allowed him to kiss me — I even kissed him back. All along he had plans with someone else? I suddenly felt so foolish, so naive.

My stomach twisted. I felt like I would vomit. I needed to turn around and leave this place here and now — to run back to the Arevale Outpost if I had to. I noted her smug look and the enjoyment she gleaned from my torture. At that moment, I decided I couldn't let this cow win and have the satisfaction of watching me turn tail and run.

I found my breath. Although my blood began to boil, I forced out my words in as normal a tone as I could summon. "I'm sure Lord Ansel was going to tell me soon enough." Not a very good response, but it was all I could do to just utter those words as she stood there twirling her hair. I fought desperately to stay in control of my temper. I added, "My congratulations to you. You two must deserve each other."

"Thank you. Actually, it will be a marriage of convenience. I'm sure I may come to love him in time. Lord Ansel is quite the talk here in South Serislan. He is exceedingly handsome, as I'm sure you've noticed." Her eyes raked my gown with disgust. "Or, perhaps you haven't. I won't fault him if he wishes to keep a *friend* on the side. You know men ..."

My breathing became shallow as my anger rose. I could hear Eshshah's warning thoughts. I would take care of Ansel later, but right now all I wanted to do was draw my dagger and shear the golden curls off of Kalonice's head. Slicing her throat wouldn't have satisfied me as much as relieving her of her prized locks — to begin with anyway — and then maybe her throat afterwards. Eshshah hummed loudly in my consciousness. My hand involuntarily made its way towards my dagger hidden in the folds of my skirt. She caught my movement and gasped. At first it looked like she was about to go for a concealed blade of her own — I fervently wished that she would.

Instead, her hand went to her throat, as she called out, "Murderer! She's trying to kill me!" She turned on her heels and hurried back the way she had come, screaming her accusation as she fled down the hallway.

This could not be happening to me. I wanted desperately to wake up and find this was another one of my nightmares.

Unfortunately, I was wide awake. Snatching up my bags, I could think of nowhere else to run but to my room.

I found my chambers and pushed in the door. Quickly slamming it shut, I locked it and leaned my back against it. My chest heaved from fear, coupled with anger — my eyes stung.

An uncontrollable rage boiled over me. Before I could stop myself, I flung my bags across the enormous room with such a force they smashed against the opposite wall, causing a wall sconce to crash to the floor. I crossed to the large ornate bed, and after swiping at the package that rested on it — sending it across the room to collide with my bags — I slumped face down and sobbed.

Without warning, a door behind me swung open. In a flash I sprung off the bed, drew my dagger and stood in a fighting stance. Prepared to defend myself, I thought Kalonice had come to my chambers to take revenge. Before me was a woman, probably in her late twenties, standing frozen in the doorway to what looked like a bathing room. Her eyes were wide, but I saw no fear in them. Nor did I detect any hostility, only surprise. Her face broke into a friendly smile as she said, "You must be Amáne."

Ugh, not again.

"Yes, and you are ...?" I snapped back.

"Pleased to meet you Mistress Amáne," she said with a deep curtsy, "I am Eulalia, pronounced yoo-LAY-lee-a, my friends sometimes call me Lali — LAY-lee —" She repeated her name slowly, as if we didn't share the same language.

"Lord Ansel enlisted me to attend you. I see he described you perfectly when he told me you had beautiful blue eyes with a fire burning inside you. Yes," she said studying my face, "I would say he was correct.

"He said you would like a long soak when you arrived and sent some herbs that would please you in your bath. Although why a gentleman like Lord Ansel would know the personal private affairs of this nature about a lady, I don't know, but that's not any of my business. I just do as I'm asked and I was asked to have a hot bath waiting for you. I expected you sooner, but was told you were delayed, but I've managed to keep it hot.

"Will you be sheathing that dagger any time soon, Mistress Amáne? Because, truthfully, it's beginning to make me a bit nervous. Not that I would ever accuse you of any attempted harm, it's just that it's not easy to help you prepare for your soak with that blade pointed directly at me. And I'm sure you understand that I am not here to harm you."

I realized I still held my fighting stance. Although it appeared she hadn't taken a single breath in this entire dialogue — that truth made me dizzy — there was nothing about her that was in any way threatening. I sheathed my blade.

Without missing a beat, she continued, "My apologies that something in your arrival has gotten you so agitated, else why would your face be wet with tears? Please tell me so I can make it right for you. Is it the bedding, or your chambers are not to your liking? I can certainly request a new location. I was told to give you anything you needed. I hope it's not me that has you upset, I know I can sometimes do that to people, but Lord Ansel assured me that you and I would get along just fine, and that I would be the one person on his staff who would be able to handle you. Oh dear — I don't really mean that in a bad way — I mean with your firey spirit. I can attest to the fact that he thinks very highly of you by the way his eyes shine when he says your name."

My heart split open just then. How could he think highly of me when he didn't even have the consideration to mention anything about Kalonice. I dropped heavily on the bed and put my face in my hands.

Eulalia rushed to my side and put her arm around me.

"Oh, now I've said something to give you grief. I'm so sorry. Please tell me what's bothering you or I'll not forgive myself."

She was so sweet, regardless of her exhausting discourse, I didn't want her to feel bad. Between sobs, I said, "It's just that I've had a run-in with one of the guests ... she told me ... er ..."

She seemed to know immediately of whom I spoke. "Oh, of course, her. I did hear some screaming in the hallway and it could be none other than Mistress Kalonice. I tell you that girl is trouble — I shouldn't speak so disrespectfully of my superiors, but I'm sorry, she is not worthy to be a guest of Lord Ansel's. I apologize if she has said something to hurt you. Just stay clear of her and you'll be fine."

If she knew what Kalonice had told me, she would know that just staying away from her would not mend my hurt.

A loud knock at the door made me leap up and draw my dagger once more.

"Amáne, it's Ansel. Are you in there?"

My heart stopped, my eyes opened wide and I looked with shock at the door and then at Eulalia. Tears filled my eyes again. I shook my head no and pointed to the bath, then rushed through the bathing room door and closed it behind me leaving her to deal with Ansel.

I threw off my clothes and jumped into the tub just in case she tried to talk me into seeing him. I could hear her open the chamber door and tell him that I was soaking and was not presentable for his visit. Of course she said it with more words than anyone else would use, but eventually I heard the large door shut and then lock. I exhaled a long sigh and started to let the hot water and the herbs wash away my misery.

CHAPTER SIXTEEN

I awoke to a loud knock. It took me a minute to figure out where I was. After my bath, Eulalia had left me to rest. I cried myself to sleep.

"Amáne, it's Ansel. May I please come in?"

"No, Ansel. I don't feel well," which was the truth. Sick to my stomach over the announcement that despicable girl had delivered, I was not ready to face him and accuse him just yet. The pain was still too great. I needed to cope with my grief before I unleashed my wrath upon him.

"Can I get you something, or send the Healer in?"

"No. I just need to be left alone."

"What's wrong, Amáne?" A hurt tone in his voice. "You sound angry, not ill. Tell me, did I do something wrong? Are you mad because I couldn't meet you at the outpost? Please, Amáne."

I turned my back to the door and didn't respond. Finally, I heard his footsteps retreat. A fresh batch of tears soaked my bedding.

A while later I was again startled awake with another sharp rap on my door.

"I told you to I wanted to be left alone!" I shouted.

"Mistress Amáne, please open the door this instant. This is the manor guard and you are under arrest."

"What?" I leaped out of bed and smoothed my crumpled gown that Eulalia had lent me. It was more suitable for a guest at this manor than the two gowns I had brought from Dorsal. I ran my fingers through my tangled hair, then yanked the door open. But not before I'd drawn my dagger and taken a defensive stance.

Sure enough, there at my door were two guards in helmets and breastplates, swords and shields.

What now? I thought, as a weight pressed down on my chest. My mouth went dry, but I succeeded in forcing out the words, "Under arrest? For what?" I threw a silent plea to Eshshah.

"I'm with you Amáne. Please watch your temper. So far it has only been to your detriment."

"For assaulting a guest," one of the guards answered as he eyed my dagger. He held out his hand for me to relinquish my blade.

"I didn't assault anyone." I said, barely keeping an even tone. I realized that standing before the guards with my weapon drawn did nothing to sway them in my plea of innocence. My shoulders dropped as I handed over my dagger, hilt first.

"Please come with us."

The two guards waited while I pulled on my boots. I closed the door behind me as I surrendered myself to them. They took an elbow on either side, escorted me to the main corridor, and then we turned left. My knees were weak, but I didn't show any emotion. *Will this nightmare of a day ever end*?

Bile rose in my throat as up ahead in the corridor, Kalonice and a woman, who could only be her mother, stood in the doorway of their chambers. Her snide look and superior attitude sparked my rage. I lunged at her and growled. I had no intention of doing anything other than to lunge and scare her. A bit surprised at my unintended growl, I was nevertheless pleased with her reaction. She actually jumped back with a little yelp, and fear showed in her eyes. Her mother matched her actions. The guards tightened their hold on my arms, but did nothing more than to keep me walking past the two women. I looked over my shoulder and gave Kalonice a smug look as she seethed behind me.

We made a few turns and then headed down some stairs. After several flights down, the air began to get damp. My smugness had worn off, replaced by concern. Is there a dungeon here in the manor? Was that where they were taking me? What was the punishment for allegedly assaulting a guest?

They opened a low wooden door and ushered me into a dim and musty room. Then releasing me in front of a long table, they left me standing there. Without a word, they exited and locked the door behind them. I surveyed the room and found myself in a wine cellar. In addition to the table in front of me, and a large chair behind it, the cellar held a great number of wine casks, stacked to the ceiling.

A spigot on one of the barrels had been left partially open and made a splashing sound as its contents dripped steadily onto the dirt floor. It filled the room with the strong fumes of wine.

Uneasiness crept up on me. Finding myself alone, I reverted to my old habit of speaking to Eshshah out loud. "Now what, Eshshah? What kind of a retched situation have I gotten myself into?"

"I am just as baffled as you, Amáne."

"How could he not tell me?" I tried to keep my voice even, but without much success. "I thought he was my friend. I'm furious — so hurt! I just want to strangle him, or at the very least knock some sense into him — maybe break his nose again.

"Eshshah, I just don't understand. Regardless of how betrayed I feel, how could he do this to himself? What could he see in that cow that would benefit his throne? It's a decision I'm sure he'll regret. Oh, Ansel," I whispered in despair. I closed my eyes as my heart bled for him ... bled for me.

"At least I don't have to guard my heart anymore, Eshshah. There's nothing left of it to give if I even wanted to — which I don't." Trying to forget my pain, I forced myself to think about the good of the kingdom. My duty remained to protect Ansel, even from himself. No matter the cost to me. I took a deep breath and made up my mind.

"I can't let him do this, Eshshah. I have Aperio's key with me." This was a key made from a scale of the late dragon, Aperio, whose name meant 'open.' It would open any lock by merely repeating the dragon's name. I kept it on a ribbon around my neck and was never without it. "I'm going to leave here, find him and tell him what a big mistake he's making. Then I'll meet you at the Arevale Outpost, even if I have to run all the way there. I wish I was back in Dorsal. This place and everything about this kind of life is not for me. If it wasn't for the Rider's Council, we would leave tonight. I'll tell the Healer that I'm ill, which is the truth, and that I must stay at the outpost until the Council. We can leave right after."

"Amáne, perhaps you just need a good rest so you can look at things with different eyes." Eshshah suggested. "You've seen too much misfortune lately."

"No, Eshshah. I've made a decision." I took a deep breath. "It's my duty. I have to find him and tell him to his face."

Just then a voice came from the chair behind the table, "What is it exactly that you need to say, Amáne?" I hadn't noticed that the chair faced the other way. It turned slowly, revealing its occupant.

"Ansel!" I jumped and grabbed the edge of the table as my heart stopped mid-beat. "What — why —" I sputtered but couldn't get any words to leave my mouth.

His expression, turned from amusement to remorse as my anger took over — of course — and my tongue was loosed.

"Is this some kind of sick joke? Who do you think you are, treating me like this? Like a common criminal. Arrested? Did Kalonice and you plan this together to torture me? I ... I ... can't even look at you right now, Ansel. I have to leave before I do something I'll regret."

I turned and headed for the door.

He jumped up and rushed around the table, repentance in his eyes. "Amáne, I'm sorry. Yes, I had you brought down here so I could talk to you, but —" He came up next to me and reached out. I deflected his arm roughly and shot him a look that warned he'd better not get any closer. He hurriedly continued his explanation, as he rubbed his bruised arm. "You wouldn't see me when I came to your room, so I thought I would be creative. It was just a little joke."

"A little joke?" I screamed.

"I received a report that Kalonice had confronted you. She made quite a scene. So, I thought I could use that, and I asked Calder and Avano to pose as guards and bring you down here. I didn't intend for you to wait long. I was going to turn around sooner. Then you started talking to Eshshah. I'm sorry, I —" he stopped mid-sentence and his eyes and mouth opened at the same time, "— did you think I planned this with Kalonice?" The look on his face after he said her name was like he had just bitten into a worm-infested apple. "Why would I have any reason to do anything with the likes of her?"

His question puzzled me. I almost started to believe that he didn't know what I was talking about. My fury rose. I couldn't make up my mind whether I wanted to punch him, or keep making my way to the door.

"Amáne?" He stood there with a bewildered look on his face. Hands out, palms up.

He was good — very convincing. I refused to look into his eyes and see the lie.

My decision made, I spun around and took another step to the door as I retrieved Aperio's key. Unfortunately, the gown that Eulalia had lent me was too long. My boot caught on the hem and sent me sprawling to the ground. I didn't bother to get up. Utterly defeated, I stayed in my prone position and sobbed, face down on the dirt floor.

Ansel rushed to my aid and tried to help me up, but I batted him away. After several attempts to get me to sit up and listen to him, he finally gave up and dropped himself down on the ground next to me. He began to stroke my hair, letting me cry while he whispered my name, along with countless apologies, and how heartless he was to pull such a prank.

I didn't want him to touch me, to soothe me, to even be near me, but I was too traumatized to try to stop him.

After he let me cry for a bit, he said softly, "Please tell me, Amáne, how did I betray you? You know I would rather die than do anything that would ever hurt you. What did that __ say to you?" He used a word that was not in my vocabulary.

I didn't look up, but kept my face buried in my arm and talked to the dirt floor. "You didn't tell me about your arrangement." I couldn't bring myself to say the word betrothal.

"What arrangement? With whom?" He truly sounded distressed, but I couldn't trust that assumption.

"Stop the game, Ansel! — With her."

"Please stop talking in riddles," he implored, "and just tell me what big mistake I'm about to make. Who's 'her?'" Frustration rose in his voice. He struggled to keep an even tone.

"Your betrothal to Kalonice that her mother was negotiating with you when I arrived, and the fact that you will be announcing it at the ball. Did you have to make me say it, Ansel? I didn't think you were that cruel. I know she's beautiful and I want you to have a beautiful wife, but she doesn't deserve you. You're making a mistake — and it's my duty to let you know." I felt as though a dagger had been thrust into my heart.

Other than the drip of the wine on the dirt floor, there was not another sound in the room. I kept my face down as my shoulders jerked with my sniffling — his silence, confirmation of my fears.

A strange sound came from Ansel's direction. Was he crying, too? When I raised my head and peeked at his face, his mouth was turned up in an odd smile. At first he began to snicker. Then when he saw me eying him, he burst into laughter. I thought he had gone mad.

"Ansel? Are you all right?" He kept laughing. I sat up and put my hand on his arm, greatly concerned. I was ready to run and find the Healer.

"Let me understand this," he said between laughing bouts, "You thought I had agreed to an arranged marriage with —? Now it's my turn to be insulted. Please give me a little credit for my intelligence. What would ever make you come to that conclusion?"

Embarrassment crashed over me like a wave. "I don't know. Her lies were so convincing. I was nervous about coming here, I felt so out of place — humiliated by my appearance. She's a beautiful rich lady. I saw no reason for her to tell me unless it was true."

My face reddened with shame. "Ansel, I'm ... I'm sorry I doubted you." I put my hand to my mouth, mortified I had been so gullible.

"Beautiful and rich do not always make an honest heart. In fact, it's a rare combination." He said as he shook his head slowly. His face reflected his forgiveness for my brash accusation. I wiped my eyes with the back of my hand. The more I thought about it, the more ridiculous the whole situation appeared. I found myself starting to giggle.

Eshshah relaxed her concern.

"Did you really try to murder her, Amáne?" Ansel asked, amused.

"No. I didn't even draw my dagger. I only thought about it ... and ... well, maybe my hand did move towards it, but I only imagined I'd cut off all her golden locks, and that was all — except maybe her throat afterwards."

"I was told the entire wing could hear her screaming that you were a murderer. I would love to have seen that. It was her demanding mother that kept me from meeting you at the Arevale Outpost. And just so you won't feel you were completely duped, there was some truth to what that — he used the same descriptive word — told you. Her conniving mother actually did try to trick me into an arrangement."

My eyebrows raised at that news. It did make me feel a little less gullible.

He smiled and traced my cheek with his finger, "Amáne, you have absolutely nothing to worry about. If I'd been available to greet you and escort you here like I should have, none of this would have happened. I'm sorry. I'll make it up to you, I promise."

"You don't have to promise anything. But Ansel, you shouldn't turn your back on that girl because, truthfully, she is not to be trusted. I caught her hand moving towards what I would guarantee was her dagger. And with the look in her eye, I'm sure she would not hesitate to use it — on anyone, at any time. Please be careful."

"She and her mother are guests here solely for diplomatic purposes, otherwise I stay clear of them. The entire family is not to be trusted."

"And speaking of trickery," I said in mock anger, "if you ever pull a prank like this on me again, you'd better be in fear for your life."

"I'm sorry, it was bad timing. I had no idea what she had said to you. But maybe next time I need to talk to you, you should open your door — especially now that you know that I'll go to extremes to get your attention."

Before I could respond, he said, "Let's get up from this cold floor and find some sunshine."

He jumped to his feet, reached for my hand and pulled me up. Facing me, he pushed my disheveled hair back, then took his sleeve and wiped my face. "You look like you've been playing in the mud."

"Maybe next time I shouldn't cry on a dirt floor."

"I hope there's not a next time that you have to cry because of me. Will you forgive me?"

"Maybe ... eventually." I tried to sound serious.

"How about we start your arrival over again? I want to prove to you that this place and everything about it can please you." He executed a low courtly bow. "Greetings, Amáne. Welcome to my home. Let me show you to your chambers, and then I'll give you a tour of the grounds."

He smoothed my hair again and then kissed my forehead. He pulled back and searched my face. His gaze rested on my lips — I knew where this would lead. This time I was ready. I gathered all my strength and took a deep breath, then put my two fingers on his lips to keep their warmth at arm's length.

"Let's go find some sunshine." I echoed his words.

He gave a small nod, yielding to my unspoken request to keep his distance.

He went to the door, and trying the latch, found that it had been locked from the other side. "I don't have a key for this door. — Avano ... I'll strangle him."

"Looks like your friends turned the tables on you. But you're in luck." I opened my hand to reveal Aperio's key.

"Is that the key you had when you ... when I ..." He didn't want to recall the nightmare we had lived through together in the tunnels of Castle Teravinea. Aperio's key was what I used to get into his cell. It had unlocked his chains and all locks that had barred our way from reaching Eshshah and safety.

I nodded, then placed it in the lock and whispered, "Aperio." The mechanism sprang and the door opened.

"How do I go about getting one of those?"

"You have to be a dragon rider." I raised a shoulder and half smiled.

"Oh, wait, I almost forgot." Ansel ran to the leaking cask and turned the spigot, stopping the noisy splash of wine on the dirt floor. My jaw dropped and my eyes widened when I figured out the reason for the dripping cask.

He grinned and shrugged, "I know how good your senses of hearing and smell are. I didn't want you to hear me breathing or catch my scent when you entered the room."

"You are evil!" I failed to suppress my smile.

CHAPTER SEVENTEEN

As Ansel and I made our way back to my chambers, he asked, "Did you like my gift?"

"Your gift?"

"I had a package left on your bed. Wasn't it there when you arrived?"

My face went red.

"Okay, let me guess." He said, sighing, "You had just experienced that unhappy encounter and you were in a mood when you got to your room. In a fit of anger, you threw the package on the floor without so much as looking at it. Am I close?"

Close? He was uncanny. "Well, it was more like I tossed it across the room." I gave him a small shrug.

Arriving at my door, I said, "I have a surprise for you if you'd like to come in." He raised his eyebrows with a sly look.

I rolled my eyes, but continued without missing a beat. "It's just a simple gift for your birthday and I want you to open it now because tomorrow you'll have so many more extravagant ones. Mine will pale in comparison."

I led the way and found Eulalia just laying down a tray of small cakes and some watered wine on the table in my chambers.

"Oh, Mistress Amáne, you're back, I was wondering where you were. There was a rumor —" she turned towards me and abruptly ceased her conversation when she saw Ansel following behind. She executed a deep curtsy, her eyes full of admiration, but a bit flustered. She looked from him to me and my muddy condition, and then back to him and was actually at a loss for words. That must have been a first.

"Lord Ansel. Good day to you ... er ... If you'll excuse me, I'll be leaving now." She started backing towards the door.

"No, Lali," I stopped her. "Please stay." In fact I was relieved that she was here as it would make it easier for me. I wouldn't have to keep my guard up.

I continued, "I came back to clean up. I seem to have gotten into some mud ... I ... um ..." Now it was my turn to be at a loss for words. How would my untidy appearance and muddy dress that she had lent me look to her as I walked in with Ansel.

"I found her in the south wine cellar," Ansel intervened. "She seemed to have gotten herself locked in somehow. It was quite muddy in there as a cask was leaking. All's well, Lali. If you could help her clean up, I'd like to show her the grounds. I'll wait."

I mouthed a thank you to him.

"Certainly, Lord Ansel. As you wish. Please have some cakes. Begging your pardon, my lord, if I had known you were going to be here I would have brought more — the raisin ones that you like so much — and another cup, and wine from the cellar, not watered. I can run and get more if it please you, Lord."

"Thank you, Lali. I'm fine. I can share Amáne's cup. Watered wine will do. Just see if you can make her presentable quickly, please." He smiled and winked. She blushed, curtsying several times as she steered me into the bathing room.

Closing the door behind her, she grabbed a linen, soaked it in the basin and began scrubbing me as she bantered on. "Make you presentable? Well that makes my job very easy indeed, as even in sack cloth, you would look presentable. You are that beautiful."

I closed my eyes and silently bore her compliments. She went on to ask what fragrance I wore that was so delightfully spicy. I didn't answer, which didn't seem to bother her, She'd already moved on to another topic.

Noticing my red eyes when she finished cleaning my face, she handed me a linen soaked in an infusion of marigold herb. She instructed me to hold it over my eyes. They were soothed immediately. She then directed her efforts to my hair and my gown.

Unaccustomed to being waited on, I kept trying to help her. She repeatedly brushed my hands away, finally admonishing, "Mistress Amáne, will you let me do my job? Lord Ansel has personally asked me to clean you up. I take his request to heart. It is my duty to oblige. Now keep your hands away and stay still so I can do as he has asked."

I gave up and obeyed her instructions. I did nothing but hold the marigold-infused linen over my eyes.

At last she stood back and admired her accomplishment. "Now you are fit to accompany Lord Ansel." She beamed. "Yes, his eyes do shine when he says your name — but his face glows when he's in your presence. I have never seen him so happy and I've worked in his household since he was a young boy."

This was not what I needed to hear right now, but I managed a smile.

Then with incredible insight, she looked into my eyes and said, "I know you will, in due time, make the right decision." My heart fluttered. I inhaled sharply, unable to respond.

She took my hand and led me back into the room, pulling me in front of Ansel. She was right, his face did glow when he looked at me. I blushed and couldn't meet his eyes. I looked down as Lali delighted in his approval.

"Lali, I marvel at your skills. You've made her even more ravishing." He was taunting me, but he knew he was safe from my wrath in front of Lali. We had an agreement that he would not offer me compliments, but since he broke his end of the of the deal, there was no call for me to keep mine. With a glare in his direction, I crossed one leg behind me in a deep curtsy.

"Thank you, my lord." I said with great emphasis, knowing he would be just as irritated. I straightened up and flashed him a 'pleased-with-myself' smile.

"Touché," he said with a slight tilt of his head.

Lali just looked from him to me. She opened her mouth to comment, but was cut short by a knock on the door.

"Amáne. It's the Healer and Gallen. Are you in there?"

Lali rushed to the door and opened it. "Lady Healer, Sir Gallen, please enter. I'm so pleased to see you again today." She backed up gesturing for them to enter.

"Oh dear," Lali looked at me and lamented, "I had no idea your chambers would be so popular." She dragged a chair from the far wall over to the table, and Gallen pulled the large chair in the corner. "Please excuse me," she said, "I must get more cakes and wine."

Thinking it was probably better than to try and stop her, I nodded my assent, as she rushed out of the room. I then turned to the Healer and Gallen and hugged them warmly.

"I'm sorry, Healer, I didn't intend to wait so long since my arrival to find you."

"It's okay, Amáne, I've spoken with Calder and Avano and I'm aware of the reason for your delay." She threw a disapproving look at Ansel who had stood up to greet them.

He looked down, genuinely contrite. "Yes ... well, poor decision and poor timing on my part ... once again. I've already apologized profusely and she may forgive me eventually. I hope you weren't too harsh on Calder and Avano. I'll take full responsibility."

At least this time his poor decision was not something that was detrimental to the throne, or to his life, I thought. Naturally, the Healer would forgive him immediately. She turned to me and read my face. Assured that I was fine, the Healer shook her head, but then smiled her forgiveness.

We sat at the table nibbling at the cakes while I told them about my encounter with Kalonice. They were not surprised at my account, as her reputation for trouble was already known to them.

Ansel changed the subject. He asked me to open my gift. Lali had placed it back upon my bed. It was a large package wrapped in a soft red fabric. I untied the ribbons and unrolled the fabric to reveal a beautiful gown in Serislan silk.

It was a rich green silk brocade overskirt, with slashing on the sleeves that were ornately decorated with ribbons and various jewels. The neckline and bodice were also adorned with jewels. It had a light green underskirt that complemented the dark green. The gown was a work of art.

I was speechless. I held it up to myself with my mouth open, looking from Ansel to the Healer to Gallen. The three of them enjoyed my various facial contortions.

"I ... ah ... Ansel ... what were you thinking? It's exquisite, but I don't want to be a showcase like I was at the Life Celebration Gathering. This is much too extravagant for me."

"Nonsense!" They all said at the same time.

"Amáne," said the Healer, "It is beautiful, but it's not too much. You have no idea of the rivalry you will be witnessing tomorrow night. Every lady will be trying to outdo the others. They will be wearing all their finest to show off their wealth."

"But I have no wealth."

"You're here as my guest, Amáne. Think of it as showing off my wealth — please — it's my birthday, after all." It was not within my power to resist those green eyes. "Open the other bag," he said, thrilled with my reaction to his gift.

I picked up a red velvet pouch that accompanied the gown. It weighed heavy in my hand. I nervously loosened the drawstring. Wrapped in a piece of silk was a magnificent necklace and matching earrings. Pearls and large green stones, cut to sparkle like nothing I'd ever seen. Emeralds. Completing the set was a circlet — which is worn around the head. A smaller emerald pendant dangled, designed to hang on the forehead.

I forgot to breathe.

"It was my mother's," Ansel said, "— my real mother."

"Queen Fiala?" My hands began to tremble. I quickly put the jewelry back in the bag and handed it to Ansel. "No, I will not accept this, Ansel. I — don't know what to say. With all due respect, thank you, but how could I ever wear this? It's not my place. Besides, I would probably lose it or break it or ..."

I looked at the Healer for help and I saw sadness in her eyes. Surely it was for her relative that now rested with her ancestors. Queen Fiala was the Healer's sister's great granddaughter. She was killed with her husband, King Emeric of the House of Drekinn, when the royal apartments at Castle Teravinea were destroyed by an explosion and fire. The work of King Galtero.

The Healer met my eyes and gave a nod to go ahead and accept the jewelry. She was apparently already aware that Ansel wanted me to have it.

"I can't ... would you agree to just let me wear it tomorrow to please you? But then I ask that you take it back and keep it in a safe place. I have no use for any such extravagance in Dorsal. I'll wear it again at your coronation or your next birthday, or whenever you want me to, but please don't make me keep it as mine."

"Such the negotiator," Ansel laughed. "I suppose I'll have to concede to your agreement, for now."

I walked over, put my hand on his shoulder and gave him a quick kiss on the cheek, "Thank you for such beautiful gifts. You're too generous. I don't deserve it, but I appreciate all of it."

I wiped a tear off my face. I carefully laid the gown back on the bed just as Lali rushed into the room bringing a large tray with more cups, wine and cakes with raisins. She eyed the gown approvingly, then proceeded to fuss over us as we caught each other up on our trips. Being mindful, of course, of what we allowed Lali to hear.

Lali showed me where she had put my satchel before she excused herself to another errand and left the room.

A wave of panic coursed through me when I recalled how rough I'd been with my bags when I first arrived. What if my angry actions had broken the goblet that I agonized over for so long — after it had actually survived the destruction of my mother's studio? I would be devastated if that were the case. I pulled it out and felt through the fabric that surrounded it. I breathed a sigh of relief that I'd wrapped it securely for the flight. It appeared to have survived even my fury. I recited a small song of thanks in my head.

Perching on the edge of the chair nearest Ansel, I handed him my package. It was my turn to be excited as I watched him open his gift. He studied the wrapping to decide how he wanted to remove it. Finally, he pulled his dagger and carefully cut the ribbon holding the fabric. The wrap fell to the table, revealing my goblet.

He inhaled sharply. "Now I'm the one that must say to you that you shouldn't have gotten me something so costly. Amáne, I can't let you spend this kind of money on me."

I laughed, "I didn't spend any money on it, Ansel. I made it."

I enjoyed the incredulous look on his boyish face. His green eyes opened wide as he tilted his head in wonder. He set the goblet on the table and leaned back to admire it.

"Look at the jewels in the dragons' eyes." He whispered in admiration.

"I got that idea from you, when you made me my walking stick."

"And this dragon with the golden eyes looks like Eshshah. Who's her friend?"

I shrugged. "I just wanted to put two dragons on it."

He leaned towards me and gave me a kiss on both cheeks. He hesitated, his eyes on my lips, but fortunately he didn't go there. Of course, the color rose in my face.

"Thank you, Amáne. It's beautiful. I love the fact that you made this for me. You have a great talent with clay."

"It's in my blood. I enjoyed making it for you."

"Let's see if this art piece is as functional as it is beautiful." He winked at me, knowing I would recognize those were the same words I'd used when he gave me the walking stick.

Pouring some wine into our cups and then his goblet, he held it up and proposed a toast. We all raised our cups to health, happiness and the throne.

Chapter Eighteen

Ansel took me on a tour of his estate, as promised. He described the activities and events planned for the guests the next day. He teased that I should enter the sword fighting competition and put all the men to shame. Truth was, none of the dragon riders would be competing. They kept a low profile and made it a point to direct no attention towards themselves. Some riders are still known for who they were when their dragons lived. But in these days not many were remembered and that was how they wished it to remain — at least until Ansel could assume his throne.

We rode to the field at the Arevale Outpost so I could see Eshshah. I missed her physical touch. It didn't feel right that she was stuck at the outpost and couldn't join me at the manor. I longed for the day when our secret would be loosed.

I kissed Eshshah goodbye. Ansel and I rode back towards the manor where he showed me the beautiful gardens and explained his new venture into sericulture — silk farming. He took pride in his new endeavor. Because of his enthusiastic explanations, I found the process of making silk fascinating. Except I did become a bit squeamish when he showed me the silkworm larvae feeding on mulberry leaves. Unlike my acquaintance, Fiona, I'd never had any interest in silk, but I could now appreciate the fabric and the beautiful silk products that Serislan is known for.

That afternoon more than made up for the horrible start of my day. There was so much to draw my attention away from my problems. I had the opportunity to relax and take in the charms of the estate, and for that matter, the charms of my host. Though my emotions were pulling me in every direction, he made no attempts to test my resolve. I could tell he tried to make up for the prank he had pulled on me.

Later that night, I went with the other riders back to the Arevale field so they could meet Eshshah. It was both heartwarming and heartbreaking as I watched them greet my dragon. Some touched her gently, some hugged her and some just stood in front of her and drank in her beauty, each lost in their own memories. Eshshah hummed with satisfaction at their compliments.

Lali woke me early on the day of the ball, as I had requested. The banquet would take place in the early part of the evening, followed by the ball.

The Healer decided she wanted to go into the township of Trivingar and speak again with the local herbalist. They had become acquainted earlier in the week and she wished to visit once more to continue their exchange in the healing arts.

I had no interest in the other activities at the manor. I didn't know how to play Pall Mall, a game where you hit a ball with a mallet through two iron arches. Nor was I interested in tennis, where you hit a ball with a racket over a net. Some of the guests were going hawking, which did interest me, but I was too shy to want to mingle with anyone. There was also the chance of accidentally running into Kalonice. I chose to accompany the Healer. On our way back, we swung by to visit Eshshah in the field. This was the first occasion that had ever required our separation for any amount of time. It helped relieve some of my anxiety, even though the visit was brief.

Lali had implored me to be back to my chambers no later than noon so she could dress me for the evening festivities. Truthfully, why she thought she needed so much time to get me ready, I had no idea. *How long could it take to throw on the green silk gown and brush and braid my hair*? But, I gave her my word that I would return in plenty of time. I found her pacing the floor when I returned to my chambers, even though I was sure I hadn't delayed.

Before the door had closed behind me, she began, "Mistress Amáne, I've drawn your bath, please go straight in and I'll be there momentarily."

I lay back, languishing in the hot aromatic water, when Lali came in to help me. In a panic I realized that my linking marks were exposed. I quickly moved my left arm across my chest to put my hand over Eshshah's linking mark, and crossed my ankles to hide my other mark. I feigned modesty and finally convinced her to leave the room.

A bit offended, she said, "It's not like you have anything that I've not already seen. It's to your advantage that you let me do my job and make you ready for Lord Ansel's banquet, but suit yourself. Just make sure you rinse your hair well, or I'll send you straight back in there and I'll do it for you." I felt badly for her, but I couldn't let her see my marks.

"Mistress Amáne, do you need help getting out?"

It was hard to leave the bath, it felt so warm, and Trivingar was much colder than Dorsal. But I took the hint and exited as quickly as I could. Drying myself, I slipped on my long sleeve chemise and left the warm steamy room.

Lali was on me immediately. She ushered me to a chair at the vanity, and taking a towel to my hair, she rubbed and blotted it until it was nearly dry.

I soon learned why she wanted me there early. It actually took quite a while to dress me. She pulled and pinched and took extra stitches where she deemed necessary — fluffing and preening until my gown was perfect.

Once satisfied, she again sat me on a stool — arranging my gown to avoid wrinkles — and turned her attentions back to my hair. Pulling it back smoothly, she gathered it into a queue. She pinned a small embroidered cap bedecked with pearls and jewels to the back of my head. Using the ribbons coming off of the cap, she wove them around my hair, creating a long tail down my back. All the while she continued her conversation, which mostly consisted of telling me how her family had been with Ansel's foster parents since before she was born. Her father a groom, and her mother was Lady Cybel, Ansel's foster mother's, waiting gentlewoman.

A knock at the door, stopped her dialog.

"Amáne," called the Healer, "Gallen and I swung by to escort you to the feast. Are you ready?"

Lali had a handful of my hair and could not let go at that moment to unlatch the door. "Lady Healer, forgive me but I'm not finished with Amáne and have my hands full at the moment. If it please you, go ahead, and I'll personally show her to the hall."

"Thank you, Lali, please let her know we'll be down the stairs and to the left once she enters the hall, then up towards the high table. We'll watch for her."

"I'll be there soon, Healer," I said.

Lali tied the final ribbon in my hair and put several more pins in my cap. I thought to myself that it would never come off, even in a Valaira. Finally, she seemed satisfied with the results.

Opening a drawer in the vanity, she said, "Now, to your make-up"

"No. I don't wear make-up," I protested.

Lali rolled her eyes as I once more resisted her efforts. "Mistress Amáne, I've prided myself in preparing a lady for a ball since you were a baby, and it is unbecoming to my dignity to do any less than I can for you. And if you won't accept it, then I must do it for Lord Ansel."

I knew then why Ansel had assigned her to attend me. I would be hard-pressed to decide who was the more stubborn, Eulalia or myself. She assuredly was the only woman on his staff that could, as she put it, 'handle me.'

Feeling she was still piqued at me for refusing her help with my bath — and with her dignity at stake — I reluctantly gave in.

"It'll not be much, as you don't need much. The current style of too much white powder never appealed to me. These ladies make themselves up to look like they walk with their ancestors. It's not flattering if you ask me. No, your light olive complexion shall not be marred with powder. A small amount of rouge and some red for your lips and you're set."

The finishing touches — Lali clasped Queen Fiala's necklace on me. I gasped at the thought of wearing such a priceless piece of jewelry. Lastly, she placed the circlet on my head with the larger square emerald floating at my forehead. She pinned it securely.

She stood me up at long last, twirling her hand for me to turn around as she scrutinized me up and down. I'd been conversing with Eshshah for the last few hours to keep my mind off of her extreme attentions. If going to a ball took this long to prepare, then I'll make a note that I never hope to be invited to another.

I caught a glimpse of myself in the glass and my jaw dropped. When I had dressed for the Life Celebration Gathering, I didn't recognize the girl in the reflection, but this time, I really couldn't find myself. I had to admit that I was a bit intrigued with the young lady who looked back at me. Strangely, it was a little less intimidating to be dressed so extravagantly here in Trivingar, as no one, or very few, knew me.

Chapter Nineteen

Eulalia ushered me to the great hall. As we reached the doors panic set in — my heart pounded in my chest. Up till now, I'd suppressed my apprehension for this moment, but it couldn't be held back any longer. The music floated out from the hall. I felt weak in the knees and on the verge of tears. I had to go in by myself and I knew I was late.

"Mistress Amáne, no! Don't cry!" Lali entreated. "Do you want streaks in your rouge, or to make your entrance with red eyes?" She began to fan my face. "Blink, Mistress, blink fast, we can't have you ruining yourself before you've even made your entrance."

Pulling myself together I gave Lali a quick hug and a thank you. She nodded at the doormen to open the doors for me as she appraised me one last time, making sure not a hair or a thread was out of place. I took a deep breath — well, as deep as I could, considering the dress I had been sewn into — and willed myself to move forward.

Through the double doors I found myself on a landing at the head of a flight of stairs that led down to the floor of the great hall. I caught my breath at the extravagance of the decor. Light blue walls decorated with yellow fleurs-de-lis. A frieze painted all around the room at the ceiling depicted stylized scenes of the various stages in producing the famous Serislan silk. Intertwined between the scenes were King Tynan's insignia and family crest. Even the beams in the ceiling were ornately decorated.

From the landing I hesitated, frozen in awe as the entire banquet hall spread out below me. It was magnificent. The tables that lined the edges of the hall were laid with fare like I've never seen. The savory aromas wafted up to greet me. The musicians played a soothing tune that contrasted the bustle of the servers who brought in trays of meats, fish and vegetables fit for a king. Of course, they had no idea they were actually serving royalty. The magicians and jesters wandered about the hall stopping at the tables to entertain.

I spotted Ansel at the high table and had to remind myself to breathe when our eyes met. He looked majestic. He wore a black shirt with billowing slashed sleeves, revealing gold satin inner sleeves. It laced up the front. His long hair was pulled back in a queue. He caught himself mid-sentence in his conversation with a gentleman next to him, and just stared at me. I saw him mouth the word, "Wow."

I rolled my eyes. Normally my following reaction to that would have been to glare back at him. Instead, I shot him a nervous smile.

Suddenly, I realized that my perfect view of the entire hall at that height meant that guests below also had a perfect view of me. My stomach leapt up to my throat and my knees threatened to buckle. I felt every eye that rested on me.

I froze on the spot, fear crept up to my chest as my smile became forced. Ansel couldn't rescue me from such attention as he had at the Life Celebration Gathering, but he could see my distress. Knowing my dread, he threw me an encouraging look and motioned to the doorman behind me. The man rushed to my side and offered his arm. I gladly took it, otherwise I would surely tumble down the stairs. Keeping my eyes locked on Ansel, we descended. I struggled to keep my mind off the dreadful fact that I was the center of attention. I held my breath the entire time. It looked like Ansel didn't take a breath, either.

I found the Healer and Gallen, but had no memory of how I actually made it to my spot at the table. Exhaling heavily, I lowered myself into the seat. They nodded their approval as they admired Lali's handiwork. I tried to catch my breath before I responded with a 'what-am-I-doing-here' look. I felt out of place, but when I saw how extraordinary the two of them looked in their finest, I began to relax. If they could do it, so could I. The Healer looked stunning in silk brocade died a beautiful deep red — I couldn't take my eyes off of her.

Once I settled in and recovered from my entrance, I began to survey the hall from the floor level. A flash of anger burned through me when I saw that Kalonice and her mother were seated at the high table. She made quite an effort to attract Ansel's attention. I caught her following his gaze in my direction and was startled at the vile look in her eyes. I immediately turned my attention elsewhere, hoping she hadn't witnessed my revulsion.

All through the feast, I snuck glances over at the high table and more often than not, I caught Ansel staring at ours — or, more accurately, at me. Each time, I looked away quickly. A couple of times our eyes met and I smiled at him — my heart fluttered.

Ansel looked miserable and bored with the nobles beside him. Several times I caught him stifling a yawn. It was obvious they occupied him in some weary conversation. My bet would be that he wished he sat in our boisterous section. All of the dragon riders had been announced as fellow citizens of Ansel's. Teravinean businessmen interested in investing in his silk business. The Healer passed as Gallen's wife and I as their ward. All of us were seated in the same area. There were about twenty-six of us, and we probably made up most of the laughter in the hall. My heart went out to him as he looked with longing in our direction each time there was an outburst.

The only rider who really looked serious was Braonàn. He sat the closest to the high table. His manner was what I would call hypervigilant. His eyes scoured the room constantly, watchful of who was near Ansel; who was approaching him; who had just entered the room — alert and guarding him, as was his duty.

I observed the other riders. Although enjoying themselves and in high spirits, they too, seemed alert to the activities in the hall. My attention rested on the Healer, who appeared to be involved in a lively conversation with Calder. But her eyes took in our surroundings. I was certain she didn't miss a thing.

In my brief time as a rider, I had only been concerned for myself, my dilemma, and ultimately my own quests. I had just shamefully recognized that it was as much my duty to make sure Ansel was safe in all circumstances, no matter the situation. Being a dragon rider was not just about the large heroic ventures of which I'd dreamed.

"Eshshah, how could I have been so selfish all this time?" I said to her in thought transference.

"Amáne, you are a young rider. All of your duties will become apparent as you train and mature. Don't be so hard on yourself."

With my guilt eating at me, my eyes searched out Ansel, who at that moment, was looking at me with concern, a furrow between his eyebrows. He mouthed, "Are you all right?"

I nodded as I hid my shame. He lifted his dragon goblet in a toast, making sure I recognized it. I was truly pleased to see him using my gift. I lifted my cup, smiled and toasted back, vowing to myself, and to Eshshah, that I would take all of my duties and tasks more seriously.

Chapter Twenty

One delectable course after another was offered. Soon I could only look at them, smile, and regretfully decline. I couldn't eat one more bite — except maybe to try just a taste of the pastries.

Ansel stood up to visit the tables and play the host. I watched the guests' faces and their hands as he graciously engaged them in small conversations. I found nothing compromising his safety. He finally reached our table, saving it for last. One-by-one he greeted the dragon riders — omitting the salute, of course.

"Calder and Avano I must warn you to beware of Amáne's retaliation for your part in my prank," he teased.

I had already spoken to the two riders, and laughed with them about it.

Avano said, "Not to worry, Lord Ansel. She's already forgiven us and promised no retribution would be forthcoming."

Ansel feigned hurt, "That hardly seems fair. She hasn't forgiven me yet." His green eyes danced as he glanced in my direction.

"I suppose I could find it in my heart to forgive you," I said. "For tonight anyway. I can't let you pass your birthday unforgiven."

We all laughed.

"If you'll pardon me," he said after spending as long as he dared at our table, but nowhere near long enough, "I have to continue my duty as host." His eyes rested on me, "Amáne, please save a dance or two for me — and then one more — the last." I could feel the heat rise in my face as I nodded. Avano looked at Ansel, then at me and let loose a low whistle under his breath that Ansel couldn't hear. I would have kicked him under the table, but that wouldn't have been polite in this company. Instead, I shot him a seething look.

The banquet concluded, and the tables were cleared and moved closer to the walls. The center of the hall was prepared for dancing as the musicians struck a new strain. Dances were performed by troupes to get the guests in the mood, and soon the floor filled with couples adept in the courtly processional dances.

Gallen sought me out for a pavane, a slow processional couples dance. He led me through it as we performed the deliberate hesitation step around the hall. He softly coached me as I watched the movements of the lady in front of me, mirroring her actions. I don't think I was too embarrassing for him. Dorjan found me for the next jig. Being from Dorsal, our particular style of dancing differed from the steps in this country. But we had a great time with it anyway, picking up some of the local movements and incorporating them into ours. Our jig was performed a little rougher than the courtly style here, but we didn't care.

I enjoyed watching as the more experienced couples processed in the galliard, a faster dance, which included leaps and skips in time to the music. Ansel was involved in many of the processional and the circle and line dances, as every lady wanted a turn with the charming host. I marveled at his grace as well as his amiable attitude towards his guests as he glided across the polished wood floors.

Even as I danced with many of the other riders, I remained watchful throughout the evening. I couldn't help but notice a certain lord — the one who had sat next to Ansel at the high table. He had been eyeing me for quite a while. I began to feel a little ill-at-ease. The dance over, my most recent partner excused himself to join a fellow rider in conversation. This left me momentarily standing by myself. The lord took the opportunity to approach. I wanted to hide. I really had no desire to converse with anyone, but that wouldn't have been courteous of me. I managed to smile at him as he sauntered over. He stood a little too close.

I thought it was only the ladies who bedecked themselves with jewels. The rotund lord must have worn half his weight in gold chains. Rings of rubies, sapphires and emeralds decorated his sausage-like fingers.

"Good evening, Amáne," he said with a small bow and a flourish of his hand. "I've been wanting to meet you all evening. Since you have not approached me, I felt the need to introduce myself to you." He had an annoyingly affected and condescending manner as he looked down his bulbous nose at me. "I am Lord Halebeorht, I own a large amount of land about a day's ride north of here."

I curtsied. "Pleased to meet you Lord Halebeorht. I see you already know my name."

"Yes, I asked Lord Ansel while we were at table. I admired your grand entrance and felt that I must get to know such a beauty as you before the evening turns to dawn." He winked at me like his statement had a hidden meaning that I was supposed to have understood.

I smiled politely through gritted teeth, wondering how he would feel if he knew how repulsed I was at his intended compliment.

It only made me wish I could leave his company immediately. I couldn't stop the red that flushed my cheeks from my discomfort and increasing irritation. I got the feeling he mistakenly took it as a blush of approval. *Ugh, how can I free myself from this pompous man?*

"Might I have the pleasure of having you as a dance partner? I've noticed you are very graceful on the floor."

I discreetly looked around for Ansel or one of the riders to help me out of this situation, but all seemed to be occupied. I really didn't know what to say to Lord Halebeorht. Not wanting to appear impolite, I just nodded. He immediately wrapped his fleshy hand around mine and escorted me to the floor where another pavane had started. I was thankful that it was not a more difficult dance.

Ansel danced a few couples ahead of us. When he twirled and faced us he lifted an eyebrow as he noticed with whom I was partnered. I shrugged my shoulders and raised a corner of my mouth.

Lord Halebeorht would not take no for an answer when I tried to decline the next dance. Ansel paid closer attention to us. I think I did pretty well hiding my discomfort. I didn't want Ansel to think I was not having a good time. In truth, I was having a wonderful time — until I met this overbearing lord.

When Lord Halebeorht asked me for the third dance, I had to think quickly how to turn down his request. He had inched his way closer and closer to me as the minutes passed, making me very uneasy. Knowing my tongue, I feared I would insult him if I remained in his presence much longer.

"Thank you Lord Halebeorht, but I'm quite tired. I need a breath of fresh air. If you would please excuse me."

I backed up, looking for an exit, when he took my arm and said, "I could use some fresh air as well. May I show you to the balcony?"

He twitched his eyebrow a couple of times. I had no idea what he tried to convey. All it did was annoy me more.

I can fight my way out of a dungeon, and escape a hideous creature, but for some reason, I could not figure out how to get away from this man. Maybe if I went with him to the balcony, I could slip away from him out there. I was trying very hard not to insult another of Ansel's guests.

Reluctantly, I allowed myself to be led away as I tried to release my arm from his grip. We reached the door to the balcony when I turned around and happened to catch Ansel's eye. He was engaged in a conversation at some distance from me. With a puzzled look, he lifted his shoulders. I pointed at the balcony, in answer to his silent question. Suddenly, his brows knit together and he gave me a serious shake of his head as he mouthed, "No!" He gestured for me to come to him as he started to make his way in my direction.

"Excuse me Lord Halebeorht, but Lord Ansel is trying to get my attention. I need to see what he needs. Would you mind waiting here and I'll be right back."

"I've been trying to get your attention all night, Love. Can't he summon someone else?" He said with a wicked smile.

My stomach turned. I bit my lower lip before I said anything I would be sorry for. With a quick curtsy, I turned and headed towards Ansel. I worked on placing a pleasant look on my face as I came up to him.

"Where are you going, Amáne?" His voice controlled, but seemed to be verging on anger.

I wanted to tell him how repulsive his guest was, but instead, I kept an even tone and said, "I was getting hot and Lord Halebeorht offered to take me out to the balcony for some fresh air."

"The balcony? You're going to the balcony with him?" He spoke louder than necessary. His attitude confused me, which of course roused my irritation. Poor Ansel, I should have made more of an effort to control myself, but his unexpected anger sparked mine.

My voice rose, "I told you I was hot and I needed some air." When I saw heads turning in our direction, I forced a smile on my face and continued in a low sweet voice, my teeth clenched, "I've been trying to decline your overbearing guest's attentions for what feels like a lifetime and since he would not take the hint I agreed to go out to get some fresh air with him in hopes I could slip away and be done with his detestable company."

"On the balcony?" He also forced a smile, as his displeasure increased.

"Ansel, what is the matter with you? Have you had too much wine? Yes, the balcony. There's fresh air out there, isn't there?" As hard as I tried to remain calm, my pitch rose. More heads turned our way. My embarrassment mixed with confusion.

His expression transformed from anger to bewildered, and finally amused.

I exhaled and my shoulders dropped as I gave up, baffled at his behavior.

"Amáne," he said gently, as he shook his head, "one of the things I love about you is your innocence. Of course you wouldn't know anything about what goes on out there. Let me get rid of the unworthy Lord Halebeorht and I'll personally escort you to the infamous balcony."

I decided not to even try to understand what he meant as he took my hand and led me through the crowd, back to where the despicable lord waited impatiently.

"My good Lord Halebeorht, I trust that you are enjoying the ball and are finding everything to your liking?" Ansel bowed.

Halebeorht returned the bow. "Why, yes, Lord Ansel, I'm finding things very much to my liking." He threw a look at me that made me cringe and want to hide behind Ansel. I could feel Ansel tense up, but he continued in an even voice, "Amáne tells me that you were going to accompany her to the balcony."

Looking a little uncomfortable, Halebeorht responded, "Yes, it was actually her suggestion. I told her that I would be happy to escort her out there."

A squeak escaped my mouth. I pressed my lips together tighter, just managing to hold inside what I really wanted to say.

"Amáne is a special guest of mine, Lord Halebeorht."

I watched Ansel's face and could see the effort it took to control his words to the beastly man.

He continued, "I will be the one to escort her. I'm sure you understand."

Halebeorht bowed with another irritating flourish of his bejeweled hand and a knowing nod at Ansel, "Of course, as you wish, it is your birthday after all." He looked at me, "Amáne." He made it sound like a statement as he tipped his head, and then turned and left — looking quite frustrated.

I breathed a long sigh of relief.

Ansel gave me his arm, "Shall we?"

We left behind the stuffy hall and moved through the colored glass doors to the balcony. The cool air hit my face, refreshing me immediately. I closed my eyes and inhaled.

The balcony was darker than I had expected, with only a few torches burning — the shadows dancing on the walls. Suddenly I gasped as I took in the scene around me. In the darkness, I saw couples settled on the benches surrounding the balcony. Each pair wrapped in varying amorous embraces — most of which I thought were not appropriate in a public setting.

In shock, I caught my breath and looked at Ansel. "He wanted to ... he thought that I ... did he...?" I stuttered, as I thought of Halebeorht and his vile intentions.

"Welcome to the balcony, Amáne."

I was so offended — shaking — livid. "That ... man!" I couldn't think of a word descriptive enough, that I was comfortable saying. "...if I had my dagger with me ..."

Ansel placed his hands on my shoulders and pressed down in the same method that Gallen had used to calm me before my first quest. He brought his face close to mine and said in a low voice, "I have no doubt that you would've been able to defend your honor, with or without your dagger. And I completely agree with you. I would be the first to throttle that man if he but lay a hand on you. But it wouldn't show me in good light in this foreign country if someone were to find a guest of mine in a heap out here when the sun comes up — whether it be your doing or mine. Don't you agree?"

I allowed a smile and nodded — his calming remedy successful. But I'd had enough of the balcony. I was ready to take his arm and rush inside when I froze at the scene behind Ansel. There, on a bench before me sat Kalonice. Her eyes blazed on me. She ignored the attentions of the young man who buried his face in the crook of her neck. Her lip curled in a snarl.

In a spontaneous reaction, I reached up, took Ansel's face and pulled it down to mine. I kissed him on the lips — hard. Then I shot a glare in Kalonice's direction. I grabbed his arm, twirled him around, and drug him inside.

Taken aback, he put his fingers to his lips and made a show of inspecting them, as though checking to see if he was bleeding. "I'm not complaining, but ow, Amáne. What was that all about?"

"Er ... I'm sorry, Ansel," I said in embarrassment. "I don't know ... that girl ... I just —"

"Oh, her again? I thought maybe it was the balcony, because if it was, I'd take you right back out there, and this time I'd be ready for you."

I rolled my eyes. "How about if I just give you that dance I promised?"

"I wouldn't oppose."

"Seriously, though, Ansel, I have a bad feeling about her. She's up to no good. You'd better watch your back."

"I have twenty-six dragon riders watching my back tonight. I feel perfectly safe. And at the risk of your wrath, I'd say that I have the most beautiful personal guard at this moment."

I exhaled. "I'll spare you my wrath this time. I owe you."

"Hmm. Good to know."

Chapter Twenty-one

Ansel led me to the dance floor. Luckily it was another of the slower processional dances. We stayed on the floor for the next dance as well. But before it was over he led me in a different direction from the other dancers. It confused the couple behind us who started to follow before they realized the procession headed the other way. I giggled as we moved on to a far corner of the hall where few guests remained. Ansel never took his eyes off of me. I was lost in the moment, completely enjoying myself and not paying attention to where we were going, nor did I care. I felt so comfortable with him. We stopped and he turned me to face him. He put his arms around me and searched my eyes.

My heart fluttered as I started to panic. Too late, I was already absorbed in his deep green eyes. I didn't even make an attempt to fight his attentions. I closed my eyes as he pressed his lips against mine. The room receded around us, as if it were just the two of us alone in the large hall. My knees went weak. If I hadn't been holding on to him, I would have been on the floor in a swoon.

He slowly released my lips. "Oops," he breathed.

"Ansel," trying to catch my breath, "you shouldn't have done that."

"You shouldn't have let me."

"I —" There was no excuse, except for my weakness.

"I'll just take the win on that round," he said smugly, as he snuck a quick kiss, and then another, before I could recover and hold him at bay.

"When are you just going to let go and admit what you know is true, Amáne?"

I let out an exasperated sigh and started to respond when something caught my eye. Off to the side, I spotted Kalonice and her mother talking to a man I hadn't seen before. She pointed in our direction. Immediately on the alert, I prepared to defend Ansel. *I'll never leave my dagger behind again*, I vowed to myself. I scanned the nearby table for anything I could use for a weapon — but would use my body to shield him if I had to. Kalonice directed her glare towards me. Our eyes locked. Icy fingers went up my spine. An involuntary shiver shook my body. I held my ground until she looked away first.

"Are you cold?" Ansel asked.

Puzzled by the look on my face, he started to follow my gaze.

I grabbed his arms. "Don't turn around. It's okay. I ... just thought I saw something." I decided right then that Kalonice's hostility was not directed at Ansel — but at me. I wasn't going to worry him unnecessarily, but would discuss it with the Healer as soon as I could. I made a mental note that it is I who would need to watch my back. When I looked again, Kalonice was gone.

"There you are, Lord Ansel!" A very old lady shuffled up to us. Dressed extravagantly, she dripped with jewels, her face powdered and painted. "I'm ready for that dance you promised. I know I can no longer match the beauty of this young lady you're with, but I don't have many dances left in me. I've been saving myself for you."

Ansel bowed deeply, took the lady's hand and kissed it, which brought a girlish giggle from her.

"Lady Daphne, my apologies that you had to be the one to seek me. I hadn't forgotten our promised dance. Please forgive me for my delay."

"I can certainly understand your delay." She eyed me approvingly.

He introduced us. I curtsied to her and she tipped her head.

"Ah, yes, you are the young one that made that marvelous entrance. Bravo to you, girl. That's the way to turn men's heads — which you certainly did. Your mother can expect an endless amount of requests for your hand starting tomorrow, I'm sure. And this young lord will be the first in line." She put her dainty hand on Ansel's arm.

A blush spread across my face, and a wave of grief passed briefly at the mention of my mother. But out of respect for Lady Daphne, I just nodded and smiled. Ansel gently touched my shoulder.

"Isn't he such a handsome young man? It seems like just yesterday when he ran around in his nappys. I've known him for that long." She pinched his cheek and I laughed as his face went red.

I took advantage of Lady Daphne's arrival. This was my chance to excuse myself before I completely lost control of my heart. Besides, I was exhausted, and tomorrow will be the Rider's Council. Or rather, later today, as it was already tomorrow, dawn just around the corner.

"Yes, he is," I answered, still laughing. "Quite handsome. And he's all yours right now, Lady Daphne. If you'll excuse me,

I'm going to my chambers before I collapse right here in front of you. I don't know how you do it. You look as fresh as if the feast had just begun. I wish I had your energy."

Lady Daphne beamed.

"You don't have to leave, Amáne." Ansel looked disappointed, but I found that if I couldn't be strong enough to resist him, then I needed to take a break from his presence. After the council I could rethink my situation.

"No, I do need to leave. It's been too long of a day for me. I'm not accustomed to dancing until dawn, which it will be shortly. Thank you, Lord Ansel, I've had a wonderful time."

"Can you wait and I'll walk you to your chambers?" I caught a desperation in his voice.

"No thank you. I'll ask Dorjan to go with me." I knew I could take care of myself, but in my tired state and with that unpredictable girl, I needed to be cautious. It also assured me that Ansel would not insist on going if he knew Dorjan would be with me.

I bid them both good night, but before I turned away, Ansel caught my eye. "I love you," he mouthed. My heart pounded as my stomach filled with butterflies. This was not going the way I had planned. I was falling in too deep before my hoped-for quest.

Closing my eyes and taking a deep breath, I swallowed, smiled and said, "Happy birthday, Lord Ansel." An arrow pierced my heart as a shadow dulled his green eyes.

CHAPTER TWENTY-TWO

I walked to my room with Dorjan and decided not to mention Kalonice tonight. Dorjan was in such high spirits, I didn't need to mar his evening with any discussion about that girl.

We arrived at my door. After thanking him, I let myself in and then latched it behind me. Expecting to see Eulalia, I found another maid in her stead. She leapt up from a corner seat and startled me. I went to draw my dagger, but of course it wasn't on me. I remained in a defensive stance as a young woman, eyes wide with fear, stood before me.

"Mistress Amáne," she curtsied and said in a shaky voice. "I am Seren, here to attend you. Eulalia has taken ill and sent me to assist you."

I nodded, greatly disappointed to see that it wasn't Lali. She said she would wait in my chambers so she could hear all about my evening the minute I returned. I knew she would have been ecstatic to learn how successful her attentions to my gown and accessories had been. It also concerned me that she was not well.

“Eulalia sent some tea that she made especially for you. She said you’d like it. Please let me to pour some for you, and then I’ll help you out of your gown.”

I smiled at her and nodded at her request. But first I went into the bathing room to remove Queen Fiala’s jewels. I placed them in the velvet bag and stashed it in a safe place. I was sure Seren was an honest person, but still didn’t feel comfortable letting her see me remove the royal jewels. Coming back into my bed chamber, I sat down at my table, no longer tired. The entire walk back to my room I could think of nothing other than falling into bed from exhaustion. But once here, I realized sleep would not arrive any time soon. The excitement of the evening still washed over me — Ansel’s warm kisses still lingered on my lips.

Eshshah was hunting. I always enjoyed sharing her flight through open thought transference, but preferred to be blocked when she killed her prey — especially when she tore it apart to eat it. We greeted each other briefly, but she had just spotted her meal. I told her I would hopefully be asleep when she was finally sated, so I would “talk” to her later in the morning. We said good night and she blocked me out.

Seren placed a cup of tea in front of me. I inhaled it’s sweet aroma as it swirled around my face invitingly. I took an experimental sip and found it so delicious I drained the cup in one toss-back of my head, then held it out for Seren to refill. The second one went down just as easily. There was something about the brew that I couldn’t get enough of. As I motioned for her to pour the third cup, she hesitated, but was obliged to do as I bid. I never finished it. My head spun, my eyes crossed and my vision blurred. I had no time to even think what was happening to me. The cup slipped from my hand and shattered into a thousand pieces. My head dropped to the table and all went black.

CHAPTER TWENTY-THREE

My entire body screamed with pain when consciousness began to wash over me. I couldn't open my eyes — what small amount of light there was in the room hurt. My chambers rolled back and forth, making me nauseous as the sound of water lapping against the walls filled my ears. *Why was there water in my chambers*? I heard sobbing as the stench of vomit, urine and salt water invaded my senses. *Maybe I'm dreaming*, I thought, but the motion of the room, the smells and sounds all seemed too real — something was dreadfully wrong — and something was missing.

"Eshshah!" I screamed, and bolted upright. My breath came in rapid gulps as I surveyed my surroundings with wild eyes. I couldn't feel Eshshah. Panic washed over me like a tidal wave. I was alone, but not in the physical sense. The eyes of several desperate people turned my way, fear on their faces — but Eshshah was absent.

"Where am I?" I asked no one in particular as I rubbed my throbbing temples.

A thick chain threaded through a ring in the manacles around my wrists. The chain began in the irons clasped to the wrists of the woman to my left, threaded through mine, then to the young girl at my right, continuing down the line of mostly women and children. I sat on a bench that went the length of the hull of the ship of which I was an unwitting passenger — along with twenty or so others.

"One more outburst like that and I'll personally come down and give you all fifteen lashes!" A harsh voice came from above.

"Slave ship." The girl to my right answered my question. She couldn't have been more than ten years old. Turning to her, I sighed in dismay at her condition — face swollen from crying, a bruise on her cheek and a haunted look in her eyes.

She wiped her nose, sniffed once and asked in a near whisper, "Are you a princess?"

"No, I'm not." I said gently, sorry that I had frightened her.

"You look like a princess. You're pretty."

"Thank you. My name is Amáne. What's yours?"

"Kira. Who's Eshshah?"

"She's a very special friend of mine." I swallowed hard and worked to keep the rising fear from showing in my face — desperate to gain control of my breathing. All the while, my mind spun as I tried to figure out where Eshshah was — and why I was here — wherever here might be. Since we linked, there was not a moment when I didn't know exactly what my dragon was doing.

Hysteria built in my chest with a pressure I'd never felt before. In all of my harrowing experiences in the last few months, nothing compared to my despair at that moment. I had to hold on to some thread of my being, because if I let go, I would snap. I couldn't bear knowing that Eshshah was not with me. I pressed my lips together as my throat closed.

Hope. There is always hope, I repeated — only half-believing what I said to myself. I took a deep breath and turned my face away from Kira. Squeezing my eyes shut, I silently screamed with all my might, "Eshshah, where are you?"

A small exclamation escaped my lips when I felt a faint answer — so far away. I screamed louder in thought transference, "Eshshah!"

"Amáne! You're alive. Are you all right? Did they hurt you?" Eshshah's relief reflected mine.

My hand shot to my mouth to stifle my shout of joy. Tears filled my eyes. I could see Kira out of the corner of my eye staring at me. She had to be wondering if she'd been chained to a lunatic.

"Yes, I'm alive. I'm fine now that I've found you. Where are you? You sound so far away, I can barely hear you."

"I'm still at the Arevale Outpost. Everyone has been searching for you since early this morning. Amáne, we're coming for you as soon as night falls."

"Early this morning?" I asked. "How long have I been missing?" It felt like only minutes since Dorjan had walked me back to my room.

"We've been looking for you for more than twelve hours. I blocked you when I hunted. When I got back to the outpost, I thought you were in a deep sleep. I'm sorry that I didn't try harder to wake you. I didn't want to disturb you. When I couldn't feel you a short time after, I asked the Healer to go to your chambers. That's when they found you missing and sounded the alarm. All of us have been beside ourselves with worry. Lord Ansel has taken this quite hard. I don't know how much longer he could have put on his brave face. Let me tell them I've found you." I listened through open thought transference.

"Eshshah, I'm on a slave ship. I don't know how I got here."

When she relayed this message, I could faintly hear the others.

"Slave ship?" They all said simultaneously. Then I heard Ansel's distraught voice as he said, "Oh, Amáne, I am so sorry."

The sound of his misery pained me.

"Eshshah, please tell Ansel that this is not his fault. I'm okay now. I'll make it out of here, I know I will."

"I did tell him, but he won't be convinced." Eshshah said, "He feels it was his responsibility — you were his guest, abducted from his home.

"It'll be dark in less than an hour, then Gallen and I will take flight and catch up to your ship. Amáne, we've found each other — this will soon be over."

I could hear arguing through Eshshah's thoughts. Ansel insisted that he be the one to fly with Eshshah. The Healer put a quash on that argument straightaway. She was not about to take any chances — this could be a trap. She allowed no more discussion. Gallen would come for me. The Healer was the only one — besides me — who could bend Ansel into acquiescence.

Kira had been watching me this whole time and I hoped that my face stayed neutral as I conversed with Eshshah. In a small voice, she asked, "What do I have to do to be a slave?"

I looked at her frightened little face, puzzled by what she meant. She rephrased her question, "What will they make me do?"

That question cut me deeply. *I will not let anything happen to this poor child.* "Kira, I have friends looking for me." I whispered. "We will get out of here. You have no need to worry about being a slave. I promise." I looked into her stricken eyes. This was a promise that I made with all my being. A smile of hope lit her face.

Just then the hatch at the front of the ship opened and a large man made his way down the ladder. He had a whip in one hand. He shouted at us, snapping the whip in the air. "Stand up you fools. Time to see what we have here before we dock."

There were three young men chained with us, maybe about my age or a little older. Two looked to be related — brothers, perhaps. The rest of us were women and children. The large man strode down the walkway connecting the butt of his whip with those who didn't rise fast enough. Cries of pain and fear echoed in the hull. Kira had trouble as she tried to stand up. I realized too late that she had an injured ankle. The man came up to her and raised his whip to beat her — as if that would help her get to her feet faster. Instinctively, I moved in front of her. With my chains I stopped his downward motion. If I had been free, I would have followed through and taken him to the ground, possibly sending him to his ancestors. *What kind of animal was he to treat this child in such a way?*

His face went livid. I knew he was furious that I dared stop his hand from beating Kira. He turned on me with murder in his eyes, thinking, I'm sure, that he would finish me off. I was ready for him, but before he struck, another man shouted at him as he descended the ladder.

"Don't touch that one!" he boomed. "Hands off of her. She is a special gift for Lord Gerik from Lady Kalonice and her mother. You know he does not accept damaged goods."

With an evil grin, he looked me up and down. "You're looking a little tired, Amáne. Perhaps you danced a bit too much at the ball?"

My stomach turned. A chill went up my spine. This man was the same whom I had seen with Kalonice and her mother as I stood with Ansel the night before.

I lifted myself to my full height, which of course was not daunting, but it helped with my confidence to face this monster.

"I will be no one's slave." I almost growled as my eyes bore into his, my teeth clenched. He stood before me, fuming at my defiance. His hand raised as if to strike. I didn't flinch. The man's face turned purple with rage. He had no choice but to follow his own orders. With a noticeable effort, he lowered his hand, turned and stomped back to ascend the ladder. The whip man followed. I slowly released my breath. A collective sigh of relief resounded as the prisoners sat back down.

I turned my thoughts back to my dragon. "Eshshah, what about Lali? Is she all right?"

"She'll be fine. The Healer treated her wounds — I heard they beat her quite badly."

"What trouble I cause to everyone that I care about, Eshshah."

"Amáne, this is none of your doing."

Facing Kira, I asked to see her ankle.

"I tried to run from them, and I fell. Then they caught me." Tears filled her eyes.

I asked Eshshah for her help as I placed my hands on Kira's injury and hummed low. The heat radiated through my hands and soon I could see by her face that her pain was relieved. The swelling subsided. She looked at me with wonder. I explained to her that I worked with a healer. She and my friend Eshshah had taught me a lot. It was only because of them that I had been able to help her. By myself, I couldn't have done so.

Darkness finally fell and Eshshah and Gallen took flight. Not knowing which direction the slave ship sailed, they first headed north. But we could feel the distance increase, so they turned and headed south. My spirit lightened the closer they came.

At last Eshshah announced, "I can see your ship, Amáne. It's reached the harbor and will arrive at the docks shortly."

The man with the whip returned and shouted, "As soon as we dock you'll get your sorry hides up to the deck, and be quick about it." With a wicked smile he cracked his whip. "I'll be happy to help you should you need it." The crack echoed like thunder in the hull. "There'll be a wagon waiting to haul you to your new owners. If you're not on it when it's ready to leave, then you'll be dragged behind it. No exceptions." He glared at me.

As soon as we docked, we were herded up the ladder. The captives at the front of the line were weighted down by those of us behind. The last of us were hard put to stay on our feet — painfully yanked ahead by the chains. The children could not keep up. They suffered. I ached for them. I kept Kira on her feet and practically carried her up the ladder while trying to help the lady who brought up the rear. The man with the whip followed close behind, cracking it repeatedly as he rushed us out of the belly of the ship, across the deck and over the gang plank to the wagon. I tried to shield Kira from his stinging lashes. I was caught several times by its cutting leather thongs. The whip man made sure the slave trader didn't catch him each time his whip tore into me.

Pulling the lady behind me, I shoved her onto the wagon. I leaped on last just as the driver shook the reins. It could not hold one more person. We were surrounded on four sides by wooden bars that rose about three hands width above my head — like a cage, but without a top. The man closed the gate behind me and locked it as the wagon began to move. There were two drivers with bows and swords up front, and two armed horsemen behind us as we left the docks and started up a lonely road.

Eshshah kept me abreast of the plan for my rescue. The first part had begun. She dropped Gallen off at a bend in the road up ahead — a perfect place for an ambush. Then she flew out over the ocean outside of the harbor. I followed her in thought transference as she banked and headed back towards the slave ship. Folding her wings, Eshshah made a silent dive at the mouth of the harbor. She swam under water to the vessel. I didn't think the crew had enough time to complete their final duties in docking their ship. Coming up under it, Eshshah used her nose as a battering ram. The huge timbers of the hull were crushed like twigs, splintering at her impact. It creaked and groaned as it took on water. In no time, the ship upended and was swallowed by the dark waters, taking part of the dock with it as well as whomever had not escaped. Eshshah swam back towards the harbor entry and exploded out of the water.

Keeping the expression off my face, I celebrated her success. That ship will never bear another captive to slavery. She flew to a spot near the ambush site to work with Gallen and myself for our timing on the next part of the plan.

I was thankful that only a small sliver of light leaked from the moon. Both Gallen and I had perfect night vision, but the guards were not so privileged. They wouldn't be aware of my actions as I pulled out Aperio's key, which I always carried around my neck. I worked to unlock my irons. It was no easy feat as I had to bend my wrist at an unnatural angle against the metal that cut into me. I guided the key into the lock, and just managed to release my shackles before we arrived at the spot where Gallen hid. Without a sound, I lowered them to the floor of the wagon, and awaited the signal from Gallen and Eshshah.

As we rounded the bend, I heard two successive swishes. Gallen's arrows quickly and accurately found their marks. The drivers slumped in their seat.

Before the remaining two guards on horseback realized what had happened, I'd already leapt the wall of the cage. In mid-air I caught my glaive that Gallen tossed. My feet barely touched the ground when I ran my blade through the guard closest to me. He dropped from his horse with a heavy thud and a loud exhale as the air left his chest.

The second guard, now alarmed, drew his sword and swung. I ducked just in time. Fighting me from horseback was to his advantage. But my small stature, as well as my gender, helped me a bit — if only to give him a false sense of dominance. I sprung back, out of his range. With a confident air, the guard leaped off of his horse to face me on foot, just as an arrow zipped by, digging a gash in his cheek. The man placed himself between the horse and Gallen, rendering the next arrows useless. I heard Gallen draw his sword and rush to my assistance.

Avoiding the frightened horse, I charged to face the guard. I thrust my glaive at him. He parried. I blocked his next series of strikes before I was able to jam and trap his sword, bringing us in close together. I could feel his hot vile breath on my face. He tried to use his weight to push me backwards. My silk gown made fighting difficult. Before he got the upper hand, I brought my knee up hard and fast into his crotch. My foot raked his unarmored shins and came down hard on the top of his foot. I leaped to the right as he doubled over in agony. At that moment Gallen arrived and executed the finishing stroke.

"May they rest with their ancestors," I whispered for all four men.

Gallen closed the gap between us. He took me in his arms and held me tightly in a fatherly embrace. Tears streamed down my face. I couldn't hide my sobs. My rescue was a success.

I unlocked the back part of the wagon and let my frightened companions out of the cage. Gallen disappeared for a moment as I used Aperio's key to release the prisoners from their irons. Amid tears and sighs of relief and an endless stream of thank you's, they were all set free. Gallen returned with several skins of water and a large bag that he opened to reveal bread and fruit. The ravenous group rushed towards the food in a free-for-all. A large woman stepped up and demanded order. She took charge as she methodically distributed the provisions. Kira came up to me and handed me a piece of her bread. With a smile and a nod of appreciation, I tore into it with as much voracity as the rest of the group. Gallen eyed us with pity.

Gallen and I gathered up the weapons from the guards, and handed one of the swords to the woman who had taken charge. She looked to me quite capable of wielding one. The other two swords were given to the two brothers. The bows and daggers we confiscated were distributed to the other male and to the women that looked well enough to use them.

I handed a dagger to Kira and said, "Take this and learn how to use it."

Suppressing my urge to vomit, we searched the guards' bodies and removed any coins they had on them. I pulled some jewels off of the sleeves of my gown that were threatening to detach and handed them to the woman with the sword.

"Use these coins and jewels and the horses to trade for safe passage back to your homes. We haven't come too far from the harbor and I'm sure you can negotiate with a ship to get you all back safely. Please take special care of Kira and see that she is delivered to her mother."

The woman nodded and promised that I need not worry about her as she would personally escort her to her home. She drew Kira to her side. I knew she meant it.

Leaving the woman's grasp, Kira ran to me and wrapped her arms around me. "Won't you be coming with us?"

"No, Kira, I have another direction I must go."

She squeezed me tighter. With tears in her eyes, she said, "Maybe we can meet again?" Somehow she knew not to ask anything else of me.

"I would like that." I held her a few more minutes, kissed her forehead, then released her as Gallen and I turned to make our way to Eshshah. I wiped my tears with the back of my sleeve as we left.

CHAPTER TWENTY-FOUR

Gallen and I wasted no time, sprinting to where Eshshah waited. I held her fangs and pressed my forehead against her nose for several moments. I kissed her and looked into her golden eyes.

"I don't ever want us to be separated like that again." I cried.

"Me either, Amáne." If dragons could cry, that's what I would have expected to see.

Exhausted, all I could think of was to get this blood, dirt and stink off of me. I mounted the double saddle and locked wrists with Gallen as he swung up behind me. He handed me a helmet and a cloak as I gave the word and Eshshah took to wing.

The flight was fast and silent and the sky was just hinting of dawn when I at last spotted the field at the Arevale Outpost. I could see several horses and riders waiting for us. Eshshah had let the Healer know when we got closer to our destination and it seemed that quite a few had come to meet us. As we approached I saw the Healer, Calder, Avano, Braonàn, Dorjan and — Ansel.

My heart beat fast and loud as I spotted him. I was taken aback as a powerful yearning washed over me — a desperation to feel his comforting embrace. I needed him with an urgency that frightened me. Only he could lessen my terror. But I also needed to stay strong. Hold my ground at least until he approved our quest — if that was even possible.

The Riders Council had, of course, been postponed since it was supposed to have happened yesterday. Gallen said if I were up to it, the riders had agreed to convene this afternoon. This was fine with me. I wanted to get it over with as quickly as possible. My hope was to get back to the manor, soak this filth off of me and get some rest before we gathered. I needed my mind to be clear in order to assist the Healer, Gallen, Dorjan and Bern in proposing our plan to procure the dragon egg — the quest for which I had been waiting for such a long time.

Eshshah barely folded her wings when Ansel rushed up to us. Gallen leaped down. I had just lowered myself to Eshshah's foreleg when Ansel, after a heartfelt greeting to Eshshah, snatched me off and wrapped me in an anguished embrace. He buried his face in my neck. I didn't fight it, but leaned my forehead against his chest, as I inhaled his scent, and let his warmth flow over me.

"Amáne, I am so sorry," he whispered.

"Ansel, please, don't apologize. This wasn't your fault." I was too weary. I wanted nothing more than to forget it all and stand there silently in his arms for a few more minutes — no matter that it went against my own rules. The Healer, along with the other riders, stood their distance, giving Ansel the time he needed.

He pulled away to take in my face. Finding the bloody welts from the whip that had bitten into my cheek, he gently put his finger on them and emitted a soft groan.

"I'm fine now, Ansel. Please don't torture yourself ... truly, I'm fine."

I started to push away so he wouldn't have to suffer any more in discovering my additional injuries. Before I could release myself from his hold, he tilted my head back and without hesitation, placed his lips gently on mine. I wrapped my arms around him and pulled him closer. I needed his attentions, his warmth for just a bit longer. Finally, with no small amount effort I managed to pull back, my heart thundered in my chest. I hoped the riders couldn't hear it.

"Ansel, please, we —" Defiantly, he kissed me once more before he released me.

He stepped back and regarded my appearance.

"Truthfully," I smiled, "I think my beautiful silk gown has seen happier times." Finding no humor in my attempt, he gently took my forearms, pulled back my tattered sleeves and studied the gashes on my wrists. He well knew the feeling of being locked in manacles. His torment over my wounds was more than I could bear.

"So ... they'll probably leave scars, don't you think?" I offered.

He met my eyes. A corner of his mouth lifted in a faint smile — if only for my benefit. He shook his head and looked at me in wonder.

"Ride back with me," he entreated.

I couldn't decide if it was an order or a desperate plea.

"You brought an extra horse for me, didn't you?"

"Please, Amáne."

How could I turn him down? I nodded, but wished he wouldn't have asked. I stepped away and headed towards the other riders.

They saluted me and I returned the gesture. The Healer wrapped her arms around me gently, uncertain of how badly I was hurt. She stepped back and searched my eyes to assess my condition. Satisfied, she released me. I graciously excused myself to take care of Eshshah. Her saddle was still wet from her underwater maneuver in sinking the slave ship. All riders know that their dragon is their first priority.

"I'll go with you to help with the saddle." Ansel said.

"Thank you, Ansel," I said gently, "but I really need a few minutes alone with her. I'm sorry."

A recognition came to his eyes. Yet once more he gave in to my stubborn insistence in declining his attentions.

Eshshah and I flew into the entry cavern of the outpost. I dismounted and rushed to my dragon's face. Leaning into her, I let my tears flow — just between her and me. They were tears of release, tears of frustration and tears of happiness that we were together.

We made our way to the library where I began to unsaddle her. It was a task that proved to be more difficult than I had anticipated. I should probably have accepted Ansel's help. The saddle was the heavy double one, made even heavier in its waterlogged state. I loosened the straps and the additional weight caused it to slip in my direction. It barely missed me as it crashed to the ground. *How ironic would that have been,* I mused, *for me to see my end because of a saddle after what I had just been through?*

After spending a few more minutes in silence with Eshshah, I proceeded to the bathing room. Wetting a cloth, I held it against my face and tried to steady my breathing. I washed the blood and grime off my hands as I stared at my disheveled reflection in the glass. Not wanting to keep the riders and Ansel waiting any longer, I took a deep breath, left the bathing room and met Eshshah in the entry. I mounted bareback and we flew back to the clearing.

Ansel and I argued whether I would sit behind him or in front, but he acquiesced to my demand to sit behind. After he mounted, Gallen gave me a leg up and I settled behind Ansel. I was so exhausted and sore that, in truth, I would have been much more comfortable on my own horse. But it would have been cruel of me if I chose not to ride with him.

When we arrived at Trivingar Manor, I slipped off the back of the horse and planned to rush inside, but Ansel followed after me.

"Amáne, I need to speak with you."

"Yes?" My heart sank. I didn't like the look on his face, and dreaded what he might say. I wasn't ready to confront him just yet, but I had a good idea what was on his mind.

"Ansel, I'm completely spent. I can't deal with one more thing right now, but only a hot soak and a needed rest. Can it please wait?"

"I need to talk to you now. No, it cannot wait."

"Then talk to me." I said abruptly. My shoulders dropped as my patience wore thin.

"Not here, can we go to your chambers?"

I nodded, spun around, and headed to my room, leaving him to catch up to me. My nerves were frayed and my mouth had gone dry in anticipation of words I didn't want to hear.

I pushed in the door to my chambers. He followed me in and closed it behind him. Turning to face him, I kept my distance. My eyes narrowed as I crossed my arms in front of me. With my jaw set, I tried to brace myself for what he was about to say.

"Amáne, this is not going to be easy for either of us."

I stopped breathing. My heart accelerated. I pressed my lips together and waited for him to continue.

"I didn't want to take you by surprise at Council, but wanted you to be prepared for my decision, so you'll have time to think about it and accept it ... time to work on your quick temper ..."

"No! Don't! We are not having this conversation right now. We can't. You have to wait until the Council. Ansel, you're not being fair."

Not heeding my plea, he said sternly, "The danger is just too great for me to allow your quest at this time. It will have to be postponed to a later date."

"A later date won't work. You can't just make that ruling right now. How can you prejudge your decision when you haven't even listened to our plan? It's unfair."

Making an effort to speak respectfully to him, I found I was failing. I had to fight for what I thought was right — the Healer needed a dragon egg. Eshshah and I were the only ones that could get it for her. *This is for his throne. Why can't he understand that?*

"It's not unfair," he remained firm, not backing down. "I'm telling you now so that you can get a grip on yourself before the Council meets. This way you can accept your orders as given, and not embarrass yourself by arguing with me in front of the other riders. You tend to run a little hot when you want something your way."

At that moment I understood. It made perfect sense. Giving me the opportunity to think it over ahead of time would save both of us from embarrassment. Truthfully, he didn't deserve the way I sometimes treated him. The other riders should never witness any disrespect, especially from a new rider. And there were some older riders who would be aghast that any disrespect towards the prince would come from ... a girl. Ansel was, of course, right. Without reason, though, this truth made me even more angry. And, as usual, I lost what little composure I had left. My tongue took over.

"Oh I get it, now! You're afraid I'll 'run hot' in the middle of Council. That they'll see the true me — my temper — my stubbornness — my double fatal flaw."

"Don't use that word, Amáne."

I didn't apologize.

" Amáne, please understand, I thought I had lost you," he said low and desperate. "I couldn't take it. I know it was terrorizing for you, and for that reason, it was torture for me as well. You're safe now and I'm not ready to put you out there again."

As well as he knew me, he should have known this was not the time to confront me with this information. He should have listened to me and let me recover. I know he thought he was saying the right thing, trying to help, but my exhaustion and torment crashed down on me at that moment. My eyes stung. My anger wrapped me in its dark hot embrace as I lashed out at him.

"You're not ready to put me out there? If you would care more about your kingdom than you do your personal desires, then maybe you would have had your throne by now — and Farvard would still be alive!" Farvard was the dragon rider, and my friend, who had been killed when Ansel was abducted by Galtero's men.

I regretted my words even as the last one left my lips. My eyes went wide. I clasped my hand over my mouth and backed up. Remorse tightened its claws around my chest.

Just as shocked at what I had said, he cursed. "Don't insult me, Amáne! You know how much I care about Teravinea. It's killing me to watch everything my father stood for be spat upon by Galtero. You also know that I accept full responsibility for Farvard's death."

I wanted nothing more in my life than to take back my angry words. But words will not retract. I stood silent.

"My personal desires?" He raged. "Because I care about your safety? I care about the safety of all the riders."

He began to pace, running his fingers through his hair. Stopping abruptly, he faced me. "I can't help feeling the way I do about you. I can't just close my eyes and pretend it will go away, which seems to be the way you deal with things. It might work in your fantasy world, but not in my world."

Ansel's eyes narrowed. "I'm no fool, Amáne. Do you think that I don't know what you've been trying to do all along? You think that if you hold me at arm's length that it will make a difference in my decisions — that I'll merrily approve your quest? How far you are from me and however often you push me away makes no difference. I can't just turn off my love. And I can't disregard your safety."

I'd pushed him too far. *Will I ever learn to hold my tongue?*

He was unable to restrain himself. Through clenched teeth, he said, "You are the most stubborn person I have ever met."

After a pause, he closed his eyes and took a deep jagged breath. When he opened them and met mine, they were filled with pain.

"Okay, you win. This round is all yours." He put his hands up, conceding defeat.

I couldn't breathe.

"I'll consent to your quest, Amáne. I promise. As you wish. Without even hearing your plan. Go. Do your duty however you see fit. Restore my throne. Save Teravinea. Save the whole world if that's what you want." Throwing in expletives at fitting intervals, he lost all sense of his manners as he cursed like the sailors in Dorsal.

"After that, you can just live your lonely life, never have anyone, or any memories of happiness, because your duty comes before anything that would ever make you happy. So be it. You can be like my aunt was for most of her life — alone." His voice shook.

Then, in a low pained tone, "Just so you know, you've sentenced me to the same fate, Amáne ... because, like it or not, you own my heart. Even if I were duty-bound to take a wife, there would be no room for her. So you see, in essence, I too will be alone."

That revelation cut me — right through my heart. My hand went involuntarily to my breast. My breath came in short gasps.

"Don't worry, Amáne," his face went hard, his eyes cold and sharp, "I will no longer bother you for your attentions. It will be strictly professional between us — allegiance and duty only. Have a nice and lonely life." With that, he turned on his heel and rushed out of the room. But not before I saw the moisture in his eyes.

My victory. I'll be allowed my quest. But at what price? This victory was not sweet, but bitter and nauseating. I loathed myself. It was unforgiveable what I had done to him. I'd lowered myself to the despicable selfish person I truly was.

Fiona's words echoed in my mind, "You're breaking that boy's heart!"

She was wrong. I didn't break it — I ripped it right out of his chest.

I turned my back to the door, bit my knuckles and moaned in anguish.

"Eshshah, maybe he's right. Maybe I am fated to be alone. But look what I've done to him. Why does love have to be so hard?"

She was with me in thought transference, but didn't answer my question. It was rhetorical — there is no answer.

"Love?" I stopped short. "Do I love him, Eshshah?"

"I've felt the strong attraction between you two, and your dedication you had to each other, though you denied it, Amáne. If that's what you humans call love, then yes."

I let out a dark laugh. "Well I've made short work of it, then, haven't I? I've lost any chance I may have had."

I paced the floor. My harsh words echoed in my head. The more I thought about what I'd done, the more angry I became with myself. My pacing increased its tempo as my despair rose. Grabbing a cup from my table, I hurled it against the wall. It smashed into a thousand pieces.

My door burst open. Bern rushed in with his sword drawn. I snatched a candle stand off the table — ready to launch it at him. Luckily for him, I realized who it was. He quickly surveyed the room and then looked at me awkwardly.

"Are you guarding my door?" I shouted as I glared at him. Bern had no idea how to handle a fifteen year old girl who had just boiled over. He stood there uncomfortably for a short time. Then he bowed his head and backed out, closing the door behind him.

That was all I could take. Like the cup I just shattered, I broke. I threw myself down on my bed and began to scream uncontrollably into the pillows.

When I'd finally quieted down, there were two small taps on the door. I heard the Healer's footsteps as she let herself in. A sweet aroma filled the air. My sensitive nose detected a combination of ginger, camomile and eleuthro, all calming herbs. I didn't give her the courtesy of acknowledging her presence. I kept my face buried in the bedding. My harrowing ordeal, my shame, the loss of my best friend all weighed heavily on me.

"Amáne," said the Healer, softly, "please have some tea. Lali will be in soon to help you remove your gown so you can have a hot soak. I'm truly sorry about what you've been through. If you can, think of the good that will come of it. A slave trade has been discovered. King Tynan is being advised and he will use his power to put an end to this despicable commerce. You, without your consent, have played a part in this. Lives will be saved. The guilty parties will be punished. Kalonice and her mother are being transported to King Tynan at this moment."

I flinched at the mention of Kalonice's name. "If good will come of this, then I'll accept it, Healer," I murmured into the pillows. But even the knowledge of Kalonice's fate did nothing to lighten my mood.

"Look at me, Amáne."

I hesitated and then reluctantly turned over to face her.

She regarded me closely, searching my face, then my eyes. "Ah ... there's more to this."

I didn't answer, but chewed my lower lip. I couldn't meet her eyes, but kept mine focused on the ceiling.

"Ansel spoke with you?"

I nodded.

"He told you that your quest will be denied?"

Again, I nodded.

After a pause, I added, "But then he changed his mind and told me that he'll consent to it."

Her eyebrows raised. "He told you he would approve your quest?"

"Yes, Healer, but it was only after I was so cruel to him. I insulted him — I'm the most horrible person in the entire kingdom. Why does my tongue always act before my head ... or my heart? Why did I have to hurt him? Healer, I never really deserved his friendship in the first place, and now I've lost it. What kind of monster am I?" I turned back over and sobbed into the pillow.

She put her hand on my head and stroked my hair, but before she could respond, there was a small knock and the door opened again. I lifted my face to find Lali. She brought in a tray of small cakes. Putting the tray down, she faced me and presented me with a sharp dragon salute.

My head jerked towards the Healer. I blinked in disbelief. The Healer nodded as if to say, 'Lali now knows.' Looking back at Lali I nodded and then leapt up from my bed and threw my arms around her gingerly, mindful of her injuries.

"I'm sorry, Lali." I looked at her bruises, touching her face gently. "This is all my fault. Please forgive me."

"Mistress Amáne, don't you for one second think that any of this was your fault. I only apologize that I was so weak and allowed those two brutes to defeat me. But I'm sure they won't forget the fight I gave them any time soon. One will have trouble for quite some time with his personals, and the other will be lamenting the use of his fingers. If only I would've had a dagger, or been quicker, they would never have gotten the better of me. We would have avoided the abuse you had to go through. I should be the one apologizing. If I ever see that girl again ... well ... she will wish she was never born."

I couldn't help but smile as she continued her prattle. The fact that Lali now shared my secret allowed me a small touch of comfort in the midst of my despair.

She released me from my gown and then drew a hot bath, placing lavender and other fragrant herbs in the steaming water. Since she knew I was a dragon rider, I no longer had to hide Eshshah's linking mark. She looked quizzically at the hideous tattoo on my ankle, but didn't insist. I decided one day I would explain it, but not now.

Chapter Twenty-Five

Twenty-six dragon riders sat around a large round table. One chair remained empty in memory of Farvard. Another empty chair sat three places to my right — to be occupied by Ansel. The room resonated with a low buzz as various conversations took place while we waited for his arrival.

This Council set my nerves on end for several reasons. The meeting included a special ceremony to officially swear Eshshah and me in as a linked pair, bound to the Royal House of Drekinn — Ansel's line. I would again be the center of attention. My stomach quaked, nauseous in anticipation.

My ultimate distress — besides the fact that Ansel would be seated only three chairs from me — was that I would have to face him after what I'd said to him. I resigned myself to the fact that I must remain detached and professional, while we proposed our plan for our quest. I couldn't begin to guess how Ansel would behave towards me.

I practiced deep and even breaths to gain composure. My head turned when the door opened. I caught my breath as Ansel entered and strode towards his chair. He carried himself in the most regal manner that I had never before seen from him. His face stern, his jaw set. Even as majestic as he had looked at the ball, it was no comparison to his princely bearing as he entered the Council room.

To my surprise, the riders all stood and saluted him. I had no idea that he merited the dragon salute. If I had bothered to give it any thought, it would have made perfect sense. He was the leader of all the riders, therefore deserving of the honor. I jumped to my feet and joined in the salute. He crisply saluted us back.

"Welcome dragon riders," he said in an authoritative voice. This was not the same Ansel I had known, and shamefully abused. This was the true Prince of Teravinea. I trembled at my insolence.

"The Dragon Rider Council will now convene." He remained standing and so did we. "We have a first order of business that has not been a part of our Councils for a great number of years. This will be the first in my lifetime. It is my honor to officially swear in a recently linked pair."

He shot a look in my direction. His eyes didn't meet mine, but fell somewhere around my lips or my chin. I swallowed hard as my heart pounded in my ears. I fought to remain in control.

Ansel continued, "I must apologize that this ceremony cannot be done properly — in an outdoor arena with rider and dragon side by side — as it should be. In these dire times, the linked pair have been essentially in hiding. We're forced to perform this ceremony behind closed doors with Eshshah present only in open thought transference."

Without further delay, he turned to me and began, "Eshshah and Amáne, have you undertaken to accept the privilege of Dragon and Chosen One as a linked pair bound to the Royal House of

Drekinn, through your own desire, and with no coercion from another party?"

"We have, your Lord — er my Grace — that is, Your Grace." My nerves were frayed This ceremony didn't start as I would have hoped, especially in front of Ansel and twenty-five riders. The blood rose in my face. He showed no emotion, but remained hard and detached. I could hear quiet snickers from a few of the other riders.

"Very well, Rider Amáne, please join me at the steps. Riders, you may be seated."

Ansel stepped away from his chair and motioned for me to walk with him to a platform against the wall, near the door he had entered. It was shaped in a half circle with three steps leading up to it — a small stage.

The short trip from my chair to the steps proved to be the most difficult walk I had ever made in my life. Right beside him, yet I couldn't look up at him, or take his arm, or find any pleasure in being by his side. A shell of myself, I blocked any feelings for him I may have had. The entire way, I concentrated on placing one foot in front of the other, lest I trip. Successfully making my way to the dais, I remained at the bottom while he took the three steps and turned to face me.

He drew his sword and held it in front of him. "Please kneel."

Lowering his sword above my head but not touching it, "Amáne, daughter of Catriona of Teravinea, you have been deemed a Chosen One by Eshshah of the Royal line of Dragons to be her rider for eternity. Do you, Eshshah, and you, Amáne now swear by your linking that you will honor and defend the Kingdom of Teravinea under the Crown of the Royal House of Drekinn?"

"We will." Eshshah and I said simultaneously.

"That you will acknowledge the additional bond to the royal family of Drekinn, due to Eshshah's line intertwined with mine?" His voice quavered.

I swallowed the lump in my throat and responded, "We will."

"That you will honor, defend and protect your Peers and those weaker than you?"

"We will."

"That you will conduct yourselves in all matters as befits a dragon and rider to the benefit of your own good name and the greater glory of the Kingdom of Teravinea?"

"Yes, we will."

"Then having sworn these solemn oaths, know that I, Ansel, son of King Emeric of the Royal House of Drekinn, true and rightful heir to the throne of Teravinea do bind you, Eshshah and you, Amáne, dragon and rider, as a linked pair to the Kingdom of Teravinea, and additionally to the Royal house of Drekinn to defend in honor and duty until you lie with your ancestors."

He lowered his sword, touching both of my shoulders.

"Please rise."

The Healer had instructed me in my response. "This day Eshshah of the Royal line of Dragons and I, Amáne, daughter of Catriona of Teravinea, as linked pair do render homage and fealty to you, Lord Ansel, son of King Emeric of the Royal House of Drekinn. We will remain true in all ways, serving faithfully. This we do swear by our lives and by our honor." My voice cracked with emotion as my eyes filled. I heard throat clearing and sniffing from some of the other riders as they, no doubt, remembered their swearing in.

"I accept your homage and fealty," Lord Ansel responded, "and I pledge to you that from this day forward I will honor and defend your rights as dragon and rider. Turn now and greet your Peers."

I met his eyes briefly and thought I saw a combination of pride, hurt and sorrow, which mirrored mine. I turned to face my fellow dragon riders. As one they stood up, saluted, clapped, whistled and shouted. Their praises welcomed me into their exclusive band of brotherhood. I smiled and nodded my appreciation for their unexpected warmth as a few tears escaped. I made my way back to my seat. The Healer hugged me and whispered her emotional congratulations in my ear.

The tragedy was that this should have been a happy moment shared with Lord Ansel. Instead, it was tense. I lacked the focus I should have had at such a momentous ceremony. It was only with Eshshah's help that I didn't break down right there.

Lord Ansel strode purposefully to his chair and restored order immediately upon taking his seat.

The Council then moved forward as each rider briefed him on the situations in their individual townships or cities. He and the Healer were well informed of the state of affairs in each locality, since they kept regular contact through the communication discs. But discussing the circumstances as a group brought out more detailed examinations and solutions to any problems they brought to the table.

I watched with admiration as Lord Ansel conducted the Dragon Rider's Council, speaking with leadership and full knowledge of their individual issues and their progress in seeking allies for our cause. He wasn't overbearing or condescending, but in full command of each rider's respect as they stood and gave their deliveries in turn. Many of these men were well over one-hundred years old. They had served under King Emeric and even King Rikkar, Lord Ansel's grandfather, yet they showed him the respect that I'm sure they had shown for his ancestors.

How could Lord Ansel have stooped so low as to show any interest in me? The whispers of those in Dorsal at the Life Celebration echoed in my head. They were right. I didn't deserve anyone of his station. I was too blind to even realize the fact that he brought himself down to my level. What a humbling sacrifice that had to have been. I shuddered when I remembered how I had assigned him the duty of slicing potatoes when we stayed at the Dorsal Outpost — and that I found it quite funny at the time. It sickened me to recall it, now.

I had pushed him away and treated him like a commoner all because of my selfishness to go on a great quest. It was all about me. I made up my own rules and he graciously went along with them, all the while waiting for me to follow my heart. Lord Ansel saw it from the start — the bond between us. He was willing to accept me no matter my station. He truly did love me and sacrificed even his love to give in to my obstinacy. What made this truth harder to bear was that I still felt the heat from our last kiss.

My mind reeled at the thought that I had lost my chance of winning back Lord Ansel's attentions. It made me sicker still when I thought of what had caused me to lose him — my temper; my stubbornness; my cruelty.

Chapter Twenty-six

Suddenly, I was drawn back into the council room by the complete silence that surrounded me, and a nudge from the Healer, as well as a prompt from Eshshah. I found I'd been staring at Lord Ansel. I don't know for how long. In looking about, I saw every eye was on me.

Fear gripped me as the Healer whispered out of the corner of her mouth, "Amáne, stand up and answer him."

Somehow I managed to pull myself to my feet. The blood rose in my face and with my eyes wide, I sputtered, "Uh ... er ... I ..."

"Do you need me to repeat my question, Rider?" Lord Ansel spoke sternly, yet with patience, as if he spoke to a young school girl.

"Yes, please, Lord Ansel."

"Were you not following any of our discussion?" He had it right once again.

Embarrassed, I was nevertheless thankful that anger didn't control me at that moment, though I did feel its heat.

Trying to find my voice, I whispered, "I'm sorry, Lord Ansel. I ... I must have gotten distracted."

"We were discussing the next order of business," he began in an even tone — again, as if I were an errant student. "Which is procuring a dragon egg from the hatching chamber at Castle Teravinea. The Healer has made it clear that a key element in our goal to overthrow Galtero is to determine how his magicians and sorcerers have controlled the dragons in their eggs.

"There are but a few eggs in the hatching chamber which are of the Royal Dragon Line — Eshshah's lineage. Galtero can't allow that line of dragons to hatch as they will have no loyalty to him. Only a dragon of that line can determine which are the Royal Eggs. Since even he can't bring himself to destroy them, of which we are thankful, keeping them from hatching is his only form of security — ensuring that he cannot be overthrown by dragon riders.

"My question to you — since I was informed that you have a plan that I must listen to before making my judgement — are you prepared to lead the discussion and convince the Council of the success of your plan?"

My first inclination was to run out of the room and be sick. I felt a cold sweat as the contents of my stomach threatened to rise. *He's asking me to reveal the details of our plan?* Bern, Dorjan, Gallen and the Healer were all part of it. *Why me? Was he punishing me*? Of course it would be less than what I deserved, but I wasn't prepared to be the one to lead the discussion. However, I would never concede to that fact.

I felt like I was back in class again with the teacher asking me to stand up in front of my classmates and sing a ballad. I used to close my eyes and pretend I was the only one in the room. But, this was not school. These were not my classmates, but seasoned, hardened dragon riders who had seen more than I could even imagine. Lord Ansel was not my teacher, but my future king.

I swallowed hard and inhaled. *I am Amáne, sworn dragon rider of Eshshah,* I said to myself. I knew Lord Ansel was purposely not making this easy for me. It had always been my habit to react by lashing out in anger. But I was no longer that girl. I just recently learned the hardest lesson in my life. Outside of losing my mother, I had just experienced a most devastating loss — that of my best friend.

Pulling my shoulders back, I drew myself to my full height — no matter that my height was insignificant. I lifted my chin, looked straight into Lord Ansel's eyes, and in a firm voice, "Yes, Your Grace. I am prepared."

I could see an eyebrow raise ever so slightly at my unexpected change in attitude, His eyes softened for just an instant. He nodded for me to continue.

"Thank you, Your Grace."

Turning to the riders around the table, I didn't waste any words. "Your Grace, my fellow riders — I have been working with the Healer, Gallen, Dorjan, and Bern, and we have a plan. We have no doubt as to its success. I'll get straight to the point — I will be walking openly through the front gates of Castle Teravinea."

The room hummed as the riders voiced their shock and disbelief. Lord Ansel gave a small jerk of his head. I was not deterred, but motioned a request for the riders' silence to let me continue.

"As you already know, Galtero has kept our tradition of the Hatching Gathering. We also know it is but a ruse. Besides Eshshah's, there hasn't been a hatching in thirty years," I looked pointedly at Avano, as he was the last linked before Eshshah and

I. "We've decided to use this to our advantage. Due to the lack of any activity in the hatching chamber, there's been a great decline in attendance, both prospective riders and spectators. The Hatching Gathering brings only a few curious onlookers, and a shameful amount of prospects. It's only six weeks away and the lack of interest will aid in my being accepted as a rider candidate."

This time, there was more than a hum throughout the room. I heard mumbling and some outright laughs. Eben, formerly Haldis, rider of the late Salama, spoke out, "Amáne, perhaps you're not aware, and the others may have forgotten, that Galtero has decreed that only males need apply as candidates."

"No, Eben, we haven't forgotten. I plan on applying as a male."

This time the room resonated as the riders expressed their disbelief. Again, Eben voiced his opinion, "No offense intended, Amáne." He tried to hide his amusement "But we all saw your grand entrance at the ball." He looked around the table as most of the men nodded or added to Eben's observations. "And many of us had the pleasure of dancing with you. We may be old, but our eyesight is as sharp as the day we woke from our dragon fever. You are the furthest example of a male that any of us have seen in quite a while. You'd no sooner pass for a candidate than Eshshah could pass for a kitten."

Laughter echoed in the room as the blush rose in my face. Eshshah even uttered her rumbling laugh, and mimicked a meow. I couldn't suppress my smile.

I inhaled slowly, and with control that surprised me, I responded, "Thank you for the compliment, Eben ..." *I never thought I would ever be able to thank a man for a compliment.* A hint of surprise showed in Lord Ansel's eyes. "... but contrary to what you might think, I can, and have successfully disguised myself as a male. There are several in this room who can attest to my success."

I threw a quick glance at Lord Ansel who suddenly found something of interest in the palm of his hand.

Gallen then came to my assistance. "Eben, you certainly have a point. If I had only just met Amáne, I would agree with you. But I can affirm the fact that she does have the skills necessary to successfully pass herself off as a male. I have no doubts that she could apply as a candidate, be accepted and enter the hatching grounds."

Another murmur around the room as the riders digested this information.

Once I regained their attention, I described our plan in more detail. How, with Eshshah's help in open thought transference, I would choose the egg. Then how I planned to escape through the tunnels and corridors under the castle that I was already familiar with. I went on to cover how I would meet up with Eshshah at the Castle Outpost, like the last time. Bern would wait there with Eshshah, staying in contact with me through her and keeping the Healer and Lord Ansel apprised of our progress. We would then leave together. Eshshah and I would drop Bern off at Anbon and then continue back to Dorsal with the egg.

"In conclusion, Lord Ansel, riders, this is a well-thought-out plan that promises to be successful. I ask that you consider this quest to be the necessary next step in the mission to secure the throne ... I ask, Lord Ansel, for your blessing upon this endeavor." His eyes remained averted.

With that I sat down and looked again at Lord Ansel, who still didn't meet my gaze. The riders began discussing and questioning elements of the plan. The Healer, Gallen, Dorjan and Bern became active in the conversation as ideas and suggestions were offered. Finally, an approving tone echoed around the table. An excitement was felt in the air as the riders recognized our forward progress in the mission to take the throne from Galtero and raise Lord Ansel to his rightful position. It had been too long since this group had any hope in achieving their goal. At this moment, Eshshah and I were their hope. I felt their enthusiasm as it lit up the room.

At last the conversation died down, everyone had given their opinions — mostly positive. Now we drew our attention to Lord Ansel who had the final say in the matter. He sat straight and stiff in his chair, eyebrows nearly touching as he stared at his father's ring on his finger. The same ring I had brought him as proof that I was sent by his aunt, to rescue him from his chains in the castle dungeon.

There was not a sound in the room. If a feather had fallen, we could have heard it hit the ground. Still Lord Ansel did not move. My heart ached at the pain in his face as he struggled to make his decision — his final ruling still bathed in doubt.

The more time that went by, the more my disappointment rose in my chest. I tried to keep a calm empty face as my shoulders started to sink. How could I have thought he truly would approve my quest? He did promise me, didn't he? I had never known him to go back on a promise. But when I thought of the circumstances in which he gave that promise, I knew that I couldn't bind him to it. There was no doubt that I had coerced him into saying what he said. His words, spoken only a short time ago, 'Okay, you win. This round is all yours. I'll consent to your quest! I promise. As you wish,' echoed in my mind. His pain. My cruelty.

I didn't deserve the honor of serving him. On my own, I considered myself as nothing. My linking to Eshshah was the only justification of my worthiness.

At last Lord Ansel took a deep breath and all eyes turned to him.

Speaking low and deliberate, "The plan is certainly one which sounds solid ... in theory. I have no doubts as to the skills and talents of this rider to pull off the disguise." *Does he loathe me so much that he can't even say my name?* My hand went to my chest as if I could stop the bleeding of my heart with that one motion.

"— However, she has just barely begun to understand and get a taste of what the world can do ... how bad it truly can be. She has bravely volunteered and even pleaded for this dangerous task, unmindful of the possible consequences. It is ultimately my decision what I can ask of you riders — the sacrifices I can bear to accept from you." He scanned the riders around the table. "I know it is my duty as a leader to make decisions for the good of the kingdom. But can I, with clear conscience, send her into peril ... again?"

Resolving that I would have to endure the inevitable denial of our quest at this time, I silently appealed to Eshshah for help.

"I'm with you Amáne," she said.

I needed her strength to be able to accept the decision that we won't be going to the Hatching Gathering. Perhaps Lord Ansel had seen the change in me — that I had taken a turn for the better in my self control. He would be correct. I can and will control my anger. I reminded myself to breathe in and out. My eyes locked on my hands. I held back any thought of tears. He had promised. But again, it was a promise that I knew he couldn't keep. I won't fault him for that. I pressed my lips together and held my breath.

"The answer to that is no — I cannot with a clear conscience send this rider into such danger. I will never get used to asking any of you such sacrifice, even though it be my duty."

His eyes swept the room again, slowly meeting each rider. He met mine for a brief instant and I barely suppressed a gasp as I saw the agony in his eyes.

He continued, "I'm fully aware of the importance of the timing of this quest. Because of our discussion and your positive support of its success ... I ... reluctantly ... will allow it." His voice trailed off at the end, barely audible.

Forgetting that I'd been holding my breath, I let it out instantly. I had prepared myself for a denial. I didn't know how to respond to his approval. My eyebrows raised in disbelief.

His saddened eyes rested on me. He proceeded in a formal manner. "Eshshah and Amáne, as dragon and rider, linked pair, do you accept the honor and privilege," he swallowed hard. I was afraid he would not be able to finish, but he cleared his throat and continued, "... of accepting a quest that will put you into extreme danger ... for the good of the Kingdom of Teravinea?"

I stood up and met his eyes. Along with Eshshah, I said softly, "We do, your Grace." On my own, I added, "Thank you. I promise you won't regret your decision."

"I already have," he said under his breath. Then, as if he had been reading my mind the last few minutes, his eyes bore into mine, and he said in a low voice only for me, "I keep my promises, Amáne."

With that he stood up, saluted, turned abruptly and exited the room by the same door he'd entered. The riders jumped from their seats and executed a hurried salute to his back. I didn't rise, but sat in shock. His decision, his defeated demeanor reeled in my head until it hurt.

This is what I had wanted; what I had begged for; what I had given up everything for. Why then was I not celebrating with the other riders as they came to congratulate me? Clapping me on the back, shaking my hand. I forced a smile, but felt empty. I'd been trying to prepare myself all along for the fact that I may have to forfeit Lord Ansel's and my relationship — that I was willing to sacrifice even that for the kingdom. I had no idea how unbearable that sacrifice would be.

I endured the conversations and laughter as the riders mingled. I wanted to escape to my chambers and be alone in my confusion of misery. But it would not have been proper to leave at this time. Everyone celebrated a positive direction in their ultimate goal. I had to remain strong as exhaustion and depression swirled around me in a dark mass.

The Healer drew her attention to me. Concern showed on her face. She glanced at my hand that held the back of the chair in front of me — knuckles white from gripping so I could stay upright. She nudged Gallen and motioned to him with a nod in my direction. The two of them came up on either side and took my elbows. The Healer excused the three of us, and led me out of the room.

We arrived at my chambers and Gallen left me with the Healer. No doubt he felt I needed the company of a female.

"Healer, please give me a few minutes by myself, and then I need to leave. I can't stay in this place any longer. Please. Eshshah and I will wait at the Arevale Outpost for dark before we ride to the Dorsal Outpost."

"As you wish, Amáne," she said with a sad, far-away look in her eyes. "The pain you're feeling can only partially heal with time. Sometime soon you must examine your feelings. Trust me. I know. I just hope it won't take you as long as it took me."

Without offering any further information, the Healer continued, "You told me your mother's dying wish for you. She said for you to remember to follow your heart, and asked that you not neglect your own happiness. Take her words seriously, Amáne."

"Healer," I cried, "the two are not possible for me. Those were words that I was never going to be able to carry out. I cannot follow my heart, and I have no choice but to neglect my happiness. My duty to the kingdom comes first."

"It is possible, my child. In time, you will see. But, I would counsel you to speak with Ansel sooner than later."

"Thank you, Healer," I wrapped my arms around her neck, "but I don't think I can do that just yet."

She kissed my forehead and excused herself to give me the time alone I requested.

As soon as she left, I ran to the desk. Rummaging through a drawer, I found a piece of parchment, a quill and some ink. I penned a letter to Lord Ansel.

My Dearest Lord Ansel,

By the time you read this note, Eshshah and I will have begun our quest. I gave Eulalia strict instructions to wait until now to give this to you, so please do not blame her for holding this letter for me. As you read this, it will be too late to stop Eshshah and me, should you change your mind.

At the time of this writing I am still a guest at your manor — I'm leaving shortly. I have made you so angry with me, and because of my cruelty, I have lost my best friend. There is now a wound in my heart with such a pain that I have never felt before — and you know I am no stranger to pain.

As to my heart, you were right all along, it did lead me to you, and I did close my eyes to my feelings, hoping that they would go away. And when they did not go away, I hid them from myself, and instead pushed you away.

I will tell you now my reasoning ~ I believed that I had to forfeit my happiness in order to excel in my obligations and my duty to you and to Teravinea. I believed that giving you my heart would have influenced your decision regarding my quest, even more than if I didn't give it. I confess now that I was wrong. You saw through me and knew the truth before I did. The Healer has tried to tell me that it is possible to have happiness and meet my obligations — that there is a fine line between the two and I must find the balance. But I don't know how.

I am so sorry that I hurt you. It was never my intention. I don't want to be the one to sentence you to a fate of being alone. I've come to the realization that I don't want to be alone, either. If I could take my angry words back, like they were never spoken, I would. I know you care about Teravinea and have carried that burden for all of your life. I was wrong to say you didn't care. I ask your forgiveness. No, I beg your forgiveness, despite the fact I don't deserve it.

Although I have a positive feeling about the success of our quest, the outcome is ultimately not in my control. Eshshah and I have discussed this at length. Should we meet with a circumstance that will send me to my ancestors and Eshshah survives, I've told her it is my desire she continue her life for the benefit of Teravinea. I have asked her to choose you as her rider. I know it is not the same as linking and I don't know if there are any rules against such a request. But then again, you know that I am not known for my capability to follow rules. I know I have been in the habit of asking so much from you so often, but please do not deny this request. Please accept Eshshah as your own. I will rest happily if I knew she would be with someone whom she and I both love.

Although it is far beyond what I deserve, my hope is that you would reconsider and not give up on me. That you will see that I've opened my eyes to what you and my heart have been telling me all along. I now know it is telling me that I love you.

May my ancestors smile upon this quest and bring me safely back to you.

With all my heart,

Amáne

I had to blot several smudges in the ink where my tears met with the parchment. Finally satisfied with what I'd written, I sealed it and impressed the dragon on the hilt of my dagger into the soft wax.

Chapter Twenty-seven

I packed the few items I came with. After instructing Lali on delivering my letter, I bid her a teary farewell. The Healer and Gallen met me in front of the manor house to wait for the stable hands to bring horses. The two would ride with me to the field where Eshshah waited. They insisted on seeing me safely to the Arevale Outpost. Along with Dorjan and his wife and son, the Healer and Gallen planned to leave for Dorsal the next day by ship.

I was numb with grief and remorse. My depression began to pull me down. Trying to maintain a tolerable disposition for those around me, I kept what I hoped was a pleasant look on my face while I controlled my urge to leave this place as fast as I could.

Gallen gave me a leg up into the saddle. As a groom adjusted my stirrups, my eyes followed a movement in the upper floors of the manor. Someone stood in a window, holding back a curtain, watching our departure. My heart stopped. It was Lord Ansel. The final stroke fell in my effort to keep myself in one piece. My eyes stung as I turned and spurred my horse. The stable boy dove out of my way. Gallen hadn't even gotten astride his horse. I gave my animal the reins. He didn't wait for a second prompting as we recklessly shot up the road. We left the Healer and Gallen behind to catch up if they were able.

The fast-paced ride didn't even come close to flying with Eshshah. But it was better than waiting for the others and enduring Lord Ansel's eyes upon me.

Eshshah waited for me in the field. I leapt off the horse before we came to a complete stop, then secured him to a tree so he wouldn't run away from fear of Eshshah. I blindly ran to my dragon and pressed my forehead to her nose. There I stayed, sobbing as she hummed softly while we waited for the Healer and Gallen.

They eventually arrived at the field, and I felt, more than saw, the Healer's disapproval of my actions. I had, in essence, turned over a new leaf in regards to my self control, but I was still Amáne, and I had a breaking point.

We said our farewells. "I'll contact you when I arrive, no matter the hour," I promised.

"We'll wait until we've heard from you," said the Healer. They watched as I mounted Eshshah and we flew into the outpost to await nightfall.

Our flight to the Dorsal Outpost went quickly. We arrived in good time — it was good to be home again. I contacted the Healer, as promised, then fell into my bed in the first chamber at our outpost. A fitful sleep soon claimed me and threw me into my old pattern of nightmares. Worse than usual — this time Lord Ansel was included in the confusion and terror. He shouted as I ran in terror from a monster beneath the castle. I couldn't tell if he was yelling for me to run faster, or for the monster to catch me. I awoke barely able to breathe.

At last the sun sent its rays through the skylights above my chamber, but I could not force myself to rise. Eshshah tried to get me to at least come out to the entry cavern to enjoy the sun and my favorite view, but I declined. My tears would not stop — my eyes, swelled from crying.

Later in the afternoon I drug myself to the chamber that Lord Ansel had occupied when we stayed here last. I slumped into his bed and inhaled as a faint scent of him still lingered.

Another series of nightmares and another morning arrived. Still I lay curled up in my bed as Eshshah hummed softly to arouse me. I felt badly for her, but I couldn't pull myself out of my despair.

By the third day, Eshshah's concern grew. Finally, in the afternoon, she decided she couldn't allow me to continue in the dark direction towards which I plummeted.

"Amáne," she nudged me forcibly until she rolled me off of the bed. "Get up! You haven't eaten or bathed since we've arrived and I cannot bear your suffering any longer. You are a dragon rider, first and foremost. Our quest that we hoped for since we linked is looming ahead of us. Are you forgetting your duty so soon? Do you want us so weak that we shall fail? What you do to yourself affects me as well."

Coaxing my body to a sitting position, I was, for the first time aware of my selfishness. I noted the distress in Eshshah's eyes and the amount of scales that she'd shed. Normally, when a dragon reached her age, scale loss was minimal, but an unhealthy amount were scattered in her sleeping spot.

"Eshshah," I groaned, "I'm sorry! Why is it that I keep hurting everyone I love?"

I struggled to get to my feet. My self abuse had left me weak, but I knew then that I must use all the strength I had left to fight my wretchedness. Standing up, I took in a deep breath, embraced her, and apologized repeatedly until she would hear it no more.

Preparing for a hot soak to help take away my gloom, I heard the communication disc buzz in the library. I walked as quickly as I could with Eshshah's help up the corridor. I placed my hand on the brass knob and watched as the Healer and Gallen's faces shimmered into view, then stared at me in shock. It took me a moment to realize what I must look like after the three days I'd spent in the dark recesses of my heart.

"Amáne! What happened? Are you ill?"

"No. I'm fine. I'm sorry, I didn't consider what I must look like. I ... I haven't been myself, but I'm okay, now. I was just getting ready to soak, and have something to eat.

"I'm glad you're home already. How was your trip?" I changed the subject.

The Healer raised an eyebrow, "We've just arrived. Our trip was fine. We'll see you here tonight. Are you sure you're well enough to fly home?"

"Yes, Healer, we'll leave shortly after dark." Uncomfortable with her scrutiny, I excused myself, saluted and released my hand from the device.

Later, after my soak and a small meal, I stood with Eshshah on the ledge at my favorite time of day. We watched as the sun lowered into the ocean. A sadness swept over me as I thought about the first time Lord Ansel had kissed me. We stood in that very spot. But the sadness only lingered for a bit before I carefully wrapped the memory of his kiss and hid it in a corner of my heart that was reserved for happier times. I gathered the last remnant of my dark cloud and blew it out the entry to be swallowed by the sea, vowing that I will never let myself get to that point again. I owed it to the ones I loved.

Chapter Twenty-Eight

The next few weeks careened towards our quest at a dizzying speed. I leaned into my practice like never before. Dorjan came over every day and worked with me on my fighting skills. He also continued to give me pointers on male behavior. They even asked Kail to come and practice some sparring bouts with me. He had been informed that I was training for a quest, but had been left out of the details. He didn't question me, but was happy to be included in any way.

"How are Fiona and her family doing?" I asked him when we took a break.

"They're still in mourning, but doing better. It'd be nice if you would call on her, Amáne. You know what it feels like to lose a parent and you may be able to cheer her."

The next day I took a break from my morning training and went to visit Fiona and her family. They still wore the customary mourning color of black. It was time for her and her sisters to start wearing colors again.

On the day he took me on a tour of his grounds, Lord Ansel had given me some colorful Serislan silk yardage and ribbons from his stocks for me to bring to Fiona, Rio and Mila. I handed her the package. Her sisters crowded in to help open it. I delighted in watching them — it was just what they needed to help them move on in their grief. Fiona recognized the quality immediately and was in awe when I told her that Lord Ansel was now a silk-grower and had sent this gift to them.

"Lord Ansel? He's a Lord?" Fiona eyes went wide. "You never told me that. It was obvious he was of a high upbringing. A Lord — Amáne, you're so fortunate to have such an admirer."

My face fell. Darkness clouded my eyes. Her hand went to her mouth. "What's happened? Did he take a turn in his affections? That wouldn't have been possible. I saw how he looked at you. Did you reject him for some insane reason?"

"I should've listened to you, Fiona. I did what you advised me not to do — I disappointed him. — No. Worse. I offended him and broke his heart with my selfishness." My lip trembled. I fought the tears.

She took hold of my hand and encouraged me to go on with my story. I decided I would tell her parts of how I had spent my time in Trivingar, leaving out, of course, how I had arrived there and my kidnapping. I chose only the fragments I could share with her — the manor, the ball and the dresses I'd seen. All the things that she could have appreciated much more than I. She held her breath when I described the gown I had worn. I even told her about the pompous Lord Halebeorht and his audacity in attempting to get me out on the balcony. Her mouth dropped open in disbelief.

"How scandalous!" She giggled.

"I won't go into details, but I insulted Lord Ansel beyond forgiveness. The remainder of my stay, which fortunately was short, he was detached and cold, for which I could not fault him. So, that's it. I deserve to be alone. But enough about me, Fiona, tell me about your wedding plans."

Surprisingly, she ignored my question about her favorite subject. "Amáne, you must write to him and beg his forgiveness. I know he must still love you and he will forgive you. Some silly angry words wouldn't be enough to nullify what I saw in him. Trust me, I didn't mistake the look in his eyes."

"I did write to him, but he hasn't yet received my letter. All I hope for is his forgiveness. I won't blame him if he doesn't resume his affections."

Fiona reached out and gave me a hug. It felt good to have shared with her. Then she turned to her new silk fabrics with a light in her eye that had not been there since she lost her father. She proceeded to tell me of her wedding plans until it was time to take my leave.

My load had been lightened on two counts. One, that I was able to lift Fiona's sadness; and two, that she helped to lift mine. Maybe my letter to Lord Ansel will be enough to warrant his pardon.

CHAPTER TWENTY-NINE

A wild racket entered my dreams. Howling wild dogs and snarling monster lizards, all chasing after me. Their only desire — to tear me apart. I awoke with a start and still the same sounds that had disturbed my sleep echoed in my ears. A full-blown Valaira whipped around outside. Our quest was to begin on this turbulent day.

"Oh no, Eshshah. How could we have a Valaira today, of all days?"

"It should be over by nightfall. We can't leave before then, anyway."

I got dressed and headed to the kitchen where the Healer and Gallen were already sitting at the table picking at some smoked fish and sipping hot watered wine. The feeling in the room was somber, which didn't give me the confidence I needed the day of our mission.

"Dorjan still has one item to deliver, Amáne," Gallen said. "He hasn't been happy with how it's been progressing, so it's taken longer than he'd hoped. He just finished it to his satisfaction, but now he has to wait until the Valaira passes before he can ride over."

"What is it? Can we be successful without it?"

"I'm afraid it's necessary. Remember, he told you that he's come up with a way that you can take an egg from the hatching grounds, yet make it look like none was missing. That's what he's been trying to perfect. Hopefully the squall will calm before evening."

"Eshshah believes it should."

I moped around all day trying to keep myself occupied so I wouldn't think too much about our quest ... or about Lord Ansel. There were a couple of occasions in the last few weeks when the Healer tried to coax me into speaking with him on the communication disc. I still wasn't ready to take that step, insisting that I needed to wait until after our journey. Although I felt physically prepared for our task, I needed to be just as mentally prepared. Contacting Lord Ansel would not help. She shook her head and didn't press the issue any further.

The Valaira continued to toss around her furious gusts throughout most of the day and didn't appear to want to let up. But finally by late afternoon, her anger was spent and all was calm.

My next dilemma was to address the problem of my long hair. The thought of cutting it all off made me shudder. No girl my age had short hair unless they had experienced an extreme case of lice — and at that, it was only as a last resort. However, cutting my hair was the only guarantee that I would not be found out.

Taking her time, the Healer brushed through my long tresses, prolonging what neither of us wanted to face. I sat on a stool with a heavy heart as she grabbed the scissors and separated a portion of my locks. I closed my eyes and held my breath. A tear escaped and the Healer hesitated, scissors poised mid air.

Before the blades closed for the first snip, I pulled away. "Wait, I have an idea."

Gathering my hair to the top of my head, I let a small amount fall evenly around my shoulders. I made a topknot with the larger amount, and held it with one hand while I pulled my cap on. The candidates would be wearing a white felt cap with no brim, free of any decoration. It had plenty of room in it to hide the rest of my hair.

"Now, you can cut what's hanging out from under the cap. There's enough hair to look like I have a short cut, but afterwards, my long hair will cover the short ones until they can grow out. I won't have to sacrifice all of it."

A collective sigh echoed in the room and then laughter as Gallen said, "You're a genius, Amáne. I was ready to stop the blades myself — I couldn't bear the thought of you losing half of your hair."

The Healer completed the task as I had instructed. After thorough scrutiny, we all agreed, it passed as a boy's haircut. What little vanity I had was saved — I was able to keep the majority of what seemed to be the only feminine part of me.

After taking a hot soak to calm my nerves, I dressed slowly for our quest, pulling on a dark heavy tunic over a dark long-sleeve chemise, and then dark tights. I retrieved my riding cloak, which always brought back memories of Lord Ansel. I thought about leaving it behind, but that would not have been wise. We would more than likely fly at the freezing altitudes that Eshshah loved as we headed for a field just outside of Anbon, where Bern now resides.

Shortly before dusk, Dorjan galloped into the courtyard. We came together around the kitchen table for final discussions before our departure. He repaired my dragon scale boots that were a gift from him and Eshshah. On our last quest one of them was destroyed by the monster I called the black creature — whose image is now etched into my ankle. Dorjan inspected my helmet and breastplate, and pronounced them flawless.

Finally, he unveiled his masterpiece. He brought out a silk satchel and made a dramatic showing as he pulled out the solution to our entire quest.

"Is that a cow's bladder?" I asked.

His face dropped in mock disappointment and then he burst out in his boisterous laugh. "Correct, Amáne. But it's not just any cow's bladder. I've been working for weeks to develop a paint that would stay on the bladder when inflated or deflated. Allow me to demonstrate."

He put his mouth on the opening and started blowing it up. "Keep going until it reaches the size egg that Eshshah chooses. You'll find their sizes vary."

"I hope she finds one of the smaller eggs of her royal line," I said.

Dorjan continued, "Once it's the same size, you tie it off like this and wrap this small weight around the knot. Place it in the exact spot as the real egg."

"Wow, Dorjan, that's ingenious. It looks exactly how I remember Eshshah's egg."

"You'll put the real egg in this satchel, throw it over your shoulder and high-tail it out of there to the Castle Outpost where Eshshah and Bern will be waiting."

We all agreed it was a fantastic plan.

Besides my personal essentials, and Dorjan's handiwork, I packed some travel cakes and a skin of water. The Healer made sure that I put in my cap and a couple of white tunics — the rider candidates were to dress only in white. My spear leaned against the kitchen wall and I had a sword on my belt in addition to my dagger. Gallen had already saddled Eshshah. Everything was ready to go.

We all met in the courtyard. The Healer helped me with my breastplate as she and I both sang a song of an ancient battle in hopes for a successful mission. I wrapped my hair on top of my head and put my helmet on, allowing my short hair to remain exposed. Standing up straight, I gave the Healer, Gallen and Dorjan a crisp salute. They returned the salute to Eshshah and I. Pride was written on their faces, although they couldn't hide the concern in their eyes.

"How do I look?" I asked.

"Like a very determined and successful young man who has hopes of becoming a dragon rider," Gallen said. "Have you thought of a name?"

"I shall be called Vann. I was studying names from far away countries and it means water ... like Amáne."

They all nodded their agreement that it was a fitting name.

I was surprised at how calm I felt — at this point in my last quest I shook in uncontrollable spasms. I expected a delayed reaction, though, and would probably feel my nerves give out sometime after we started our flight. Which was fine with me — that way I wouldn't upset those I loved.

Chapter Thirty

The night was lit with countless stars, the moon was a crescent in the sky — like the smile of one who has a secret to tell ... but won't.

Eshshah and I spiraled up from the courtyard and swung east over the water. It was then I began to unravel. My teeth chattered, my body shook and a cold sweat came over me. I expected it, but did not welcome it. With Eshshah's help, I gained control, and after a few deep breaths and some concentration, my heart finally found its beat.

As to my heart, the long flight gave me time to think and discuss my situation with Eshshah. At any moment Lord Ansel would be unsealing the letter that I had left for him. I wished I were a tapestry on the wall so I could see his reaction. I couldn't predict if he would be angry, sad or remorseful. My guess was all three at once.

"Eshshah, do you think I should even have written that note — was it the right thing to do? My only hope is that he'll find joy in the fact that I've finally admitted my love for him — but I'm afraid to hope. What if I won't be able to salvage anything? What if he truly meant every word when he said, 'I will no longer bother you for your attentions?' I won't be able to bear it — even though I've resigned myself to the fact that I must."

"Amáne, don't torture yourself. You did what you thought was right at the time. He needed to know. I'm not able to predict human sentiments, but I can't foresee him relinquishing the feelings he had for you."

"How could he forgive me for what I said? I don't deserve his forgiveness, much less his friendship."

"You will do better in preparing yourself for your upcoming task. Let's get the egg first, then we can discuss this on the way home."

"Thank you, Eshshah."

For most of the flight, we didn't soar as high as we did when Lord Ansel was with us. With just my weight and a single saddle, Eshshah didn't need the higher altitude, but I convinced her to do so. I knew that she enjoyed the frigid air. She acquiesced and flew high for a short time, as I pulled my cloak around me.

At last I saw the lights of Anbon approach. We passed silently over the town. Flying a little further, we found the spot where we were to meet up with the dragon riders involved in our quest ... in a field outside the town walls. Spiraling down, Eshshah and I landed and were greeted by Bern, Avano and Eben. I dismounted and saluted the three, unable to contain my smirk at the incredulity in their faces as they stared at me.

"Well, Amáne —" Eben started.

"— Call me Vann, please, from now until we all return safely."

"Okay, Vann. I have to admit, you were right. You look like you could be Bern's son." A curse escaped his lips before he could stop himself. "Sorry."

"Don't apologize, Eben. I'm going to have to get used to it if I expect to keep company with males, right?"

They had set up tents for a two nights' stay in the field before we would leave for the City of Teravinea.

The following day we spent in training. We practiced with various weapons, but they also showed me some wrestling moves, and constantly gave me tips and pointers to improve my ruse.

They didn't hold back — in their manners or their fighting. They actually treated me like I was Bern's son.

After some experimentation, cursing still didn't taste right on my tongue. I gave up on it, but I at least got my ears used to it.

Eshshah found it amusing when they taught me how to spit. But then she became defensive as they took pleasure in slapping me on the back, and friendly-punching me every chance they could. I assured her that I was fine with it, even though they certainly enjoyed themselves at my expense. She kept her displeasure to herself, noting I didn't protest their treatment. I added more and more pins to my hair to keep it up and figured out how to make sure my cap would stay on, no matter how they assailed me. I think they actually forgot I was a female.

Later that afternoon I sat at a distance from the men, as I leaned against Eshshah. I started to drift into sadness as my thoughts went to Lord Ansel. I tried to imagine how he would have reacted to my letter. Out of the corner of my eye I could see Avano watching me. He approached and asked permission to sit with me near Eshshah. I quickly wiped a stray tear from my face and nodded.

Avano was the youngest living dragon rider until Eshshah and I linked. I was told he was nineteen when he linked with Cira. My heart went out to him at the early loss of his dragon — they had only been together for about eight years when she met with a tragic accident. I'm convinced that it was not an accident, but the same treachery that took many other dragons. I connected their deaths to Galtero. Cira was the last dragon to pass before Torin, the Healer's dragon, met his death. Avano looked like he was in his mid twenties, but was probably closer to fifty. A good looking man. I felt comfortable around him.

"Vann — or if I may break the rule for just a few minutes — Amáne, I need to talk to you. I can't help but notice your sadness, and at the risk of being bold, I believe I know why."

How could he know why I was sad? It annoyed me that he thought he could read me that easily, but I kept my thoughts to myself.

"I'd like to tell you a little something about Lord Ansel," he began.

Ugh, I thought, *why would he want to do this to me now?*

Ignoring the look I shot him, he began, "As you know, it's an age-old tradition in Teravinea for parents to arrange marriage for their children. Times are changing, but this practice has always been particularly strong in royal circles. For years Lord Ansel's foster parents tried several times to arrange a betrothal. They were never successful because Lord Ansel would always devise a way to get out of the agreement. Once, he succeeded only by running away on the day when the final betrothal contract was to be signed. Since he was fifteen and of age, he needed to be present to complete the arrangement.

"Always a romantic, he swore he would never even consider spending his life with someone he didn't fall in love with first. It must have been hereditary as that was the same cast of mind as his true parents, King Emeric and Queen Fiala.

"I was the one Lord Ansel always confided in when he had a love interest. I won't ease up on the truth, Amáne, when I tell you that he had quite a few."

If Avano's intentions were to make me feel better, he's failed miserably. The dark cloud grew thicker over me. I pressed my lips together and let him continue.

"But they never lasted. He could find no one who could hold his interest — that is until he came back from his ordeal in the dungeons. He was a changed man. I was more than a little concerned, thinking he had been so traumatized by his experience that he was ... well ... damaged somehow. Then I discovered what had changed him when he confided in me that he'd found someone he was seriously interested in."

My chest felt like a weight had been dropped on it. "That's what he told you about me?"

Avano continued, "Let me see if I can remember his words — they were quite poetic."

He closed his eyes and recited, "'I've met someone who has put color into my day. She has the scent of cinnamon and exotic spice, a spirit that soars and a fire in her blue eyes that can't be extinguished. She is my reason for hope.'"

My throat closed. My eyes filled.

"I asked him about the family and background of this person of whom he spoke." Avano's eyes met mine. "But he waved me off and told me family and station made no difference to him when it came to this special girl. He assured me she was royalty in his eyes."

My eyes spilled over as Avano went on with his narrative. "I'd never before seen him in such high spirits as when he spoke about you, Amáne. When he came back from the Life Celebration Gathering, I think that his boots didn't touch the ground — he was that smitten.

"As his birthday ball approached, he was as nervous as a race horse. He hoped everything would be perfect for your arrival.

I'm sorry that didn't turn out quite as planned and I'm also sorry I played a part in ruining your first impression."

I smiled and put my hand on his arm.

"I'm telling you all of this because I've been one of Lord Ansel's guardians since he was a baby, and his happiness is important to me. It's my duty.

"I know something unfortunate happened before the Dragon Rider Council." Avano looked into my eyes and became more serious. "And I'm not talking about your abduction. I know words were exchanged between you two that were regretted. I felt the weight of it as soon as he walked into the Council room ... many of us did. We know him that well. I wish you hadn't left so quickly. This misunderstanding shouldn't have gone on this long.

"Amáne, Lord Ansel has no knowledge that I'm telling you this, but he needs to know that you forgive him."

"He's asking for my forgiveness?!"

"I'm sorry, Amáne, but I've found that forgiveness is a powerful remedy. You're going into a dangerous quest. When I prepared to go into battle or a quest, I made sure that there was no one that needed my mercy before I left. If I were to meet with my ancestors, I knew forgiveness would make my journey easier."

"You don't understand, Avano. It is I who need his forgiveness. He's done nothing that he needs to be sorry for. It was my fault. I was the one who said angry, unforgiveable things, not him. I don't deserve his attentions."

I dropped my face into my hands and trembled in silent sobs. He put his arm around my shoulder and held me in silence for a while.

"See how it gets to this? This suffering on both of your parts was unnecessary." He sounded a bit angry.

"As soon as Bern gets to the Castle Outpost," I said between sobs, "I'll ask him to contact Lord Ansel and beg his pardon. I know I should have done it earlier, I just didn't know how. I wrote him a letter, but I made Lali wait until I left Dorsal to give it to him. That was wrong, too."

"We'll make it right, don't worry. He needs you, Amáne."

"Thank you, Avano. I owe you."

"You owe me nothing." Then with a mischievous smile, he punched my arm — hard, then said, "And by the way, Vann, boys don't cry." He leapt to his feet and strode away.

I picked up a small stone and bounced it off of his head as he retreated.

Chapter Thirty-one

The sun shone gently through the trees as we broke camp and left for the City of Teravinea. Eshshah stayed at the Anbon field that day and waited for nightfall, then flew to the Castle Outpost. We would stay in contact through open thought transference.

After a relatively pleasant ride, we reached the gates of the walled City of Teravinea as the sun lowered in the sky. I made the mistake of looking up just before entering the arch of the portcullis. With a jerk, I pulled my horse to a stop. A wave of revulsion and nausea swept through me. Above me were a number of pikes sticking out from the walls, and on the ends, staring blankly at us were severed heads in various states of decay. The flies buzzed thick around them. I leaned over and vomited.

"Ah, yes," said Eben, "a very understandable message from our king. These unfortunate heads, I can assure you, belonged to citizens who had in some way earned King Galtero's displeasure. This is his way to let all those who enter his gates, regardless of the festive occasion, know that he will punish those who anger him in any way."

I spurred my horse to remove myself from that macabre sight.

As we rode, I willed my stomach to settle. The city began to wake to its night life. Light poured out the windows of the taverns and inns that lined the road. Vendors were just setting up their booths for the next several days of festivities. The fourth day held the Hatching Ceremony, and if our plans went well, we would be far from here by that day.

Although the Hatching Ceremony had sadly lost its importance, there was still a festive air at this gathering. It had transformed into an event of feasting and merrymaking — more of a general festival, where wares were sold, and music and dancing took the place of the original significance of riders and dragons linking. I was saddened knowing that the Hatching Ceremony had so devastatingly declined.

Many travelers were arriving from all directions, so no one paid us any heed. We rode to an inn off the main road. Bern negotiated with the proprietor for three nights for he and I, knowing we would not need the room for the third night. Eben and Avano separated from us and took two rooms at an inn down the lane.

We woke up early and walked the streets of the city. I took in the sights, the smells, the crowds of colorfully dressed people — like none I had ever experienced. This city meant something to me as it was where my mother grew up. I convinced Bern to take me to the potter's district so I could see the shop where she had been raised. Her family had run the potter's guild which was now headed up by another family — my mother being the last of the direct line of potters in her family. I had a desire to meet those who had taken over, imagining that maybe we were related in some way. A need for some kind of family connection was strong, but I had to fight it. This was not what I was here for.

Soon it was time for the candidates to assemble in the market square, accompanied by their fathers. I counted only nine of us. In earlier times, there were many who signed up, from which only a certain amount were selected. From those, only a very few were chosen by dragons.

While we waited in the square for my turn to sign up, Bern related various stories of dragon lore. This place and its history brought back memories for him. A favorite of his was told to him by his father in this very square. It was about Leyna, rider of the late Sitara — the same dragon of the light shields in the outposts. Leyna had disappeared a few years before Nara and Torin had linked. The legend was that she had gone looking for the Valley of Dragons. A far-away, almost mythical place where the ancient dragons resided.

Before he could finish his fascinating tale, we arrived at the front of the line and stood before a large red-faced man seated behind a table.

He looked me up and down and couldn't contain his laughter. "Your father must think highly of you, boy, to imagine you would ever be acceptable as a dragon rider. You're too scrawny to even dream you could qualify." He looked at Bern with disgust and shook his head. "I suppose I'll have to approve you as a prospect, seeing we have so few applying. You're lucky, boy. Better prove you're worthy or we'll throw you out before the Hatching"

"Yes, sir, thank you sir." I imagined what his pompous face would look like if I summoned Eshshah to the market square just then, and she landed right in front of his table. I felt Eshshah's rumbling laugh and only with great effort was I able to suppress my smile.

The candidates would be reporting to this same man at dawn to begin our initiation on the Hatching Grounds. The first rite would last until the following dawn, with no sleep in between. Part of that time involved walking on the grounds, allowing the dragons in the eggs to feel our presence. The other part would be spent in a classroom where we'd be taught the process of linking, dragon lore, and other related subjects. At the end of this initiation period we'd spend twenty-four hours with our fathers, which would be a time of preparation. Lastly, the prospects gather again for the Hatching Ceremony on the third dawn. If our plans come to fruition, I'd be gone before the third dawn — with an egg.

Dorjan's contact informed us the best time for me to slip away would be during one of the later classroom periods. Because the instructors had little interest in their students, nor in the subject matter, they usually ended up falling asleep instead of lecturing, leaving the candidates with no supervision.

Chapter Thirty-two

Before the sun came up, I'd already donned my white tights and tunic. Bern helped me with my breastplate, which the Healer insisted I wear. I didn't protest because I knew I needed it for my disguise. It helped me look more like a male, covering what slight curves I might have. I pulled two more tunics over my breastplate which gave the illusion I had a little more weight to me. I topped it with a wide leather belt — white, of course. We were not allowed weapons. As much as I wanted to have my dagger with me, I thought it best not to take any chances. Dorjan's man was given my sword and glaive and had hidden them where I could retrieve them on my way out of the hatching grounds ... just in case I had need of them.

My chest tightened, my heart beat faster. I could feel Eshshah's comforting humming as I tried to gain control of my breathing.

Bern steadied me by pressing down on my shoulders. He looked into my eyes. Making sure he had my full attention, he said, "Vann, I know exactly how you are feeling. I remember vividly all the missions my dragon and I completed. It's normal to feel anxious, tense, fearful. But this next short period of your life will be far from normal. You must use your head to rule your decisions and your actions. I've heard about your temper — Vann, there will be no room for it in what you are about to do. Your life, as well as the success of our ultimate mission, depends upon your control."

"I know, Bern. I can control my temper, now." I may have sounded a little more confident than I felt.

He tipped his head, a bit doubtful.

We walked together to where the red-faced man waited, and said goodbye. He punched my arm. Pride shown on his face.

Bern was to meet Eshshah on a deserted beach on the other side of the castle. From there the two will fly north, low over the water on the coastal side of the castle, where it is no longer guarded. At the mouth of the river, they will fly inland. After following the river a short distance, Eshshah will turn left towards the castle cliffs which would bring them to the entrance of the Castle Outpost — the same outpost we visited for our last quest. I will meet them there at the completion of my task.

We'll stay in contact with a chain of communication the Healer devised. Eshshah will convey my progress in open thought transference to Bern. Bern will be stationed at the communication disc and pass on her information to the Healer. The plan was of quite some comfort to me.

Eben and Avano were to be stationed nearby in the city and be available in case Dorjan's man tried to get in touch with them — and to assist in the unlikely event our plans would go awry.

The nine dragon rider candidates lined up in front of the red-faced man as he looked us over with disdain. That is, until his eyes rested on a large boy who looked to be older than any of us. He was obviously from a notable family. The guide gave a barely noticeable tip of his head. It was clear he approved of this one. I glanced over at the boy and was repulsed by the arrogant look on his face. Even that look couldn't hide the fact that he obviously didn't want to be here. I made a mental note to keep my eye on him as one who could not be trusted.

We entered the castle and the man led us in several turns through the hallways, and down a couple of levels to the hatching grounds. I paid attention to the path we took. Although I knew the way, following a parchment map was never the same as actually walking the real thing.

I felt Eshshah's heart sink with mine when he opened the large doors to the hatching grounds. I fought the tears in my eyes as I took in the neglect of the arena, the grounds and the eggs.

We gathered in the large oval indoor amphitheater. I felt the warmth radiate from the sand beneath my feet. The arena must have once been magnificent. Rows of benches rose in tiers to our left. The entire stadium could probably seat about a thousand people. The bleachers were expertly crafted out of a beautiful dark wood, but were now in a sorry state of disrepair. The railings of fine brass, were tarnished. But the most painful sight was the disrespect shown to the dragon eggs — a layer of dust covered them, the sand strewn with rodent excrement and dead rats. Cobwebs looked like they held the eggs to the sand. My heart broke.

"Boys don't cry." I heard Avano's warning in my head. I glanced around to make sure no one had caught my unintended emotion.

"Your first job as candidates," the guide said, "is to clean this place up. We still have a number of esteemed guests who desire to be present at the Hatching Ceremony." And then under his breath, "Why, I'll never guess, nothing ever happens in here."

He pointed to cloths, brooms and rakes on one side of the room. "I'll be back in a few hours and I better see these grounds shining!"

We all went about in our own way of cleaning. I discretely studied my fellow rider hopefuls and could pick out two or three other boys who looked like they really believed — who truly had hopes of becoming dragon riders. The rest were there, I guessed, because their parents forced them into it for various reasons. Possibly the parents still had hope that a dragon may hatch, desiring the prestige that a dragon rider brought to their family.

I was happy to show my respect to the unhatched dragons. This also gave reason for me to spend some time with each egg. There were about sixteen eggs waiting for their Chosen One. What a crime to have deprived them for so many years. Eshshah followed with me in open thought transference. At about the third egg I started to wipe down, she stopped me.

I felt a flicker of excitement from Eshshah. "Amáne, put both hands on the one you are in front of now." Eshshah was not going to call me Vann. I remained Amáne to her.

I did as she asked and after a few seconds, she said, "That's the one."

My heart skipped a beat. I wanted to jump, rejoice and cry out, but I kept my emotions in check, not allowing any facial expression. I sang a silent song of thanksgiving. The fact that it was one of the smaller eggs added to my joy. I noted my bearings and mentally marked which egg Eshshah had chosen, then kept moving through the hatching grounds cleaning and observing.

"Amáne, we have a problem." Eshshah said with concern. "Dorjan's contact was ordered on an unexpected errand for the king and he will not be available to assist you, should you need him. He managed to stash your sword and spear before he left."

"It can't be helped, I guess." My disappointment was difficult to hold in. I took in a deep controlled breath. The thought of someone on my side in here had given me some peace of mind, even if I didn't know who he was. At least the Healer had thought to keep us connected through Eshshah, Bern and the communication disc. But the loss of an inside contact was nearly devastating.

The hours passed while I waited for the opportune moment to arrive — when I could grab the egg and be out of there. The nine of us moved around the grounds cleaning or lounging depending on how serious each boy took this opportunity.

Later in the afternoon the arrogant boy, I learned his name was Kemp, proved my suspicions to be true. He reclined near one of the eggs, unable to hide his boredom. When another boy approached that egg, Kemp became defensive. He actually jumped to his feet and pushed the other down. The offended boy retaliated and pushed back. Typical of a male confrontation, a fight ensued. The other boys gathered around them and shouted for their favorite, urging them both on. I was appalled at their behavior, but had to join in and mimic their actions so I wouldn't stand out.

Suddenly, Kemp drew a dagger. He looked very adept at handling a blade, as was expected of someone of his station. All of the candidates went silent at the unexpected turn of events. Kemp's stance showed an aggressive edge as he faced the boy. Shocked at the murderous look in his eye, I refused to stand by and watch him finish off the unarmed candidate. Kemp made his move and lunged. Reacting instantly, I swept my foot around. He fell forward, landing heavily on his stomach. As he crashed to the ground, the blade jolted free from his hand. It flew several paces away. The other boy dove for it and stood up defensively just as the door flew open. The innocent boy was caught with the dagger in his hand.

Kemp didn't miss the opportunity. He complained to the guide that the boy had smuggled in a blade and tried to attack him. I stepped forward and protested, with a few of the braver boys backing me up. The guide would not hear it. He immediately escorted the other boy out roughly, and turned a deaf ear to our protests. I felt badly for that boy — I sensed that he was one who did believe he could become a rider.

The heat rose in my face as my anger threatened to take over. I wanted to punish that ruffian for what he had done. My eyes must have flashed daggers as I faced him, because for just one second, a hint of fear shown in his eyes. It was abruptly replaced by hatred. If he still had his blade, I had no doubt it would have been pointed in my direction. I summoned all of my strength to quench my desire for justice for the boy that was evicted. Eshshah was ready to step in to calm me, but I succeeded without her help. Breathing in deeply, I turned my back to him and walked away. I actually hoped he would attack me while my back was turned, but I kept walking until I cooled off.

"Good job, Amáne," Eshshah said.

A short time later we gathered in a room off the arena for a class on what to expect during linking. The instructor didn't have all his facts straight, but I was not about to point that out.

Afterwards, we found ourselves back on the hatching grounds to continue our cleaning duties. I polished the brass railings as I allowed my mind to wander. Eshshah had informed me, just moments ago in the classroom, that Bern had contacted Lord Ansel. Bern was to ask for his forgiveness on my behalf. I had made it clear that I did not want any dialog with Lord Ansel through open thought transference — I couldn't bear anything other than, was

I forgiven, yes or no. Lord Ansel had thankfully forgiven me, but wanted further conversation. I wouldn't have expected anything other than that from him. Eshshah and Bern had honored my desire and told him I was unable to have contact with him at this time. Truthfully, I was afraid of what he might say. I had to keep my hope alive that I could revive at least a portion of what we had shared. It would take all my energy to accomplish this quest, and I wanted to keep the unknown ... unknown at this time. In my mind that was the best solution. With his forgiveness, I knew I could continue my quest with a clear conscience.

While I was occupied with my thoughts, one of the candidates came up and began to polish the railings beside me.

"Hi, I am Gavril." He was a good looking young man and I could see in his eyes that he was another who believed he could become a dragon rider — I could see hope. "That was impressive, what you did. I'm glad you were able to bring Kemp to the ground. He doesn't deserve to be a rider and I hope there's no unhatched dragon who would think that he does."

"It was just luck that I was close enough to help that poor boy. My name is Vann."

"What do you think will happen to him?" he asked.

"They'll probably just send him home in shame, although you and I both know, he doesn't deserve the shame. Did you know him?"

"No, only that he was Spero, from Nunn."

His eyebrows knit and he hesitated. Finally, I think he realized that I was of like mind. "Do you think a dragon will ever hatch again? I mean, there hasn't been a dragon living in Teravinea since Torin met his end. Do you know of Torin? He was linked to Nara."

"Yes, I'm familiar with both of them," I said casually. "And to answer your question, Torin will not be the last dragon to live. You must continue to hope. I believe there will again be dragons in the skies of Teravinea in our lifetime. I'm not sure if this ceremony will see any hatchings, but I trust that soon the spell, or whatever it is that keeps them from linking, will be broken and we will again see our dragons fly freely."

I was so fervent in my answer, a satisfied smile lit his face. He nodded, as if to say he knew his dragon dreams were not just a fantasy.

Throughout our conversation, I could feel Kemp's eyes upon us. I glanced quickly and caught his glare. I'd embarrassed him and I was sure he wasn't going to let it go.

The day drug on without another incident. We alternated between cleaning the hatching grounds and instruction on dragon lore. It was already late evening, and time to go back into the classroom.

All of us had been up since before dawn, and besides being tired from the polishing and cleaning, we suffered from lack of sleep and food. This was also a day of fasting. Most of us found it nearly impossible to keep our eyes open.

I had hidden two vials of the Healer's dark liquid concoction in the folds of my layered tunics. The same potion I had used for Lord Ansel to give him strength during his rescue. The moment had arrived for me to drink one. My time for action quickly approached. I lagged behind as we headed for class. Making sure no one was looking, I downed one vial. Scrunching my face at the horrible taste, I could barely keep from choking. Immediately I felt it's warmth flow down my throat and a wave of alertness surged through me. I made sure to retain the same bored and tired expression as everyone else.

The instructor had feigned an effort to teach the next portion of our training, and after a quarter of an hour he fell asleep, just as Dorjan's man had predicted. I looked at the other boys, and most of them dozed as well. A couple of them quietly talked among themselves. Kemp slumped back against the wall with his head lolled against his chest. My chance had arrived.

"Eshshah, it's time."

"Okay, Amáne. Be safe. The Healer, Gallen and Bern will stay in contact until you are safely here at the outpost."

It was comforting to know they would essentially be here with me throughout our mission. I breathed in a few deep breaths to calm my racing heart. After one last look to confirm that everyone was either asleep or occupied, and that no one would notice my departure, I got up and snuck toward the exit.

Silently, I eased myself out the door. I'd opened it just enough for me to squeeze through. I walked across the grounds and knelt in front of the egg that Eshshah had chosen. Reaching in my tunic, I removed the silk satchel and took out the cow's bladder. Reverently, I lifted the egg that was no larger than my head.

Pulling off my top tunic, I used it to wrap the egg carefully. Dragon eggs, by nature, are very strong. It was not likely that it would break, but I wasn't going to take any chances. I put the wrapped egg in the silk bag, slung it over my head and put one arm through the strap so it crossed my chest.

I quietly blew up the cow's bladder to match the size of the egg, and placed it exactly where the real one had been. I was pleased with how smoothly and quickly the procedure had gone.

Adrenaline pumped through my body as I made sure everything looked right. I stood up and adjusted the silk satchel so the egg hung behind my left hip. Tightening the strap, I turned to head out of the grounds.

Just as I reached the exit to begin my journey to the Castle Outpost, the classroom door opened behind me. I looked over my shoulder, and there stood Kemp. My stomach lurched as I fought my panic — I could not allow fear to show. It would have been easy to outrun him, but I had no doubt that he would alert the instructor or the guide.

"Hey, you, what do you think you're doing?" he bellowed as he strode toward me.

I cringed. *He'd better not wake everyone up.*

"It was too boring in there," I answered. "All those lies and fairy tales were putting me to sleep. I'm going for a walk. No one is going to miss me, especially that dull-witted instructor — if he even wakes up. Why? What business is it of yours?"

He seemed to relax a bit. I probably reflected his own sentiments.

"What's in the bag?" He eyed it suspiciously. I was glad I had wrapped the egg, which distorted the shape.

"Some food I had stashed. Again, what business is it of yours?" I had put some of the Healer's travel cakes in the sack. I was thankful I didn't need to lie — it was something I did not do well.

My anger began to radiate. Coupled with my impatience to leave the arena, I was afraid something would show in my eyes to alert him.

"I'm with you, Amáne, take it easy," Eshshah hummed.

I drew in a silent breath and kept my voice even.

"Just go back to sleep and leave me alone." I waived a dismissal and turned to leave.

Kemp's hand clamped on my shoulder with an iron grip. "I'll let you go, but I owe you one first, boy. This is for interfering with my fight."

He pulled his ham-sized fist back, ready to deliver a brutal blow. I was quicker. I grabbed the hand gripping my shoulder, pivoted to the side, brought my other hand down on the back of his arm as I twisted his wrist. Kemp dropped to his knees. I gave him a quick hard kick. He sprawled sideways, gasping for air. Spinning around, I rushed out the door.

I sprinted down the corridor. Finding the alcove where Dorjan's man had hidden my weapons, I ducked in. Besides my glaive and sword, I was elated to see he managed to smuggle in one of Dorjan's lighting balls — an ingenious explosive device I had used on the guards when I last came here to rescue Lord Ansel. I hastily hooked it to a loop on my belt, then attached the scabbard and sheathed my sword. Grabbing my glaive, I continued on to find the stairs down into the bowels of the castle where I would make my way back to Eshshah.

My heart sank when I heard a commotion behind me. Kemp had shouted for the guards. I didn't think he had discovered my theft, but sought revenge — I had shamed him ... again. The candidates were not allowed to leave the area of the Hatching Grounds. My infraction was enough reason to call the guards.

Chapter Thirty-three

I bolted down the stairs as quickly as I could. These were cut in the same uneven pattern as the tower stairs I'd previously used — it felt like so long ago. Each castle has a pattern in which the heights of the risers in the stairs vary. This is to slow down an enemy who doesn't know the pattern. I, fortunately did, thanks to Dorjan. I still didn't want to take them too quickly as sometimes I lost count and missed a step. The last thing I wanted was to tumble headlong to the bottom.

Arriving at the lower level, I sprinted again until I found the cross corridor. Veering right, I raced quite a distance to the hallway I sought. I turned left. A clamor up ahead caught my attention. Two guards turned the corner and headed straight for me with their pole axes at the ready. I turned on my heels and darted in the opposite direction. Passing the corridor I had just come from, heavy footsteps resounded ahead. My mouth went dry as two more soldiers turned the corner with their weapons readied.

I stopped abruptly and doubled back again, hoping to make the corridor I had just passed. The other two had already reached it and blocked my way. There was no way out. I felt like a trapped animal, which was exactly what I was.

Finding no other alternative, I had to fight — I was ready with my spear.

"Eshshah!" I shouted in thought transference.

"I'm with you, Amáne. Take your time. Use your head." I felt a surge of her strength flow through me.

Concerned about the egg slung over my shoulder, I knew it was essentially unbreakable, but somehow it didn't feel right that I was going to have to jostle it. I wished it didn't have to be present in a fight. But I had no choice.

The first soldier to reach me obviously did not put much effort into his attack. He had sized me up. There were four of them and only one of me — and not very much of me, considering my size. He showed no doubt that I would be taken without much resistance. Pity for him. He went down easier than he should have. As he lunged at me with his halberd, I dodged, stepped aside and ran him through.

"May you rest with your ancestors," I had the presence to say.

Pulling my spear free, I faced the second guard. He was now too close to use my blade. I jumped clear as he swung. Ending up behind him, I turned and tripped him up with the butt-end of my spear. Finding his ribs between his loosely buckled breastplate, I thrust my blade in. He fell.

In an instant I turned to face the other two men. The lead guard brought his halberd down heavily. I dove to my right. Cradling the egg, I rolled to my feet. His axe head stuck in the dirt floor. Abandoning it, he drew his sword. Before I could parry, he thrust it at my chest. Had I not worn Eshshah's dragonscale breastplate, I would have been run through. The air forced out of my lungs and

I stumbled backwards a couple steps. I recovered my breath and gained my balance. He'd made his move too soon. The distance he kept proved to my advantage. The force of his thrust was not enough to make me lose my footing. *That's going to leave a nasty bruise* I thought, but the alternative would have been disastrous.

My opponent hesitated, incredulity on his face. It should have been a fatal blow. In the next breath, I hooked his sword with my glaive. As it flew from his hand, I finished him off. I turned to face my fourth and last adversary — ready for his attack.

Behind him, further down the hallway, a door flew open. I caught a swift glimpse of a high ranking official. He shouted, "Garritt! Stay your weapon! We need the boy alive."

"He's taken out three of us," Garritt shouted back. "He does not deserve to live, Lord Duer, he shall see his ancestors this moment." Garritt pulled his halberd back for the blow — death glinted in his eyes.

The name by which he addressed this new arrival stunned me. I froze.

Garritt did not follow orders, but swung his halberd. I bent forward, barely in time, ducking as his blade came around. I wasn't quick enough to evade his strike. His axe-head caught the top of my hat, ripping it off, along with a handful of my hair. The rest of my hair was loosened. It tumbled down in a tangled mass. In a fluid motion his blade traced a graceful arc and came back at me from the opposite direction. I had just straightened up — the halberd leveled at my neck. My weight on my back leg allowed me to bend backwards. I threw my head back and to the left as the blade whizzed by, taking a nick out of my jaw.

Duer drew his sword and rushed at me. In an instant I reformulated my strategy to fight the two. To my shock Duer did not set upon me, but struck Garritt down.

I turned towards him and readied my spear, but found him with his mouth agape. The bloodied sword in his hand hung limp at his side. I stared at the man, shaking my head in denial. My heart stopped. My eyes went wide as I recognized a familiarity about his face. Similar features had stared at me from the looking glass. That truth, and his name left me no doubt — this man was my father.

A hatred, like a poison, burned through me — a fury I had never known. Red flashed before my eyes, wanting nothing more than to see this man's head roll. More than ready to bring my lifelong desire to fruition, I lunged. But I stayed my blade before it struck. He didn't counter. I hesitated, waiting for him to make a move. But he just stood there.

"Are you going to fight or be the coward I always knew you were?"

Duer ignored my taunt.

I kept my eye on him, and said through gritted teeth, "Raise your sword, Duer, so I can finish you without conscience."

"Amáne," warned Eshshah in my thoughts, "show mercy. Don't let hatred guide a poor decision."

"Mercy, Eshshah?" I silently screamed in thought transference. "Like he showed to my mother and me?"

Without any more deliberation, I raised my spear high and brought the point down with as much force as I could — driving it into the ground, just a hair's breadth from his foot. I stood in front of him, shaking from anger and a host of other emotions that fought for dominance.

"Catriona," he whispered as he stared at me. "You have her eyes and the same crease between them when she got angry."

I didn't respond. My jaw hurt from clenching my teeth.

"So ... she remarried?" He asked slowly.

I huffed a contemptuous laugh. "No!" — *No, you idiot, she loved only you.* I thought to myself.

As sudden as a Valaira, comprehension hit him. "Then you are ... my ..."

Nothing would come out of my mouth. All these years — all my life — I've wanted to find this man. I'd first let him know what he missed, and let it sink in. Then I would send him to his ancestors. I had gone over and over it in my mind. I had rehearsed it. I had dreamed it. Trained for it when I used to fight with Kail. But now, here he stood. My glaive still vibrated from the force I had just used to bury the point at his feet. I could say nothing — or do nothing.

"What did she name you?"

"Amáne."

"Amáne," he said slowly, dream-like, as if it were a pleasant taste on his tongue "... a very beautiful name. You have your mother's voice."

"Don't call me Amáne, here. I came as Vann and must remain Vann, until my job is done."

"And Catriona — how is she?" He asked with a far-away look in his eye — memories of a happier time.

I bit my lip to keep it from trembling.

His sword clattered to the floor. Falling to his knees, he sat back on his heels, and put his hands to his face. I felt foolish standing in front of this broken man with my hand on the hilt of my sword. I slowly worked the blade of my glaive from the dirt, knowing he was not going to move against me — he was a guilt-ridden wreck of a man. Another episode in my life where I got exactly what I had wished for. But again, my victory was bitter. I felt no satisfaction whatsoever. My desire to end his life faded.

He pressed his lips together briefly, then whispered. "May she rest with her ancestors and may she forgive me if I even deserve to find her there."

Wiping the blood from my jaw, I started wrapping my hair again, securing it back to the top of my head. I winced when a pin found the raw spot where my hair had been ripped out. Picking up my hat, I pinned it on, becoming Vann again. All the while not taking my eye off of Duer.

He stood up slowly and picked up his sword. After wiping it clean, he sheathed it. Opening the door from which he had come, he motioned for me to enter.

"Come Vann, it's my duty to get you out of here."

I looked at him, puzzled. "You're Dorjan's man inside?"

Chapter Thirty-Four

Duer rushed me through a series of rooms, and hallways, locking the doors behind us. I finally had the chance to ask, "Why are you here? I was told you were called away on an errand."

"I was. No one knows I've not yet left. I knew how important this mission was going to be, and I felt it necessary to stay, until the egg was safely out."

We traveled quickly through the corridors beneath the castle and although it was not the route I'd planned on taking, I had a good idea of where I was. I started to relax — we were making good time to the Castle Outpost where Eshshah and Bern waited.

I felt Eshshah's relief as the situation came under control. And I knew that relief spread back to the Healer and Gallen.

"Why are you doing this, Duer?"

He ushered me into what looked like a supply room. Chairs stacked in one corner, large casks of wine crowded most of the small space.

Locking the door behind him, he turned to me. "We'll be safe in here for a bit. Sit down and catch your breath." He pulled a chair over, then reached in his sleeve and handed me his handkerchief.

"I can't deliver you to your friends with blood all over your face." His blue eyes crinkled at the edges.

For lack of water, I used my saliva to wet the cloth and blotted the gash on my jaw.

Duer lowered himself wearily into a chair in front of me. "The answer to your question is a long one. I'll make it short."

Taking a deep breath, he hesitated, trying to formulate his words. He exhaled slowly. "When I met your mother, she was just a bit older than you — you look so much like her. Her family ran the pottery guild and she usually worked their booth at the marketplace. I found myself at that booth often — vying for her attention. Her parents had other plans — a betrothal arrangement — but I had her heart.

"I was foolish and wanted a position in Galtero's court so I could have something to offer Catriona. I didn't realize at the time, who Galtero really was — a tyrant greedy for wealth and power — the one who orchestrated the deaths of the Royal Family. After he assumed the throne, he cared for his subjects for the sole purpose of obtaining more treasure. Then he heard about the prophecy. Are you familiar with it?"

"Not very. I've only just recently heard about it."

"It starts, '*From the Guild of Clay she shall emerge.*

The Kingdom's bane in hopes to purge...'

"Galtero had his sorcerers and wise men working on interpreting the meaning for quite some time. They came to the conclusion that it had something to do with Catriona. Knowing I was anxious to prove myself to him, Galtero ordered me to send her to her ancestors."

I gasped.

"Yes, and he knew I had an interest in her, so it was that much more evil of him to choose me for the deed. Galtero's decision worked against him, for it enabled me to protect her. I had a plan and told him I would be gone for some time as I could not take her life here in the City of Teravinea.

"I didn't tell her of the plot, but pleaded my love to her and convinced her to run away with me. She didn't oppose. She loved me and didn't want to marry whom her parents had chosen. We married privately and stole out in the middle of the night. I felt she would be safest at the furthest point of the kingdom — Dorsal.

"We traveled for several days. Those were the best days of my life. Catriona loved the outdoors, sleeping under the stars and angling. She must have fished every body of water between here and Dorsal."

I nodded, "It always was one of her favorite things to do. She taught me to love it just as much as she did."

A faint smile curved his lips. "I stayed as long as I dared in Dorsal. I didn't want to leave, but felt she would be safer without me, until Galtero was dethroned. I told her I had to go back to the City of Teravinea, but would return as soon as I could. Truthfully, I meant it. But the days turned to months and the months to years.

"There hasn't been a day gone by that I didn't want to run back to your mother. But if I did, her safety would have been in jeopardy. I did the next best thing I could — I protected her from this distance. I stayed in Galtero's court and secretly joined in the cause of the dragon riders to overthrow Galtero and crown a new king.

"Once a new king gained the throne, I could go back to Dorsal — to my Catriona. I didn't think it would take this long, and now I'm too late. I should have taken her to Serislan or somewhere further, and never come back." His voice trailed off.

My heart broke at his anguish and my tears flowed freely, the salt stinging the gash in my jaw.

"Dorjan recently told me they now have someone qualified to take the throne."

My heart skipped a beat.

He continued, "I now have renewed hope. I'll continue to work with the riders — for you." He stopped as comprehension dawned. Looking at me, his eyebrows raised, he said, "You ... you're a Chosen One."

I gave a slight nod. He saluted me with pride, which brought more tears to my eyes as I acknowledged his respect.

"The prophecy, was true, then," he said. "Galtero's wise men were correct in fearing your mother. Although it was not Catriona that became the rider, but her daughter ... our daughter."

Duer paused, then sighed heavily and rose from his chair. "I could gaze at you forever, but we both have our duties. I will see you safely to the outpost and you will deliver the egg to your leader. Come, we've tarried long enough."

He unlocked the door, then moved slowly into the corridor. His hand raised to signal that I wait. Duer surveyed the area and then motioned for me to follow. We made our way quickly through another succession of turns.

Nearing the outpost, I marveled at how quickly this quest had gone. I would be back in Dorsal sooner than I'd expected. My relief was short-lived — a commotion echoed further ahead. I grabbed Duer's arm and whispered, "Several men are heading this way."

"Go then! That way." He pointed back towards the way we had come. "Left at the corridor we just passed and then left again and you will be heading in the correct direction. I'll take care of these men."

I'd just met my father, and wasn't yet ready to separate from him. There was so much I needed to ask him. So much to know about my mother and about him. In my wildest dreams this scenario would never have happened. It was almost impossible to tear myself away, until I heard bootsteps and the clink of weapons drawing nearer. I couldn't afford to get caught — my quest was nearly accomplished. It would also put Duer's life in danger. I couldn't chance that.

"Thank you." I said through my tears. I turned to run.

"Amáne —"

I stopped short and spun around to face him.

"I'm calling you by the name she gave you — Amáne," he repeated. "There is one thing I ask of you."

"Yes?"

"Will you sometime in the future find it in your heart to forgive me?"

"No, Father. I forgive you now." Holding my spear in one hand, I threw my free arm around his neck and gave him a kiss on his cheek. With one last look, I turned and raced towards the other corridor.

Chapter Thirty-five

Without delay I found the alternate route and sprinted towards safety. I could taste victory. I would soon be returning to face Lord Ansel. If he didn't wish to continue our friendship, at least I will have proven to him that he made the right decision to send me.

My heart sank when I heard the clashing of weapons. I stopped in my tracks and turned back.

"Eshshah, I need to go back and help my father!"

"No, Amáne. He has his duty and you have yours. An alarm has been sounded and they're searching for you. Continue to the outpost. You're almost here."

"I've only just found him. I can't lose him so soon."

"Head this way, Amáne," she repeated. "Healer's orders."

I'd learned my lesson some time ago about obeying the Healer's orders. I didn't want to abandon my father, but I had my duty. I had no choice but to comply.

I exhaled, "Tell the Healer I'm on my way."

I spun back around and rushed towards the safety of the outpost and Eshshah, but froze mid-step as a door ahead of me flew open and several men poured out. They turned, spotted me, drew their weapons and rushed in my direction.

My delay had cost me dearly. I surprised myself when a curse left my lips.

I came upon a door to my left. I dove for it and hoped to find it unlocked. Even though I had Aperio's key, I wouldn't have the time to use it — the guards were closing on me.

Thankfully, it opened. I stumbled into a large room. Turning, I drove my body against the door. But not in time. The butt end of a spear was thrust in the crack. I pushed with all my might to keep the man from entering, but with no luck — I could feel another join him. There was nothing within reach to put in front of the door to secure it, nor would I be able to hold it much longer.

My head spun — panic threatened. I felt Eshshah's concern as she tried to calm me. Transferring the satchel to my front side, I put my back to the door and pushed with my legs. I couldn't allow the egg to be captured and brought back to the hatching grounds.

To my right, and just out of reach, stood a tall crate, the lid ajar. I pulled the silk satchel off over my head, and wrapped it tightly around the egg. Using my glaive, I strained to open the top of the crate, while still keeping pressure against the door. My legs shook from the effort, sweat dripped into my eyes. I had one chance to save the egg.

Breathing in, I tried to keep my balance as I struggled with my spear to lift the lid. I needed more leverage, but out of sheer willpower, and Eshshah's help, I managed to raise it. I tossed the egg and held my breath as it arced into the opening in the crate. The lid slammed shut. Letting my breath out, I begged for the unhatched dragon's forgiveness for this show of disrespect. Maybe Bern, Eben or Avano could make their way here and retrieve it — if I didn't make it.

My legs gave way. I stumbled but managed to jump clear. The door flew open. Three guards tumbled into the room. I quickly dispatched one of them. More rushed in. I had to look for another way out. Charging towards the other end of the chamber, I realized there was no other exit. I was trapped ... again. I ducked behind a crate and listened in horror as the storeroom filled with the sound of pounding boots.

Someone bellowed in a rough voice, "The boy stays alive! D'you hear me? If any of you send him to his ancestors I'll be sure to oversee your torture and slow death."

"Eshshah!" I cried in thought transference.

"I'm with you Amáne." Her strength spread through my body as I made the decision to stand and fight sooner rather than later. It was my only chance.

"Eshshah, if these men obey their orders, this may not be my last day in this life." I had to give her hope, but could not fully trust that those orders would be followed.

Bursting from behind the crate, I engaged the first man. I knew he'd underestimate me because of my size. This was always to my advantage. Coming in too close, he didn't know what hit him when I thrust my spear into his neck. He dropped quickly. The others approached with a little more caution. They stepped back out of reach.

I retreated towards a corner. I'd make my stand there, with the walls to my back. Before I reached my goal, the men had advanced and started to fan around me. My hopes of escape faded.

My mind raced for a solution. Glancing down, I spotted a crate with its lid askew. It was packed with daggers. I moved my glaive to my other hand. Before the soldiers realized what was happening, I began grabbing and hurling daggers. Their shields stopped most of them, but the ones I threw low found flesh. My opponents weren't in full armor. They had no greaves, poleyn, or cuisses to protect their shins, knees, or their thighs. When they lowered their shields to protect their legs, I threw high — again with some success.

The guards were dropping or backing up. But it didn't increase my chances of escape. There were now too many of them. More than likely, it would increase the chances that they would disobey their orders. I decided to stop throwing the daggers.

It looked hopeless, but I had one more weapon on my belt. It was time to use Dorjan's lightning ball. I wished he'd had time to assemble more than just the one. I had to make the best of it. Removing it from my belt, I pulled the brass ring and whispered "Torin, Unule, Salama" as I tossed it in the middle of the group moving towards me. I ducked behind a crate from the flash and explosion. Bodies went flying. Screams and yells were cut short as the flash overtook them. I had less remorse with this device — it didn't take lives, but only incapacitated for several hours.

My outlook brightened again. I jumped to my feet to head for the exit. As I began to feel my escape was imminent, I saw a movement to my left. A quick glance revealed a man sneaking up between crates, holding something in his arms. He must have been shielded from the blast, although he did look a little disoriented. Unfortunately, he had enough awareness to be able to carry out his intentions. With a fluid motion, he threw the object at me. Alarmed, I watched as it opened up into a large round net, edged with weights. It looked like a giant jelly fish turning in the air above, as it hurled down towards me. I scrambled to get out of its way, but too late. It landed on me. With the momentum of its spin, it wrapped tightly around my body, down to my feet, rendering me helpless.

I could feel Eshshah's distress. I convinced her I was not hurt, but couldn't hide my fear. There was nothing she could do for me, but only stay with me for comfort and support.

Chapter Thirty-six

The sound of the key unlocking my cell door woke me. I was still wrapped in the net, having given my captors such a such a struggle when they had tried to remove it. In the end they threw me in the cell, net and all. They did manage to secure the manacles around my ankles before they left.

I recalled my exhaustion as they slammed the cell door. I had fought the claustrophobia that began to take hold of me. With Eshshah's help, I allowed my body some rest. She did her best to console me, assuring me that the riders were working to get me out.

Now, four men stood over me, fully armed. They were taking no chances. My surroundings brought back frightening memories — it was identical to, if not the same cell where I'd found Lord Ansel. That night seemed like another lifetime ago, but the stench of death, vomit and urine brought it back quickly.

The head guard glared down at me and laughed. "King Galtero wants to use you as an example, boy. An example of what happens when ya don't respect his hospitality. You're dirt, boy — not worthy of a candidate. You'll soon be wishing you already met your ancestors. The king is in the mood for a little sport." The other guards broke into hideous laughter.

"So, what's it gonna be? You want the net off and you'll come easy, or do we carry you out of here and deliver you in the arena wrapped up?"

Arena? That didn't sound good. I stared angrily through the ropes. Maybe it would improve my situation if I started cooperating just a bit. At least until I found out what they were going to do with me. I was ready to have this net off and that wasn't going to happen if I kept fighting them.

I gritted my teeth, "I'll cooperate."

"Strong ... and smart. This is gonna be a good show," another guard said.

After releasing the net, they shackled my wrists and my feet. With a chain they led me out of the cell. We went up a few levels and down a corridor. They threw me into another cell. I heard a murmur coming from the other side of the wall. Excited voices drifted towards me. *A cheering crowd?*

The last vial of the Healer's dark liquid was still intact in my tunic. I would be needing all the help I could get. Making sure no one was watching, I retrieved it with my chained hands, uncorked it and drained the last of the energizing concoction. I closed my eyes and held back a choking cough as I felt its warmth travel down my throat.

Eshshah continued to relay my situation to Bern, who was on the communication disc to the Healer. I didn't want my loved ones to know everything that would be happening to me — it wasn't fair to put the Healer and Gallen through that kind of anguish. Bern, Avano and Eben had to be at their wits end trying to save me. Time had run out. If things went poorly, I didn't want the details shared.

I conveyed this to Eshshah, who understood, but repeated that she was following the Healer's orders. She did her best to console me, as I in turn tried to console her. I reminded her one more time that she will need to carry on without me if the outcome would be as we feared — I wanted assurance that she give herself over to Lord Ansel. She promised me she'd do as I asked, but added, "Amáne, I have hope that we will see a positive outcome."

"So I will, too, Eshshah."

A burly man came to collect me. He led me out a door and through a tunnel. As we headed toward a large metal door, he took out a small vial and shook the viscous contents onto his finger, then spread the pungent salve under his nose. I had only a second to wonder about his actions before the door opened onto a large oval indoor arena. The smell of blood and death assailed me. I gagged. The sand on the floor, meant to absorb blood and whatever foulness took place in this cavern, was so saturated with gore and rotting tissue, that it no longer served its purpose. The stench was overwhelming. I wrestled to control my urge to retch.

I squinted as we came into to the brightness. The walls were lined with light shields, like the ones in the outposts. The light they shed made it seem like we were in full daylight, although we were somewhere deep within the castle.

Similar to the hatching grounds, there were tiers of seating around half of the arena — complete with spectators. Unlike the hatching grounds, the seating started high above the ground level where I stood. My guess was that it kept the spectators safe from whatever vile activity the arena hosted. I swallowed hard, and silently sang a battle song to build up my courage. Eshshah hummed with me.

The guard pushed me to the center of the dirt grounds and spun me roughly to face the small crowd. There were probably a couple hundred people. The fabrics and colors of their clothing showed the majority came from high stations — nobles and well-to-do merchants. Men made up most of the crowd, but there were plenty of women as well. They held handkerchiefs over their noses, or used fans to dispel the fetid odor. I had no doubt they made good use of the salve as well. All were in a seemingly festive mood as if they had come to enjoy a bit of fine entertainment. I knew they were not here for any benign recreation.

My eyes surveyed the stands. Horror froze my heart when I spotted a small group in the far corner — the candidates. They huddled together with terror-stricken faces as they were forced to watch one of their number take part in some barbaric form of amusement. Even Kemp, the bully from the hatching grounds, looked uncomfortable. My eyes locked on his. He lowered his eyes immediately.

Standing in chains facing the crowd, my heart beat fast, but I didn't let any emotion show on my face. A door opened high in the top tier in front of where I stood. Several armed guards came out first, and then a sourness rose from the pit of my stomach as I watched King Galtero enter the stadium. The crowd stood and bowed to him as he descended the stairs to his seat in the front row.

I stood up straight. My jaw set, I glared at the man as he came down. My guard grabbed me by the back of the neck and shoved me down to my knees. I squeezed my eyes shut to avoid seeing what writhed in the sand beneath me.

"Bow to the king, you insolent boy!" He growled. He held me down with his powerful hand. I could have broken his hold, if I so wished, but this was not the time. I let him hold me down, knowing this was no show of respect on my part. I hoped Galtero noticed.

The crowd settled in their seats as the king arranged himself in his. He then directed his full attention to me.

"Welcome to our little game, Vann of Anbon," he said. "You grieve me by the disrespect you've shown for my generosity. I invited you, along with your small band of candidates," he waved his hand towards the corner of the stands, "to participate in the great honor of a Hatching. I expected courtesy in return, not an ill-mannered boy running through my halls cutting down my men for amusement."

I breathed a sigh of relief because this accusation meant they hadn't yet discovered the missing egg. *Why such the extravagant efforts to punish me, a simple candidate? Was this intended as a demonstration to set me as an example for anyone who dared to cross him, or was there more to it?*

I recalled the heads on the stakes at the city gate and a morbid thought came to mind. *I wonder if my head will be joining those.*

"Amáne!" Eshshah pleaded.

"I'm sorry, Eshshah. I'd be willing to wager, though, that a few of the nobles and merchants here were required to be present for just this lesson."

Galtero continued, "You've disgraced your fellow candidates and will now pay the price. You will be the example of my displeasure of anyone who wishes to take my hospitality for granted." He scanned the spectators. Quiet fell upon the crowd as the festive mood became somber.

I stood silent — meeting his eyes with as much defiance as I could summon. I hoped the fear I felt didn't show. Silently, I thanked Eshshah. She was my strength.

"Have you nothing to say to me boy? Will you not plead for your life?"

Still I remained silent. My eyes blazed at him.

My guard smacked me in the back of the head. It took a great deal of control to keep from using the irons and chains around my wrists to strangle him.

Besides leaving Eshshah, my biggest heartbreak, should I not survive this ordeal, would be that I'd never see Lord Ansel again. No matter if he wanted nothing more to do with me. Missing his gaze one last time was a regret almost too heavy for me to bear.

"Eshshah, I love you. If I meet my ancestors today, please let Lord Ansel know that I did love him." My throat tightened.

"And you are a part of my heart, Amáne." I could feel her struggle to maintain her composure. She knew I needed her to stay calm. "Please forgive me for not being able to come to your rescue. These corridors were not made to accommodate my size and your location will not allow breaking down any walls — you would be crushed." She was distraught — inconsolable, but she held on bravely for me.

I breathed in deeply, swallowing the lump in my throat. "Hope, Eshshah. There is always that. It does not disappoint." A peace came over me. My body relaxed. I resigned myself to my fate — ready to face whatever foul amusement the king had planned.

Galtero stood up and ordered the game to begin.

"And to show that I am a fair king, I'll allow you more of an advantage than you deserve." A sickening grin distorted his face. "Unchain the boy, give him a weapon and release my pet!"

My guard turned to me and quickly unlocked my irons. I was relieved in a strange sort of way to see in his eyes that he was not in agreement with whatever was in store for me. He handed me a small dagger and whispered, "I'm sorry, but this is the weapon I was instructed to give you. It'll do you no good. May you rest in peace with your ancestors."

I took the dagger and hefted it. The balance felt good in my hand. The blade was true and sharp. The man turned to leave the stadium but before he took two steps, the grating sound of wheels turning and chains clanking echoed through the arena. The massive metal doors behind us opened. The burly guard shouted in terror as he realized that they didn't give him time to exit before releasing whatever lay behind that door. He bolted towards the stands.

Growling, scratching and an additional, yet familiar putrid smell preceded the monster that emerged. Out slithered a lizard-like creature. It was similar to the one that had bitten me when I had rescued Lord Ansel from the dungeons of the castle. Its tattoo-like mark remained on my ankle as a reminder. This one was not the same black creature, but a mottled dirty brown — the color that runs in the gutters of the streets in the mornings. Its large head weaved back an forth on its long neck. The bulbous eyes searched for prey.

The movement of the guard fleeing for his life attracted the creature's attention. With remarkable speed for such a large misshapen beast, he fell upon the unfortunate man before he could even swing the sword he had drawn. It wouldn't have been of much use, anyway. The monster opened his jaws, dripping with venom. In one snap, half of the man was gone, leaving his shield and sword to drop to the dirt.

I turned and retched as the crowd cheered.

"Eshshah." I whispered.

"I'm with you, Amáne. Do not make any sudden movements. When he gets close to you, lock eyes with him, just as you did with the black one."

I surveyed the arena and thought perhaps I could escape the same way Lord Ansel and I had done when the black lizard stalked us. There were some barrels against the wall under the stands and if I could get a running start, I could use them to scale the wall into the stands, jump the railing and take my chances with the guards.

My escape route was behind the creature, who had just finished feeding. Blood dripped from its maw. He turned his yellow eyes to me. He began to stalk me slowly ... deliberately. I backed up steadily and met his eyes. They were powerful, trying to draw me in, but its pull was not as strong as the black one's. I had Eshshah's venom running in my veins, which is what kept me from being drawn in. I planned to lead him in a circle so my back would be towards the barrels. Then when my position was right, I would turn and run for the wall. It worked before — more or less — there was no reason it would not work again.

In the next breath, fear exploded in my chest. My head thundered and my tattooed ankle began to burn. *Not now! Why was this happening?* It was the same pain that had assailed me in Dorsal, when a sorcerer came in search of me many months ago. The timing of this attack was crucial. Any sudden movement would cause me to break contact with the beast's eyes.

My pain increased, but I managed to continue in my path, turning the beast. I realized that now, because of the pain in my ankle, it would not be possible for me to run to safety. Arriving at the spot where the guard's life had ended, I spotted his shield. I blocked from my mind the repulsiveness of what I was about to do. Not leaving the creature's eyes, I bent over slowly and grabbed the bloody shield. The guard's hand still clung to the grip, blood still flowed from the severed end. I moved my arm back slowly as the creature turned its attention to the motion of the shield. Then I flung it as hard as I could across the arena. Like a dog that chases a stick, the monster charged after the shield. As soon as it hit the ground, the brown creature snapped it up and began to devour it.

Something prompted me to look in the direction of the king, who had all this while been shouting encouragements to his "pet." While the creature occupied himself with his grotesque snack, I allowed myself that glance. My head felt like it would burst. Flashes, like lightning, went off behind my eyes. There, seated next to Galtero, staring intently at me, was another sorcerer — evil twisted his countenance. He looked to be a relation to the one who had met his end in Dorsal.

I couldn't mask the agony written on my face. Galtero nodded appreciatively at the sorcerer. I would have no chance against the monster with the excruciating pain the mage inflicted upon me. That certainly added to the king's pleasure.

The king stood up, stabbed a forefinger at me and shouted, "So, my sorcerer was correct. He felt your presence in the castle. You are the boy that entered my dungeon several months ago and stole my esteemed prisoner!"

I was taken aback. *How did he know?*

As if to answer my question, he continued, "You were bitten by my black pet, were you not? Why you weren't killed? I don't know. But I'm pleased that you have been very helpful with our experiments. We'll soon have replacements for the useless dragons that are all but fairy tales. There will be a new breed of lizard that will answer only to me. With them, I will bring power to my monarchy. Even the Kingdom of Serislan will fall to me."

Some vile link existed between the sorcerer and the black creature's venom running in my veins. I heard Eshshah's menacing growl. Her pain joined her anger as she tried to accept the fact that she remained helpless.

The sorcerer intensified his attack. My torture increased. I sunk to my knees, holding my head. My teeth clamped shut, stifling my scream.

"Eshshah, I need you to increase your power in me."

"But you'll be unable to breathe. Remember what happened last time? I could have ended your life."

"It'll be ended sooner if I don't stop this agony. He's increasing his dark magic." I fought the nausea and the urge to scratch out my eyes to get to the pain. "I have a plan. Please, when I give you the word, I'll need more than you gave me the last time we fought off the sorcerer. It's my only chance."

"As you wish, Amáne. Tell me when you're ready."

I immediately made my calculations, and then inhaled deeply. I held my breath and silently yelled, "Now, Eshshah!"

I felt her power surge through me like never before. Fighting to control my body, I leaped up, spotted my mark and let my dagger fly with lightning speed.

Before anyone knew what had happened the dagger buried itself past its hilt in the sorcerer's neck, impaling him in his seat. A crimson spray pulsed from the wound. A bright red bloom spread on the front of his robe. Pink foam bubbled from his mouth — his eyes wide in a grotesque stare. I wished his evil spirit to wherever evil spirits go.

Galtero screamed. The crowd went silent.

Eshshah relieved me of the extra surge. I spun to my right to face the creature who now charged towards me, attracted by my sudden movement. My timing was off. I leaped to my left — almost avoiding his attack. His teeth missed me. But as he stormed by, he struck at me with his front claws. Raking my right arm, he sent me flying backwards. I couldn't control my landing. When I hit the dirt, I heard the sickening pop of my right wrist. Pain set fire to my arm from the strike of his filthy talons. That and the agony of my broken wrist threatened to send me into shock. My hand now hung at an unnatural angle. A cold sweat went through me. My stomach twisted.

On natural instinct, I grabbed my wrist as I slowly rose to my feet, thankful that my bone had not broken through the skin. "Eshshah," I whispered as heat radiated from my hand that held my wrist tightly. Disbelief washed over me as I felt the bone begin to mend under my burning touch. Light-headedness took me for a brief moment. With Eshshah's help, my body urged itself back to fight-ready.

There was no time to question what just occurred with my wrist. The creature had run to the other end of the arena before he could stop his bulk and turn back to face me. He approached with slow deliberate steps. I remained completely still — my eyes locked with his. I would attempt my original plan to break for the barrels and safety. I had to turn him almost completely around before the barrels would be at my back.

My concentration threatened to break as Galtero screamed something about The Prophecy. I saw him out of the corner of my eye — his arms flailing wildly. I gasped. My sleeve had been ripped to shreds, exposing Eshshah's linking mark. My hat had been torn off. My hair fell around my shoulders. The crowd whipped itself into a state of frenzy.

"Release my black pet!" Galtero howled at the top of his lungs. A combination of fury, incredulity and terror sounded in his voice.

But another sound came to me that moment.

"Eshshah, who's calling me?" It was a guttural sound, in a language I did not recognize, but I could tell it was my name.

"I don't know, Amáne, I hear it, too."

"Where is it coming from?"

A grating sound filled the arena. Another massive door began to open somewhere behind me. My heart froze as I felt the vile black beast emerge — the very same brute I had encountered on my last visit. The brown broke his gaze with me, his attention drawn to the movement of the nightmare creature that emerged. I used that opportunity to turn slowly. My eyes rested on the black monster lizard. His short legs that supported his distended belly; the undersized wings; bulbous eyes and long snout; fangs that dripped with venom. He had grown in size half again from what I remembered. Charging into the arena, he headed straight at me.

I tried not to be disheartened. I was not a quitter, but now I had two beasts to face. And my right arm was almost useless. My end was forthcoming. Galtero screamed like a mad man, urging the creatures on — a wicked note of victory in his voice. I wished I had another dagger to stop his despicable ranting.

Hope. There is always hope. I cannot let it slip away. I must not leave my dragon to mourn me. I must see Lord Ansel's green eyes again. The Healer. Gallen. All marched before me in my mind.

"Amáne, jump to your right — now!" Eshshah cried.

I did as she commanded. I dove to my right as the black lizard bolted past me, not even looking at me. He fell upon the brown one. Both tumbled to the other end of the arena. The black one clamped his jaws on the neck of the brown and picked it up shaking it like a dog would shake a squirrel. I stood frozen as he launched it into the stands high above us. The brute crashed lifelessly into the seats, crushing several spectators. It sailed over Galtero, who was instantly surrounded by his protectors. They ushered him out of the arena through another exit. The crowd screamed in a panic, trampling each other to leave the stands.

"The black one wants to help you, Amáne." Eshshah informed me. "He speaks the ancient language, and calls himself

Charna Yash-churka, Black Lizard. You are linked to him, just as we suspected. But contrary to what we thought, his only desire is to serve you. It's a very primitive linking and he can't communicate with you from any distance. That's why you couldn't hear him until now. He's telling you to leap onto his back. He'll take you out of the castle. Go, Amáne! It is safe."

Chapter Thirty-seven

With my good hand I grabbed the metal collar around his neck and swung onto Charna Yash-churka. The mutant dragon turned back, exiting through the open door he had just entered. We rushed through the tunnels under the castle. I tried to comprehend what had happened. A creature that a few months ago was ready to have me for his meal, now saved my life. I had his venom in my veins, as well as Eshshah's. All this time I was disgusted at the thought of being linked to him. Now, I rode him to safety. My head reeled.

Eshshah directed him to where I'd hidden the egg. Wasting no time, I moved to the crate where I'd stashed it. Breathing a sigh of relief, I found it exactly how I left it — it had not been discovered. I threw the satchel over my shoulder, then leaped back on the black creature's shoulders. Leaning forward, I held tight to his metal collar as we bounded towards our escape.

I heard his harsh-sounding speech, but couldn't understand what he said, except when he said my name.

Eshshah translated, "He says there is a gate on the river side of the castle where he will take you. I'll meet you there, but it may be locked."

I had Aperio's key at the ready. The gold chain kept it hidden under my tunic, close to my heart.

We were almost there — my beautiful dragon waiting on the other side.

A commotion behind me told me that the guards had discovered our position and raced in our direction.

We made the gate. I leaped off and hurried the key in the lock, whispering, "Aperio." The gate unlatched. I threw it open and we rushed out. The sunlight — the glorious sunlight — drenched my face as the sound of pounding boots increased behind me.

Eshshah was there, ready for a wing mount, but I hesitated. I turned and thanked the black lizard, Charna Yash-churka. My eyes rested on the cruel metal collar around his neck. I needed to remove it for him in thanks for saving my life.

"Amáne," Eshshah called, "hurry, there is no time for that."

In my stubbornness I put Aperio's key in the lock and relieved him of the cumbersome device. All at once arrows whizzed past me. I had no weapon. Whirling around, the black lizard shot flames at the soldiers that poured out the door.

From out of nowhere, Avano rushed up. "Amáne! Go. I'll handle this."

"Avano!" My heart leaped to see him. "Give me your other sword."

"No! You have your duty. I have mine. Go — do yours. Don't make my efforts be in vain. Get our boy on the throne. Farewell, Amáne. I'm proud of you." He turned to deal with the soldiers that managed to get through. Charna Yash-churka stood with him.

Tears in my eyes, Avano's brave stand ingrained in my memory, I spun and ran towards Eshshah. Using my left hand, I got hold of her wing "finger." She raised her wing and catapulted me into the saddle. With her powerful hind legs, she launched off the ground. A perfect execution of the wing mount maneuver Gallen had taught us so long ago.

There were no words to describe my feelings. Too many emotions swirled in my head — in my heart. My chest was ready to burst.

Eshshah flew to the Castle Outpost entrance. Bern sprung onto the saddle behind me as Eshshah barely touched the ground. Immediately, she leaped off the ledge and soared towards the ocean. The battlements above us showed some action, as men mustered to their positions. But Eshshah was too quick. We outpaced the arrows they released.

We flew swiftly over the ocean, my adrenaline still pumping. I closed my eyes and breathed deeply the briny air. We took in the reality that our mission was accomplished. It was at that moment I lost control. The pain and torment of what we had just been through flooded through me and my body shook. I let it all out as Bern put his arms around me in comfort.

Turning inland, Eshshah took a longer route, flying over forests and uninhabited areas so we wouldn't be spotted. Darkness had just fallen when we landed in the field outside of Anbon where Bern's friends waited.

Eshshah treated my arm. She breathed her warm soothing breath, fighting the infection that had set in from the creature's foul claws. The oozing gashes would need more treatment to ensure they were free of all contamination — but that would have to wait until we got home. She attended to my wrist, and did a better job at mending it than I had done.

I turned my attention to my clothing. I smelled so badly, even I couldn't stand myself. I didn't know if the putrid stench could ever be washed out — or, if it would ever leave my nostrils. My once-white tunic held no memory of ever having been white. It was covered in blood and the unimaginable filth from the arena.

I grabbed a large pot of water that heated on the fire and retreated to the far side of the field. With Eshshah as my screen, I scrubbed myself until my skin burned. After which I donned a fresh change of clothes from my pack. Pulling the egg satchel back over my head, I made sure it hung securely. Feeling much better, I headed back towards Bern and his companions.

Rolling up my filthy garments, I tied them into a ball. With an exaggerated motion I cast them into the fire and watched the flames consume them. My eyes remained on the fire until there was nothing left of them but glowing embers. Relief washed over me as the embers died and blended in the ashes. If it were only that easy to rid my memories from the horrors of the arena.

Bern offered me a plate of steaming meat. I was ravenous, not remembering the last time I'd eaten. His friends were shocked at the amount I consumed. I'd never tasted anything so delicious, whatever it was that they'd roasted over the fire — I didn't ask.

It was time for me to get back to Dorsal to deliver the dragon egg to the Healer. Bern would head towards Anbon to wait for word from Eben. I was distraught at the thought that I may never see Avano again. I was also anxious for word on my father.

We said our good-byes. I put on my helmet and my riding cape. With one last salute, I mounted, and Eshshah took flight.

Chapter Thirty-eight

Dawn just hinted when I spotted the coast of Dorsal. My heart beat noisily in my chest. I was never more happy to be arriving home than at that moment. As exhausted as I was, I didn't get any sleep as we flew. I wanted to just be with Eshshah. Our minds melded as we comforted each other. We both admitted how terrorized we'd been. However, our atmosphere of terror turned to elation as we rejoiced at our triumphant quest.

Eshshah and I discussed my options for contacting Lord Ansel to report our success. Although we knew he would already have been informed, I thought it would be more proper if I told him myself through the communication disc. My only concern was that I wasn't sure I'd be ready to face him — to encounter his flashing eyes should he still be angry with me. I knew he had forgiven me, but that wasn't a guarantee that he would give me a second chance.

Our spirits lifted. We spotted the Healer's home growing larger as we neared it. Eshshah contacted her that we were coming in. The first thing I'd do — after I see to Eshshah, of course —

would be rush to the bathing room for a long hot soak. My body ached like never before.

Eshshah's wings whipped the air around the Healer and Gallen as they stood watching our approach, making them look even more impressive. We hardly touched down before I slid off and wrapped my arms around the Healer. We kissed both cheeks — her tears flowed freely, as did mine.

I turned to Gallen, who had just greeted Eshshah with the scratch between her eyes that she loved so much. He kissed my forehead, then put his arms around me and swung me in a circle. It hurt a bit, but it was well worth the pain. I was home safely, with the egg slung over my shoulder under my riding cape. I had adjusted the strap so the egg hung at my back — protected and out of the way.

Eshshah and I hoped this quest proved fruitful. If the Healer could decipher the evil the sorcerers had committed on the eggs, it would help our cause.

"You have a gift in the kitchen, Amáne." Gallen broke into my thoughts, barely able to hide his excitement. "Why don't you go in and see what it is?"

How important was this gift, that Gallen couldn't wait to tell me about? Only minutes had passed since I'd been on the ground.

"From whom? What is it?" I was afraid to hope it was from Lord Ansel. He was the only one that had ever sent me a gift. If it were he who sent this one, then possibly it meant that I still stood a chance.

"Go in and find out."

"Let me take care of Eshshah first."

"I'm sure Eshshah won't mind if the Healer and I do that for you. You'd probably end up pulling the saddle down on yourself, or some such thing," Gallen said with a laugh.

“Go open your present, Amáne. I’m fine with the Healer and Gallen.” Eshshah assured me.

I took Eshshah’s fangs, pulled her head to mine and kissed her nose. I thanked her, then turned and rushed inside to find my package, hoping that it would be from Lord Ansel.

I didn’t bother to remove my riding cape or the egg satchel, but hastened to the kitchen. I stopped at the table. There was no package there. I stood puzzled, staring at the empty spot.

Footsteps sounded behind me. Spinning around in alarm, I almost lost my balance.

I gasped, lowered my eyes and dipped in a deep, but painful, curtsy. “Lord Ansel! Your Grace.”

His voice filled with pain, “Get up, Amáne, please. What are you doing? It’s Ansel. Just ... plain ... Ansel.”

He took my hands and helped me up. I hesitated to look at him, afraid to face the disappointment that may come. But I had to know. I gazed up to search the cool green depths of his eyes. My eyes melted into his. My eyebrows lifted and a smile turned my lips. Still holding my hands, he put them gently on his shoulders, then he pulled me close and kissed my forehead. I pressed my head on his chest and listened to the beat of his heart, content to remain there and not move.

Feeling his warm breath on my neck, he whispered, still with a note of distress, “You weren’t listening when I told you that I keep my promises.” I looked up at him, confused. He pulled me closer and pressed his lips against mine.

As my heart beat against his, I recalled the promise of which he spoke so long ago. He told me he would not give up on me. That truth demonstrated in his kiss.

He pulled back and gazed into my eyes — I saw his deep unconditional love. I saw his forgiveness. I saw the person whom I loved most in this world. We stood in silence, drinking each other in — no words needed. I raised up on my toes and invited another kiss just to make sure this wasn't a dream. It was not.

"I see you found your gift." Gallen said as he and the Healer entered. They were holding hands and looked quite pleased at finding us in an embrace.

I pulled away quickly. The heat rose in my face. Ansel reached for my hand and clasped it tightly, as if he feared he would lose me if he let go.

"I have water heating for you Amáne," said the Healer. "A hot soak with soothing herbs is what I recommend straightaway. You must be exhausted."

"I am, Healer, but I don't think sleep will find me any time soon." My heart still raced. I glanced up at Ansel. He hadn't taken his eyes off me.

Ansel smiled and reached to pull me back to his side, but unknowingly grabbed my injured arm. A stab of pain ripped through me.

Grimacing, I drew in my breath and stifled a cry.

"Your injuries! How thoughtless of me. I'm sorry." He winced.

Ansel unclasped my riding cloak, took it from my shoulders, and gently lifted my sleeve. The three of them gasped at the same time at the sight of the angry red grooves the brown creature had left in my arm — infection showing once again.

Trying to ease the pressure in the room, I offered, "Do you think that's going to leave a scar?"

Ansel just closed his eyes and shook his head.

The Healer acted at once. "Bring her to her chambers, we'll need Eshshah's help." She poured some hot water in a bowl, grabbed a linen and we all moved down the corridor to my quarters.

"You need to open your gift, Healer," I said as they ushered me along. I touched the satchel that hung at my back — the egg safely tucked inside.

"Let's take care of your arm first, then you can have your soak. We'll all enjoy your prize afterwards ... and after that, you need to rest. I am eager to see it, of course, but now that it's here safely, it's not going anywhere. It can wait."

A hot soak and rest. I could think of nothing sweeter — except Ansel's kisses. I realized I had missed two night's sleep. How I could even remain upright was a question I couldn't answer. When I was finally ready to succumb, I knew I would fall into bed like a stone.

Entering my chambers, I breathed a sigh of relief. The day's new light was shining through the skylights above, and the room was bright and inviting. It seemed like I'd been gone for much longer than five days, but here I was back again, delighted with my surroundings. I sang a silent song of thanksgiving. Eshshah and I were home. Our quest was successful. And ... Ansel still loved me. Life could get no better.

I lowered myself into a chair at my table. Ansel pulled up another one close to me and rested his hand on my shoulder. A ripple of warmth spread through my body at his touch.

The Healer placed a hot cloth on my arm. The scent of healing herbs rose as I began to relax. Eshshah breathed her warm healing breath, soothing the pain instantly. I felt the infection withdraw. The heat increased with their treatment. My arm improved noticeably. I exhaled a long sigh.

With my free hand, I pulled the satchel over my head. A jolt brought my attention to the egg. *Did I knock it on the table, trying to take it off with one hand?*

"Did you feel that?" asked Eshshah.

"Eshshah, the egg!" I said out loud.

There was no doubt that it had moved, a small quiver, nothing more, but something had happened. The egg gave off an unmistakable heat — a slight vibration grew.

The Healer and Gallen knew immediately, but Ansel stiffened in alarm, not knowing what to make of our concern.

"Is everything all right? Is the dragon egg broken?"

"Quickly, Amáne, unwrap it and set it on your bed," said the Healer

I did as instructed. When I turned back to explain to Ansel, his eyes were drawn to the egg in a glassy stare.

Eshshah, the Healer, Gallen and I divided our attention between the egg and Ansel. Its vibrations increased — it began to hum. Ansel walked towards it like one who walks in his sleep, unaware of anything in the room, other than the object that pulled him in. He made his way up onto the bed and kneeled before the dragon egg. Sitting back on his heels, his hands reached towards it. Watching him place his palms upon the vibrating ovoid, I was entranced with the glow upon his face. I wondered if I had looked like that when Eshshah began her hatching ritual.

The egg hummed louder. Eshshah hummed with it. The Healer and Gallen held hands and watched enraptured. I guessed that they, like myself, were reliving their linkings. I melded with Eshshah as we observed the incredible event.

The humming rose to a feverish pitch, and suddenly a crack appeared in the shell. My heart stopped. I stood frozen, lest I interrupt the wonder before me. Tears came to my eyes as I watched a tiny dragon nose emerge from the crack. At last the dragon broke free and toppled out, landing at Ansel's knees.

It was about the size of a full-grown cat. A beautiful golden creature, shining wet from the moisture in its egg. Small graceful legs held up his short body which tapered to a long tail that ended in a sharp barb. Horns protruded from the top of his perfectly-shaped head on a long graceful neck — a miniature version of Eshshah. If I hadn't known my dragon, I would have said it was the most exquisite being I'd ever seen. His scales shone with luminescence. He glowed in his own light. Immediately, he locked eyes with Ansel whose face lit with the reflections of the light bouncing off of his little dragon. I found it difficult to decide who was the most magnificent of the two.

The little one swayed. His golden eyes spun — Ansel followed his every move. Suddenly, the dragon blinked. Ansel looked confused — shocked. Knowing what was coming next, I pressed my lips together and put my hand to my mouth so I wouldn't scream. I wished I could have protected Ansel from the pain and agony that was about to come, but I couldn't — it was part of the process and he must endure it.

The radiant dragon pulled his head back and quicker than lightning, he struck. His fangs buried deep into Ansel's shoulder. The force threw Ansel back on the bed. He shouted in pain. His eyes went wide and his face almost purple. The Healer put her hand on my shoulder and held me back. With her touch, I managed to remain where I stood, watching Ansel burn in agony as the venom traveled through his body. I vaguely remembered this part in my own experience.

The Healer kept an eye on his condition, but did not assist him. Her job was only to keep Ansel alive, and nothing more at this time. His dragon walked towards Ansel's face, and watched him as he writhed. I marveled at the love and concern I saw glowing in his eyes as he gazed at his Chosen One. He placed his nose on Ansel's forehead and hummed in an effort to help him. I clenched my teeth and squeezed my fists as Ansel's body stiffened, arched in convulsions — and then, thankfully, he lost consciousness. The little creature looked at each of us, distressed for his rider. He let out a low whine then curled up on Ansel's chest and closed his eyes to wait.

My heart pounded. My breath came in sharp gasps. The Healer motioned to Gallen. He came over to me and led me out of the room. At first I resisted — I wanted to stay with Ansel. But then I gave in, suddenly overcome with fatigue.

Gallen led me to the bathing room. "Healer's orders, Amáne. Take a long hot soak. Lord Ansel will be fine. It was a good linking. There's nothing you can do for him now. You need to get some rest and then you can take a turn to watch over him. Now, go." He opened the door and gently pushed me in.

Chapter Thirty-nine

Hardly lucid after my hot soak, I headed back to my chambers. Grabbing some blankets I drug myself into my room. With my eyes half lidded, I noted that Ansel lay in good hands — the Healer watching over him.

"Please wake me, Healer, when it's my turn to sit with him," I mumbled. Then I staggered over to Eshshah, who slept in her indent on the stone floor. I threw the blankets down, crawled under the covers, and succumbed to exhaustion.

My rest was fraught with nightmares — lizards, dungeons, evil kings — all made up from my recent reality, which was ... a nightmare. Avano and my father wove in and out in confusion as I thrashed and tangled myself in my bedding.

At last, my dark dreams took an uncharacteristic turn toward the light. Ansel had wandered into my torment and in a daring rescue, lifted me from a dark hole in which I'd been trapped. He carried me in his strong arms and gently placed me on a bed of soft flowers in a bright field, then kissed my forehead. It felt so real. Finally, I fell into a comforting sleep.

Still dreaming, I found myself gazing at Ansel as he pushed my hair out of my face, smiling at me. I smiled back and reached out to touch him. My movement must have awoken me. My eyes snapped open.

Where am I? Momentarily disoriented, I tensed as my recent peril came back to me. Eshshah touched my consciousness. She slumbered outside sunning herself in the courtyard. I was in my own bed — two sets of eyes stared at me.

Ansel reclined in front of me on my bed — elbow bent with his head propped in his hand. The little golden dragon, who had doubled in size since his hatching, looked over Ansel's shoulder. Their gazes locked upon me.

"We didn't mean to wake you," Ansel said. "Your hair fell forward and we couldn't see your face anymore. I had to push it back."

"You have a bad habit of watching me sleep," I murmured, recalling the Dorsal Outpost after his rescue.

"It's one of my favorite pastimes."

I rolled my eyes.

"How's your arm?" he asked.

I flexed my wrist and winced slightly. "A couple more treatments from Eshshah, and I'll be ready to test that venom running in your veins. We'll see if it's improved your swordwork. Deal?"

"Deal." He gave me a smile that lit up the room.

Then, remembering my manners, I propped myself up on my elbow and saluted them both. It was a sideways, half-awake salute. A little stiff with my sore wrist, but they both nodded in response. "Permission to speak to your dragon."

"Granted. Any time. No need to ask." Ansel nodded in my direction. "Amáne, rider of Eshshah, this is Sovann. Sovann, meet Amáne."

"Greetings, Sovann, dragon of gold, you shine more brightly than the sun." He dipped his head, his eyes whirled, pleased at my compliment. I found myself instantly in love with him.

Ansel laughed responding to something Sovann conveyed. "Yes, you're right. She is, I agree wholeheartedly."

I grinned, noticing that he spoke to his dragon out loud. He realized it at that moment as well, and said, "I guess I'm going to have to practice thought transference before I get myself into trouble."

"I highly recommend it. But by the look on your face, I'd say you're already in trouble. What did he say?" Mock suspicion in my voice.

"He thinks you're beautiful."

"Hmm, yes, the worst kind of trouble." I blushed.

"Ansel, wow ... you're a dragon rider ..." I shook my head at how unbelievable, yet fantastic was this turn of events.

With a smug twist of his mouth, Ansel asked, "So, tell me, Amáne how do you feel now about the fact that you won't have to watch me grow old while you stay young?"

I let out an exasperated sigh. Dragon riders do not age the same as normal humans. It had been an excuse I gave him so long ago for why I couldn't give my heart to him. I told him I couldn't bear to see him grow old and meet his ancestors while I stayed young. It was a weak excuse. We'd come a long way since I'd made that statement.

"I think I'll have to come up with another excuse — or not."

"I think you're completely out of excuses."

"I think you're right."

His dragon hummed. I wondered what Ansel said to him.

"I can't believe your dragon fever is over after just a few

hours," I said. Noting the light in the room, it looked to be just around noon, and we had flown in at dawn.

"Twenty-four hours could hardly be considered 'just a few hours' when I'm writhing in pain and agony," he said.

Shock flashed through me. "Twenty-four hours? I've been asleep that long? Why didn't someone wake me? I was supposed to take a turn sitting with you." I exhaled in remorse.

"It's fine, Amáne, truly. The Healer and Gallen took turns. You needed to rest."

My eyebrows knit. "I thought I fell asleep on the floor with Eshshah. How did I get here, in my bed?"

"You were thrashing on the floor — nightmares again?"

I nodded. He shook his head, in sympathy.

"Since I was up and about, the Healer allowed me to put you into your bed where you belonged. I think it helped. You relaxed and got in a couple more hours sleep."

I felt the heat rise in my face. It wasn't just a dream, then.

"It was my fault you were forced to sleep on the floor. It was the least I could do."

"Ansel, you had no control over that. Besides, I don't mind sleeping on the floor. Unless, of course, it's in a filthy dungeon cell. The difference between that and sleeping in Eshshah's bed is like moon and sun. You, of all people can attest to that."

A shadow crossed his face. His eyes filled with pain. Sovann moaned in response.

"Ansel, I'm sorry for bringing that up."

In the most heart-wrenching tone, "No, Amáne — I'm sorry."

We lay propped on our elbows facing each other. He reached his free hand out to me, palm out. I pressed my palm in his. We intertwined our fingers and squeezed tight. For several moments we remained in that position, each feeling the other's pain. I guessed that his distress was not only about his painful experience in the dungeon, but more than that.

Ansel and I shared a bond, that no matter what happened, it would never break. We were linked to each other as surely as we were linked to our dragons. I could feel the anguish of the contradictions burning in his eyes. I knew he regretted sending us on our quest, yet if he had not, he would not now be linked to Sovann.

"Because of me, your life has been endangered ... twice. It was my fault you had to return to the castle," he said with a tremor in his voice.

"Ansel," I whispered, "it's over. We're home. We're safe. You have Sovann. Let's concentrate on that. What I went through is all behind us, now."

"Don't speak so lightly of it, Amáne. I'm fully aware of what you went through to bring back Sovann's egg."

"What do you mean?" My eyes went wide. "Did the Healer tell you everything?"

"No, I was here. I arrived the day you entered the Hatching Grounds."

I groaned.

"I followed you the whole time, through Eshshah and Bern — on the communication disc with the Healer and Gallen."

I couldn't breathe. The thought of Ansel here suffering through my ordeal pulled at my heart.

"Ansel, it was my duty. I did it willingly. Eshshah and I would do whatever it takes to help win your throne. Mark our quest as a victory. Hold tight to our hope of several more victories, until we're no longer in danger. Just so you know — it's more than duty. We do it for love. Just as you would do it for us."

He leaned in toward me. We were only inches apart. I felt the heat of his breath on my face. My heart accelerated.

His eyes settled on my lips. He seemed to struggle with some internal argument. Biting his lip, he moved back, brows furrowed. My hand still in his, he brought it to his lips, then set it gently on the bed. His finger traced my cheek as he gazed deeply in my eyes.

"It's best I leave you to your rest. The Healer's probably just about ready to send Gallen in here to drag me out."

Ansel rolled off my bed. With a longing glance over his shoulder, he strolled out of the room, Sovann trailing behind.

Chapter Forty

After Ansel left my chambers, there wasn't any rest left in me. The abundance of sleep left me feeling refreshed, and my heart still beat wildly. I crawled out of bed and threw on some tights and a long shirt. I wrapped a belt around me and padded to kitchen where I found Ansel sitting at the table picking at some smoked fish.

Eshshah informed me the Healer had left the house to make her rounds. Gallen minded the apothecary shop. She and Sovann lay in the courtyard soaking the sun.

I slid onto the bench next to Ansel. "I can't believe I didn't ask you earlier, Ansel, but may I see your linking mark?"

He untied the neckline of his shirt and let it fall over his shoulder. I'd never seen his bare chest and shoulders before. Taken aback at his muscular build, my eyes widened. He caught my reaction. As my face reddened, his mouth curved up in a crooked smile. I hoped maybe he mistook my expression as a response to his linking mark and not his body. I think I hoped in vain.

Recovering my composure, I studied the tattoo-like design that Sovann had left as a permanent reminder that they were forever linked. It was beautiful. So different than mine, yet similar. I studied the stylized likeness of his dragon with swirls and symbols, including a crown. All incorporated into a perfect device.

"I've been doing a little research of my own on linking marks. I know how interested you are in them, so I tried to learn more. Did you ever think you would have one of your own?" It allowed us one more thing to share with each other.

"Never in my wildest dreams. Well, I take that back. When I was a young boy, I used to wish to be a candidate at a Hatching, and couldn't wait until I was old enough. But of course, my foster parents or my aunt would never have let me near the castle, so I stopped dreaming."

"You should never have stopped dreaming."

I moved closer to examine the fascinating mark. I became very aware of the heat that radiated from his body. Captivated by the elements in the design, I barely managed to ignore his warmth.

"Oh, I think I've found your name, right here." Tracing the area, I tried to sound it out. "Protector? I didn't know that's what your name meant." His muscles tensed slightly as I moved my finger over the tattoo.

I was thoroughly absorbed in the intricate pattern. This was better than the drawings in the books, and an entirely different angle than trying to study mine. Even though I lived with two dragon riders, I'd only seen the Healer's linking mark once. Gallen's, I had seen a few times when he had his shirt off working around the property, but I never wanted to bother him about it. Nor did I want to stir up any grief for him. This was the first time I had such a perfect view of a linking mark.

"I should copy this on to parchment and have you and the Healer explain the symbols I don't understand. This part right here," I spoke — more or less to myself — as I followed the lines, tracing lightly with my finger. "... that flows so perfectly into this section over here, I —"

In a lightning move he clamped his hand over mine. The action abruptly brought me back into the room. I looked up in surprise and found his eyes smoldering.

"Amáne," he said in a low whisper, "you're driving me crazy."

"I'm sorry, Ansel, I didn't mean to annoy you."

"I didn't say you were annoying me, I said you were driving me crazy."

"Oh ... I ... uh ..." I tried to remove my hand, but he held it tightly to his arm. His heart beat loudly, competing with the sound of mine. He brought his free hand behind my neck and ran his fingers through my hair. Drawing my face towards his, he brought his mouth to mine. Time stood still as I melted into the fire of his kiss.

Reluctantly pulling back, he studied my face, beginning at my forehead, then moving to my eyes, my nose, my lips.

Shaking his head slowly, he said in a controlled voice, "I think you should save your studies of my linking mark for a time when the Healer can accompany you."

"I ... I think that's good advice."

Chapter Forty-One

The Healer, Gallen and Ansel were in the library on the communication disc, contacting the riders throughout the kingdom, gathering news. The Healer's library had been rebuilt since that horrible night when the sorcerer had destroyed it. She was in the process of replacing what she could of her maps and books that had been caught up in the fire. We had brought some books home from Ansel's manor in Trivingar. She also picked up some apothecary books from the shop in that town and the nearby town of Arevale, when she was up there for Ansel's birthday.

I had just gotten out of the bath for the second time in the same day. I knew the stench from the arena no longer remained on my skin, but wanted one more aromatic soak to try to rid myself of the memory of the smell.

"Amáne!" the Healer called. "We need you in here for a moment."

I entered the library to find the three of them with eyebrows raised and barely-suppressed smiles. I tilted my head and looked at them suspiciously, "What is it?"

Gallen held his hand on the brass knob of the communication disc and announced, "A rider has a question that only you could answer. Would you mind helping him out?"

I noticed there was no image of a rider in the disc. It showed only a blank wall. Stepping hesitantly up to the device, I wondered what they found so amusing. More than likely it was some kind of joke at my expense.

Gallen said, "Rider, what is it you needed to know?"

A voice resonated from the disc, "Amáne, or Vann — whichever — I need to know how you feel about yourself. Are you angry you left me with all the fun of finishing off the guards you riled up?"

My hand flew to my mouth to stifle my scream. My eyes filled as the speaker stepped into view. "Avano! You're alive. Of course you are — you're too much of a scoundrel for your ancestors to even want you. And, you forget, I offered you my help, but you insisted on keeping the fun for yourself!" I laughed as I blinked away my tears.

"I couldn't have done it without the help of that nightmare monster that you're linked to ... and the excellent swordwork of your father."

"My father? You saw my father?"

"Yes, he's some fighter. He took down those on one side of the door and Charna Yash-churka — however you pronounce his name — and I took care of the ones that got through. He left after that, before anyone spotted him."

Relief shot through me once more, hearing that my father lived. I swelled with pride at the compliment that came from Avano, a master swordsman himself.

Avano then updated us with the goings on in the townships from which he had information. We spoke for a bit before he signed off. The Healer excused herself to do some work in her shop. She was still laughing at my reaction, although, I'm sure she was as elated as I that Avano made it out.

Gallen announced that Dorjan was waiting for him at the Dragon's Fang Tavern. Before leaving, he asked Ansel to update me on the rest of the news they had heard while I was soaking.

Ansel spread out some maps on the library table, and began his instruction, "Word is Galtero will be on the move soon. He declared he would seek out and destroy every dragon rider in the kingdom — especially 'the girl of the prophecy and her dragon.'" He looked at me pointedly.

We all knew this would be coming.

He drew my attention to the map of the kingdom, pointing out the cities where the dragon riders were stationed, and which rider resided where.

I tried to pay attention but found myself distracted. There was an aroma in the air that I couldn't ignore. Did the Healer bring home a new herb, or did she have something cooking in her kitchen?

"... and this is where Eben has settled for the last few years." I glanced to where Ansel pointed, but my attention diverted again. I lifted my nose in the air and inhaled. I felt like an animal, but I had to find out where that delicious scent came from. Exotic, spicy, musky.

As Ansel bent over the map, his hair hung across his shoulder on my side. He usually wore his long wavy hair pulled back in a queue, tied at the nape of his neck with a leather thong. Sometimes he added several ties down its length, but at this moment, there was just the one. My nose led me to turn in his direction. Without thinking, I took his dark locks in my hand and brought a handful to my face, inhaling the source of the fragrance. It was the aroma of his dragon, infused in his hair. My eyes closed as I absorbed the scent, losing myself in it.

When he turned to see what I was doing, his hair yanked out of my hand. My eyes sprung open to his amused expression. I couldn't hide my guilty look as I grinned self-consciously, my hand still poised in front of my face — empty.

"What are you doing, Amáne?"

"I ... er ..."

"You were smelling my hair, weren't you?"

"It smells nice ..." *Feeble answer.* I felt the heat rise to my cheeks. He burst out laughing.

I couldn't help but laugh with him. "I guess I owe you an apology, Ansel. More than once you told me you loved the scent of my hair — that it smelled like my dragon. It annoyed me, and I always pulled it away from you. Now I understand. I didn't realize it was so ... so ..."

"Enticing?"

"Yes ..."

Our eyes met. I lost myself in his cool green eyes.

Chapter Forty-Two

Every day Sovann grew in stature and beauty. Eshshah offered her support from the start. She showed him where the tastiest game could be found, the best place to sun, and I'm sure she told him all the quirks to which we humans are prone. Like Eshshah, he was of the Royal Dragon line and a bond was shared between them similar to Ansel's and mine — unexplainable, yet undeniably present.

I felt badly for Eshshah that we didn't have the same privileges of support when she hatched. But maybe our linking would be less powerful if we'd had witnesses. The Healer once told me that there were linkings where they had to extract venom from a Chosen One. In their dragon's excitement, a deadly amount had been forced into the rider's veins — similar to what had happened when I linked with Eshshah. Only because of my dragon's healing powers, did I live. Our bond proved unusually strong.

"Amáne, I can't believe how much Sovann eats." Eshshah confided in me one evening. "He's hungry most of the time. I don't recall eating more than one or two goats during a night's hunt. I think last night, he still wasn't sated after five. Two more days of that and he'll be nearly my size."

Although very young for a dragon, Eshshah had reached her full size. She once told me that dragons grow in relation to their rider. She would naturally be a smaller dragon because of my size.

I laughed. "He is growing fast. I remember how surprised I used to be at the speed you grew."

Besides his rapid growth, we were shocked to find the truth about his scales. Dragon scales exhibit the properties of the dragon from which they came. For instance, Eshshah's name meant fire. Whisper her name when holding one of her shed scales and it would flame up. We were not sure what to expect with Sovann's luminescent scales. His name meant gold. We found they did, in fact, turn to gold at the whispering of his name. Gallen tested a transformed scale by rubbing it on an unglazed porcelain tile. The result was a golden yellow — no black streak. It was pure gold.

Our dreams were realized. We needed to raise an army to fight Galtero, and although Ansel's silk farming showed excellent profit, and he had some treasure remaining from his father, supporting an army did not come cheaply. We all kept our eyes open for any of Sovann's shed scales. Even Eshshah and Sovann were helpful, should they notice any had fallen during their hunts or their wanderings. They brought us those they had found, spitting them out at our feet.

Ansel had no choice but to stay at the Healer's for their training. It would take about a week for Sovann to grow strong enough to fly with him, and a few weeks before his dragon could make the long flight to Trivingar with a rider. Ansel couldn't hide his pleasure when the Healer informed him.

Although not as overprotective as Ansel — he could easily have kept me no farther than arm's length at all times — I wished I could have spent more time by his side, but we were both quite busy.

As Ansel and Sovann worked with Gallen and the Healer, I trained on my own. I was ready to pour myself into my practice — my wrist had healed and the talon marks were nearly gone, thanks to Eshshah. I spent a good deal of time practicing on the pell — a large tree trunk that simulated a man's height. It was planted in the ground on the other side of the barn. I worked on my strikes, concentrating on my precision and technique. The sun beat down mercilessly on that side of the Healer's extensive property. My body was drenched in sweat, but I pushed myself. When I became weary of my practice sword, I switched to my glaive.

Later, sitting at the kitchen table for our midday meal, the Healer and Gallen announced it was time to implement their plan.

"We are at last seeing a positive direction from our efforts. Our next step is to raise an army of elite soldiers. We'll need a contingent of highly skilled troops," Gallen said. "We will seek out the best of Dorsal. Bern, Eben and the other riders will do the same in their locations."

He turned to me, "You'll be pleased to know, we plan to include eligible girls on a case-by-case basis."

I smiled and nodded. Females were forbidden to participate in weapons training in anything other than the bow. It was a law with which we would take liberties.

"Amáne," said the Healer, "We've practically abandoned you to work on your own. You've done well. Your weapons skills are exceptional. We'd like you to take a group to lead in their training."

I made an effort to close my gaping mouth. Ansel looked at me with pride.

"If you feel I've reached that level, I ... I'd be honored."

"With a little more work, you can start training with Dorjan and Avano, to work towards swordmaster."

"Thank you, Healer," I managed to whisper.

CHAPTER FORTY-THREE

The morning came when the Healer announced, "Ansel, Sovann is now strong enough and large enough to fly with you. We can begin tonight." Sovann was a week old and towered above us. He had reached Eshshah's size.

I screamed in delight.

Sovann had been pleading with Ansel to fly with him, but Ansel, trying to live by the rules, told his dragon that they would have to wait until the Healer gave the okay. The wait was over. But this would be a long day, waiting for nightfall.

As if she read my mind, the Healer said, "Amáne, why don't you and Ansel take the day for yourselves. You've been working hard all week. The evening will come quicker if you enjoy some diversion. It's a market day. You should go into town."

"Thanks, Healer," I said. "That's a perfect idea."

I turned to Ansel, "I need an hour before we go. The herb garden is in serious need of my attention. After that, I'm all yours."

He shot me a devious look. I rolled my eyes.

The weather was perfect, as I headed to the herb garden at the far end of the courtyard. I loved the warm dirt on my hands and the smell of the herbs as I pruned and collected them in my basket.

I glanced over at Eshshah and Sovann who sunned themselves in the field between the courtyard and the barn. I smiled thinking how content Eshshah had been since Sovann had hatched. Maybe when they both matured, they would accept each other as mates. Just because they were the only two dragons alive now did not guarantee they would be attracted to each other. Dragons are monogamous and pair for life. Considering how long they lived, their choice was not regarded lightly.

Eshshah used to chide me about my reluctance to follow my heart in regards to Ansel. I did feel badly that I held off a suitor who was meant to be with me, while she remained alone — the only one of her species in all of Teravinea. Undoubtedly, there will be more dragons in our future. So even if Sovann were not *the one*, she at least had some companionship. For that I was thankful.

In the midst of my musing, I suddenly needed to find Ansel. I didn't know why, or if I felt there was something wrong. All I knew was I had to see him.

Wiping my hands on my tunic, I left the garden and headed across the field to the barn. He mentioned he would be sharpening and polishing his sword.

I passed our dragons and my urgency increased. Quickening my pace, I arrived at the door of the barn and saw him at a workbench engaged in his task. I stood there for a short time watching. My heart skipped a few beats. Gazing at the way his dark hair fell over his shoulders, and how he held his mouth in a pucker while concentrating on his work, my need to be closer to him escalated. Hearing my footsteps, he turned towards me. Our eyes met. My heart accelerated and threatened to leave my chest as I moved across the floor to where he stood.

Tilting his head, his deep green eyes met mine. I noted a recognition of something he caught in my gaze, although I don't know how. I certainly didn't know what urged me to close the gap between us. I slid right up to him. Close enough to inhale his scent.

Ansel put his sword down. He raised an eyebrow. His mouth turned up in an inviting smile. I wrapped my arms around his neck, stood on my toes and pulled his face down to meet my lips. He clasped his hands around my waist and pulled me closer. I felt I couldn't get close enough. My heart beat against his.

At that moment, my unexplained emotion turned to shock as I realized the source of my behavior. I pushed away from him, stunned. My shame washed over me. He stood there, confused, his eyes still burning, as were my lips.

"Eshshah!" I said out loud, and then continued in thought transference. "Stop that! Block me out. I don't need to be a part of your thoughts now. This is embarrassing!"

"I'm sorry, Amáne. I'm just thinking about Sovann. I know he has only recently hatched, but his egg was laid many years before mine. I find myself quite attracted to him. He is drawn to me as well. If dragons felt love for each other like you humans, I believe this would be love."

"I believe that's a little more than love! Block me now, please."

I heard her rumbling laugh-like sound before she excluded me from her thoughts.

Turning back to Ansel — his face like a child who had just gotten a sweet taken from him, mid bite. I swallowed hard and tried to extricate myself from this predicament.

"Ansel," I brought my hand to my mouth, my face hot with embarrassment as well as emotion. "I am so sorry. I'm ashamed of myself."

"Sorry? For what?" he said in a low voice as he took a step towards me.

I took a step back. "No, you don't understand. It was Eshshah. She was ... er ... admiring Sovann. I ... I got tangled in her ... feelings for him. I told her to block me out once I figured out what had come over me."

"I think that kiss wasn't only about Eshshah's attraction to Sovann." He smiled, as if daring me to deny it.

I felt even more self conscious. I couldn't completely disagree with his assumption, but I wouldn't admit it out loud.

"It was improper behavior on my part. Please forgive me. I feel like one of those ladies down by the shipping docks."

"Truthfully, Amáne, you're nothing like those ladies." His eyes glazed and I recognized he was communicating with Sovann. Focusing back on me, his eyes heating up again, he took another step towards me.

I took one back.

"Ansel, tell him to block you!"

"Why?" He moved towards me.

Stepping back once more, I began to think we'd been caught up in a strange dance.

"Ansel!"

"Okay, okay, you win — like always. Blocked." He didn't hide his frustration.

I breathed a sigh of relief. "Thank you, Ansel."

With a bewildered look, he shook his head and exhaled, "Wow!"

Embarrassment still ruled my emotions. But very much aware of the heat we had just generated, I had to agree with him. I nodded slowly.

"Well ... so ... er ..." I tried to think of something to say to ease the tension, but found myself at a loss for words.

"Come on," he said. I think he recognized I was still mortified. "Let's go see what the Healer has in the kitchen. I hope she has some strong ale stashed somewhere."

He put his arm around my shoulder, and we made our way back to the house. I lost myself in the thought of the powerful link the four of us shared.

Mid stride, I came to a halt. "Hey, what did you mean when you said I'm nothing like those ladies at the docks? How would you know what they're like?"

He pursed his lips, shook his head and kept walking.

We stopped at the laver outside of the kitchen to wash up. Feeling his gaze, I turned to him — his eyes still smoldered. I filled my cupped hands with water and splashed it in his face.

Laughing, I said, "You need to cool down, my friend."

He splashed me back. "Well, you started the fire, my love."

"Then allow me to put it out." I found a bowl, filled it and doused him.

He found a pot and the fight was on.

Drenched, laughing and out of breath, we finally called a truce.

The fire still burned in his eyes.

Chapter Forty-Four

Ansel and I left before noon for the marketplace, deciding to walk, instead of going by horseback. We were in no hurry — having the rest of the day to ourselves. It was a long-needed diversion, giving us a chance to just be together and talk.

It had been a week since Ansel and Sovann had linked and not only was he was so busy with his new role, but we were both too tired by the end of the day to be able to stay awake long enough for any kind of meaningful conversation.

At last I had the opportunity to ask, "Ansel, you never told me what made you decide to come to the Healer's when Eshshah and I began our quest."

His eyes darkened. After a moment of silence, he answered, "Eulalia came to me the evening you left Dorsal for Anbon. She handed me your letter and apologized profusely for keeping it from me. She said it was upon your orders that she held it until you left, and it was upon my orders that she obey you. You can understand her dilemma."

"Oh, poor Lali," I said, wishing I hadn't put such a strain on her. "It never occurred to me that it would have been so hard to follow my orders."

"I opened it," Ansel continued, his voice thick with emotion. "I must have read it and reread it a hundred times. I would have gone mad if Lali hadn't been there."

My heart sank, "Ansel, I'm sorry, I shouldn't have brought this up. I should have left it alone. I know now that leaving you that letter was a heartless thing to do. I wish I hadn't." I wanted to change the conversation. It seemed, though, that he needed to get it out, so I let him talk.

"It wasn't heartless," he said. "But, you were right. I would have tried to stop you after reading it. It was too late to catch you on the communication device. I tried, but Gallen said you'd already left. Lali urged me to leave immediately for Dorsal. She must have sensed that being with my aunt and at your home was the only thing that would have kept me sound during your ordeal."

His brows furrowed and he bit his lower lip.

I stopped and turned to face him. I wanted only to smooth his creased brow and ease his memories of what I had been through at the castle. I put my hand to his cheek. "It's over. Look at me. I'm here with you now. Besides a few new scars, I'm fine."

I smiled up at him as a thought came to mind. "Ansel, I concede. You've won the final round."

"The final round of what?"

"You've won. You've captured my heart. I surrender. My little white flag is waving." I stood on my toes and pulled his lips close. I kissed him to seal this truth.

He put one hand on my waist, and the other held my face. He drew me closer. I melted into his lips. Heat radiated up my body. I left him no doubt that at last I've listened to my heart. This time I didn't need any help from my dragon's thoughts.

We parted and gazed into each other's eyes, then joined lips once more.

"Hmm," he breathed. You've surrendered."

I nodded.

"I have a captive." His eyebrows raised. His smile lit up his face. With a mischievous look, he said, "Maybe we really don't need to go to the marketplace. We can just stay here, and I can enjoy my spoils."

I rolled my eyes and pulled him back on our way, shaking my head.

"Your spoils are going to the marketplace." I laughed.

But truthfully, my heart beat out of control. My knees nearly gave in. I put my arm in his. Not only to stay close, but to make sure I stayed on my feet.

Chapter Forty-Five

We enjoyed ourselves as we wandered up and down the aisles between the colorful stalls. Just the two of us. Thankful we didn't run into any of my acquaintances, we still drew a lot of attention from the townspeople. They'd all known me my entire life. I'm sure they wanted to know who Ansel was and why he would be in the company of a commoner like me.

The attention didn't affect Ansel. He acted like I was the only person in town. I, on the other hand, became very self conscious, especially after the whispered snide remarks. With his newly enhanced hearing, Ansel caught the same rude comments I did — a repeat of the ones I'd heard at the Life Celebration Gathering.

"What does she have to offer for him to accompany her."

"He is obviously of a much higher class than she. How embarrassing for him."

He squeezed my hand and helped me to ignore them. I made up my mind to tune them out and just relish my time with Ansel.

The afternoon went quickly. Too soon it was time to head back to the Healer's. We walked slowly arm in arm.

Back at home, the anticipation of Ansel and Sovann's first flight together made waiting for dark very difficult. We sat at the kitchen table with the Healer and Gallen. Taking our time with our evening meal, I glanced outside often at the slowly waning light — willing it to hurry and leave us.

Gallen broke the silence. "So, Amáne, I heard you found out Eshshah has an attraction to Sovann." He and Ansel exchanged glances.

I inhaled sharply and jerked my head towards Ansel, who sat on the bench to my right. He deliberately didn't look at me, but suddenly found something of interest on his plate.

"Is there nothing private around here?" I asked.

"Come on, Amáne," Gallen said. "Feeling our dragons' emotions and having the urge to act on them is as old as the stars." He glanced sideways at the Healer.

This time I really did turn on Ansel, "You ... you told him what I did?" Livid, the heat rose in my face — a combination of anger and embarrassment. "Ansel, how could you?" My eyes welled up.

Ansel concentrated on his plate and shrugged his shoulders, not daring to meet my eyes.

The Healer spoke up, "Gallen, when are you going to learn to think before you blurt things out like that?"

"Why does everyone feel a need to share everything I do?" My voice broke.

Ansel turned to face me. When he saw my eyes spilling over, his remorse was immediate. He put his arm around my shoulders. I pushed him away.

"Amáne," he pleaded, reaching for me again. This time I let him pull me to him. "I'm sorry, I didn't mean to make you cry." He stroked my hair back from my face and kissed my forehead.

"I'll know next time not to share anything with Gallen." Ansel looked accusingly at him across the table.

I almost felt sorry for Gallen — the repentant look on his face was pitiful. But I wasn't going to let him off that easily. I glared daggers at him. He shifted uncomfortably.

"Okay," the Healer interjected "— we are a family. Amáne, you don't ever have to be self-conscious about anything around us. Gallen and I understand everything you're going through. We've been through the same thing. A family shares with each other." She looked pointedly at Gallen .

He nodded almost imperceptibly. "Speaking of sharing, we have an announcement we'd like to share."

I picked my head up from Ansel's shoulder and raised my eyebrows looking first at Gallen and then the Healer.

"We decided," the Healer said, "that after a hundred years of being each other's friend and companion ... and more," she looked at Gallen almost shyly, but with a hint of pain that she couldn't hide, "we've denied ourselves for duty long enough. We want to finally make it official and to pledge our troth in a gathering of friends."

Forgetting my anger, I screamed with joy. Jumping up from the bench, nearly toppling Ansel over, I ran to the other side of the table and threw my arms around the Healer. I laughed and cried at the same time. I felt guilty over my little temper tantrum — how trivial my concern became when they shared their exciting news.

Once I released the Healer, I moved to Gallen, instantly forgiving him as I gave him a formidable hug. Rising from the bench with me still clinging to him, he swung me around in a circle. Ansel had stood up and embraced his aunt, then gave Gallen a hardy shake, as they pounded each other on the back.

Caught up in the moment, Ansel wrapped me up in his strong arms and lifted me off of my feet. Our eyes met. Behind the happiness for his aunt and Gallen, was a shadow of envy. Did he wish it was us making this announcement?

CHAPTER FORTY-SIX

Darkness fell heavily — no moon in the sky — perfect conditions. I stepped into the courtyard and watched Ansel saddle Sovann. Gallen oversaw the procedure. Ansel looked magnificent, his face glowed with excitement.

Dorjan joined us. He brought Ansel a gift from himself and Sovann — a riding helmet similar to mine, but made out of Sovann's scales. The scales were attached to a leather cap-like piece. Another layer of leather was stitched over the scales. It buckled under the chin. Like my riding helmet, there was a lever on the side, near the temple. When flipped down, a pair of transparent highly-polished scales emerged from the top of the helmet — eye shields to protect from wind, dust and glare.

"Whatever you do, Lord Ansel," Dorjan joked, "do not whisper Sovann's name to turn these scales into gold. You'll end up on your face, pinned to the ground by your helmet." We all laughed.

Watching Ansel prepare for his first flight brought to mind Eshshah's and my painful first try. I broke my nose the moment Eshshah left the ground. I was hopeful that Ansel and Sovann were trained enough to avoid that injury. Eshshah gave Sovann pointers for a smooth take off.

Ansel mounted and strapped himself in. He used the larger, basic saddle with the thigh straps that buckled at the hips. He lowered his eye shields and then looked at us with an unbridled joy. We all saluted him. He gave Sovann the go-ahead. Ansel had an advantage over most newly-trained riders in the fact that he'd already taken several flights with Eshshah and I, and was accustomed to the powerful thrust when a dragon launches into the air. Sovann, under Eshshah's direction executed a perfect take-off and they were airborne without even a jolt — of course. I was a little envious, but Eshshah had to remind me that we were on our own when we took our first flight. Besides the lack of proper equipment, we had no way of anticipating the problems we faced. We did, however, remember the feeling we had once we were airborne — just Eshshah and me. There was nothing in this world more thrilling.

The Healer wanted Ansel and Sovann to share this moment alone for a while. She told Ansel that after they had flown for a bit — and if Sovann wasn't too tired when they returned — then Eshshah and I could fly with them. We were beside ourselves, hoping that we would be able to join them.

Heading back inside, we expected them to be gone for quite a while, enjoying the thrill on their own. Before I reached the kitchen door, Eshshah told me they were on their way back. At first I thought something was wrong, but I didn't get that feeling from Eshshah. She told me Sovann and Ansel wanted to share their flight with us without delay.

Sovann's powerful wings backstroked, whipping up the wind around the courtyard as he and Ansel came down in a perfect landing — of course.

"Healer, we're ready for Eshshah and Amáne to join us." Ansel called out.

The Healer raised her eyebrows and tilted her head, looking a bit surprised. She already knew how her nephew felt about me. Smiling, she nodded her assent. Without delay, I ran to my chambers to change out of my gown. I pulled my boots over my tights and raced back out to the courtyard, helmet in hand. Gallen had saddled Eshshah for me and gave me a leg up. I put on my helmet and strapped myself in the saddle. In my eagerness, I wanted to give Eshshah the go-ahead before I finished buckling in, as was my habit. But this was Ansel's night, so I forced myself to wait for his signal. Being a gentleman and always so calm, he waited before he gave Sovann the okay.

"Don't be gone too long or go too far, you two." The Healer got in while we could still hear her.

Eshshah launched and with a powerful downstroke we were airborne and following closely behind Sovann. Tears of joy streamed from my eyes, I could barely keep the shout in my throat. I hoped they headed towards the water and far from land so I could scream out my elation.

Eshshah soared up abreast of Sovann. Ansel and I turned towards each other. Our eyes locked, his face reflected my joy. We saluted simultaneously, and then laughed that we both had the same impulse at the same time. My heart swelled to the point of bursting. Our bond, that had already been strong, was now profound.

Amazement washed over me. *How is it that I, a common girl from Dorsal — whose dreams and aspirations had been exceeded by far — be so fortunate as to have the love and attention of this dragon rider who flew by my side?* The heir to the throne of Teravinea, no less.

I made a mental correction. I used to think there was nothing in this world more thrilling than Eshshah and me airborne. I was wrong. We had found a new thrill — Eshshah and me airborne with Ansel and Sovann. I sang a silent song of thanksgiving and reveled at the thought that I was in love with my best friend.

Chapter Forty-Seven

Three weeks passed since Ansel and Sovann linked. Their training progressed quickly. Like Eshshah and me, they were fast learners.

I took time out of my practice to watch. They worked on their tail mount and wing mount. Both were escape mounts. If a rider was being chased and needed to get into the saddle quickly, both methods would get us in the air faster than the standard of climbing up the dragon's foreleg.

For their tail mount, Sovann held his tail straight behind him. On his first try, Ansel ran up his dragon's tail and in three bounds he traveled over Sovann's back towards the saddle. Before he got past his wings, he slipped and slid down behind Sovann. I cringed as I heard him hit the ground with a thud. On only his second try, he reached the saddle and leaped into it. He buckled in as Sovann brought his wings in a downward stroke to take-off.

The thought of my first try that ended in a crotch-drop on Eshshah's tail still made me wince. I'm sure Ansel was very thankful that he avoided my unfortunate mishap.

I lingered a bit longer as Gallen instructed Ansel on the wing mount. I used this method when I escaped the castle with Sovann's egg. Ansel started at a distance from Sovann, who held his wing at the height where Ansel could just reach it. Ansel ran towards Sovann's wing and grabbed the bony "finger" that protrudes from the bend in his wing. Sovann lifted his wing too quickly and Ansel swung too forcefully. Instead of landing in the saddle, he catapulted over it, landing in a heap on the far side of his dragon. Executing a wing mount correctly was not an easy maneuver.

I only had the heart to watch a few more unsuccessful attempts. I left their practice to take up my own on the other side of the barn.

That evening, Ansel trudged into the kitchen late, disheartened. He hadn't mastered the wing mount by the end of his first day — and I had. I gave him a smug look. It was unkind. My competitive edge got the best of me. When I saw how disappointed he truly looked, I regretted my taunt. I put my hand on his arm as he started to walk past me.

"I'm sorry, Ansel. That was rude. But you always made everything else look so easy. Finally, there's one thing that I could do better than you."

He still didn't look at me. I tilted my face under his so he had no choice but to meet my eyes. "Ansel?" He focused on my face and I smiled, trying to cheer him.

"Here's what I think: You two are trying too hard. You're using too much muscle trying to swing into the saddle, and Sovann is using too much power to catapult you to it. If you would swing with less force and Sovann slow his uplift — relax and just let your natural momentum get you there, you'll hit your mark."

"We're trying too hard?"

"Yes, you two powerful males think it's all about muscle and strength." I said in a gruff male voice, "But it's timing and grace." This time, in a soft voice.

I could see his eyes light up as my advice sunk in.

"I'm surprised Gallen didn't give you that pointer. Eshshah and I did the same thing. Gallen had to keep telling us that it shouldn't take that much effort. Once we finally listened to him, we got it."

He kissed my forehead and turned abruptly to head back to the courtyard. "Sovann," he said out loud, "I'm sorry my friend, but can we just try it one more time?"

"Aren't you tired?" I couldn't believe he wanted to go back out.

"Truthfully, I'm exhausted, but I won't sleep tonight unless I try it once more with your suggestion."

I walked outside and watched as Ansel ran towards Sovann, who was in the ready position, his wing at the right height for his rider. Ansel reached up for the wing "finger" and with just his forward momentum, he swung upwards as Sovann raised his wing. Just like that, first try, he landed in the saddle. They took flight, Ansel whooping at his success.

Watching from the courtyard, I jumped up and down and clapped. I shook my head as I thought about the fact that he succeeded on his first try after my tip.

"I'm going to strangle Gallen," he said laughing as they landed.

"I'm sure he was just as tired of your constant successes as I was. He probably planned to make you work for this one. You'd better not tell him that I was the one that let you in on the secret."

He slid off his dragon and gathered me up in his arms, swinging me around as he buried his face in my hair. He stopped and put me down. His eyes turned serious, his brows furrowed.

"What?" I stiffened at his sudden change in attitude.

He sighed, "Like you said at the Dorsal Outpost so long ago, how quickly time goes by, but all things must come to an end."

My throat tightened.

" I've been here for too long," Ansel continued. "I can't deny that it has been, so far, the best part of my life. Linking with Sovann. Seeing you every day." His eyes softened as he pushed a strand of hair out of my face.

I fought the panic that rose in my chest.

"My life keeps getting better, but I have a manor that I need to run, a silk business to oversee, an army to raise. Too many responsibilities, and it's time I take them up again. Sovann and I must leave at dark tomorrow."

The wind sucked out of my sails, my spirit sank. I didn't want him to see how disappointed I truly was, because I knew he felt badly, too. So, I forced a smile, "You mean we can't just continue to live here in bliss for the rest of our lives? Close our eyes to everything out there?"

His mouth curved up in a half smile. "In our dreams, yes. I know that's how you prefer to go through life — with your eyes closed. But I'm afraid I'm not capable of thinking that way."

I abandoned my effort to hide my distress. My eyes welled up. He pulled me closer and whispered. "Soon, Amáne. Soon all of our efforts will come to fruition. Because of you — my girl of the prophecy — and Eshshah, we're closer to our goal. But ... we're not there yet. We have no choice but to continue the fight."

He gazed into my eyes and said, "When it's all over, we can look into the living-in-bliss part, and you can teach me how to close my eyes to everything else."

He leaned over and brushed my lips with his. I pressed my forehead to his chest as we stood, in silence.

Chapter Forty-Eight

While waiting for night to fall, I tried not to be depressed, but it took all of my effort. Eshshah moped around, miserable at the thought of having to part with Sovann for the first time. Our only consolation was that we were only four hours away. Ansel told me it was Eshshah's and my turn to come to Trivingar. I agreed and promised we would visit soon.

Night time arrived too quickly. Why is it that when it is anticipated with great expectations, it approaches slowly; yet when it is rejected and unbidden, it arrives prematurely?

We all gathered in the courtyard to see Ansel and Sovann off. Eshshah and Sovann touched noses and exchanged sad farewells.

Ansel held me close, his lips lingered on mine. We stood in silence staring into each other's eyes. Previously, I would have been uncomfortable with this affectionate display in front of the Healer and Gallen, but not any longer. Especially when the Healer had reminded me that we're family. Besides, the two of them behaved like love-sick adolescents now that their announcement was out.

Releasing me after one last kiss, Ansel wiped the tear that escaped the corner of my eye. He kissed my forehead and both cheeks, then turned and mounted his dragon. He gave the word as we all saluted. Sovann launched himself into the air with a powerful leap and a mighty downstroke of his wings. We stood watching until they became a tiny golden speck in the sky, blending in with the countless desert stars.

The Healer, Gallen and I turned and walked slowly back into the house. I felt its vast emptiness now. Sadness wrapped around me. I already missed them. I couldn't give in to depression — Eshshah needed my support. The separation between her and Sovann strongly affected her.

A short time later the communication device buzzed in the library and the Healer went to see who was contacting her. I startled when her urgent voice called out for Gallen and me to join her.

Inhaling sharply, I gaped in shock at the face that stared out at us from the glass disc. It was Bern, battle-worn and weary.

With a raspy voice, he said, "Anbon was the first on Galtero's list. He's making good on his oath to hunt out and destroy every dragon rider. Since I'd signed Amáne up as Vann, a citizen of Anbon, we were the first to get hit." He ran his fingers through his hair, pushing it out of his face.

His hand was wrapped in a bandage — the blood seeping through.

"We've been able to hold the town gates so far. But against Galtero's army, I don't believe we can hold it much longer. If it doesn't look like we can stave them off soon, I'm going to call a retreat. We'll pull back and take cover in the mountains. Galtero's army doesn't stand a chance against us there."

Bern's eyes reflected his anguish as he gave us this news. We knew war was coming — we had been preparing for it. But the reality of it whipped through my mind like a Valaira. I couldn't help feeling that it was my fault that Anbon had been the first to suffer.

However I looked at it, there was only one truth ... Galtero's assault had begun ...

Acknowledgments

Wow, book two is now behind me. What a ride that was. Once again, my family and friends supporting me, encouraging me, is what kept me on track.

My husband, Lloyd, my daughters April and Alanna, their daughters, Rio, Mila and now Kira (possibly future dragon riders) were inspirations. Son-in-law, Jason, offered contagious enthusiasm. My sister, Doreen won't let me rest until the throne is won.

Once again, my "Battle Consultant," Scott Saunders, added his suggestions to make Amáne's fight scenes believable. The dancers of Linda Armstrong's School of Highland Dance were my target market support team. Forrest Vess, again, gave his input for the cover art ... and saved me from a major typo! Tattoo artist, Pete Walker, added his expertise for the awesome linking mark for Charna Yash-churka. Michael Clark offered a helpful critique and some great suggestions that I couldn't resist. I stayed focused and to the point thanks to the generous input from my Tuesday night writer's meet-up group, including, but not limited to Al, Candace, Craig, Devon, Donna, Pam and Van.

To all whose uplifting words in person or through my facebook page and email inspired me to fly higher, thank you again and again!

... we fight on to win the crown ...

CHARACTER NAMES AND THEIR MEANINGS

Some of these names I've taken liberties with their spellings and full meanings. But most are not far from the original.

AMÁNE - Water - derived from Native American

ANSEL DREKINN - Protector - German; Drekinn - Dragon - Icelandic

BERN - Brave and gallant - German. Formerly known as Koen (Brave - French) - Rider of the late Heulwen

BRAONÁN - Sorrow/tear drop - Irish/Gaelic. Formerly known as Yaron (to sing or shout - Hebrew) - Rider of the late Volkan

CALDER - Violent Stream - Welsh. Formerly known as Vahe (strong - Armenian) - Rider of the late Bade

CATRIONA - Pure - Old Greek

DORJAN - Dark man - Hungarian. Formerly known as Ruiter (rider - Afrikaan) - Rider of the late Unule

DUER - Heroic - Scottish

EBEN - Rock - Hebrew. Formerly known as Haldis (Stone Spirit - Greek) - Rider of the late Salama

ESHSHAH - (Pronounced ESHAW) Fire - Hebrew

EULALIA - To talk well - Greek

KING EMERIC DREKINN - Leader - German. Ansel's father.

FARVARD - Guardian. Formerly known as Kei (sand - African) - Rider of the late Okeanos

QUEEN FIALA DREKINN - Violet - Czechoslovakian

FIONA - White/Fair - Gaelic

GALLEN- derived from Galen - Healer/Calm - Greek. Formerly known as Kaelem (honest) - Rider of the late Gyan

GALTERO - Ruler of the Army - German

GAVRIL - Believer - Slavic

HALEBEORHT - Proud - English

THE HEALER - Formerly known as Nara - Happy - Greek. Rider of the late Torin

JESLYN - Blessed with wealth and beauty - American

KEMP - Fighter - English

KAIL - Mighty One - Celtic/Gaelic

KALONICE - Beauty's Victory - Greek

KIRA - Dark Lady - Celtic/Gaelic

MILA - Favor, Glory - Slavic

KING RIKKAR DREKINN - Strong Ruler - Nordic form of Richard. Ansel's Grandfather

RIO - Water - Spanish

KING TYNAN - Dark - Gaelic

SEREN - Star - Welsh

SPERO - Believe - Latin

D. María Trimble lives in Carlsbad, California with her husband. Her days are spent as a graphic artist at a local company. She has been a student of dragonology from a very young age.

Made in the USA
Charleston, SC
28 January 2013